Praise for the *Wendy Dar*

"For readers craving a whimsical adventure and an unforgettable sequel to the first *Wendy Darling*, this swashbuckling plot will leave readers stunned well beyond the last page."

—*The Reading Room*

"In this extraordinary, stunningly written adventure, readers will encounter a darkly suspenseful twist on an old tale which reminds readers of every age of a Neverland-lesson: we never truly grow up."

Redbook magazine

"Top 10 YA Fall Reads by Authors We Love."

—*Culturalist*

"A dark twist on a familiar tale that readers will have difficulty putting down."

—*School Library Journal*

"Oakes superbly crafts both a story with wings and a Neverland with teeth, a story that will tempt any reader into never growing up."

—Brianna Shrum, author of *Never and Never* and *How to Make Out*

"If the first *Wendy Darling* pulled me away from familiar adventures in Neverland, Book 2 has me sprinting away from them... and I didn't know how badly I wanted that deviancy until it was too late. Oakes' delicious plot twists and rich revelations leave you just the right amount of full, but they mostly leave you crying out for the final installment in this micro-epic where Wendy's authenticity is the unquestionable star. Oakes' signature style of dark fantasy retellings is intoxicating, and the much awaited Captain Hook does not disappoint."

—Mason J. Torall, author of *The Dark Element*

"This twisted spinoff of a famous children's tale is filled with richly developed characters and fast-paced, eloquent writing. With *Seas*, Oakes delivers a stunning sequel to her *Wendy Darling* series. Stuck on board a pirate ship with the infamous Captain Hook, Wendy must quickly learn to face her true nature, and choose what kind of heroine she will be: sappy or strong, as she is swept inexorably toward a showdown with a chilling and maniacal Peter Pan. Oakes does a marvelous job slowly chipping away at her characters' exteriors to reveal what lies beneath, be it true heroism or malignant evil."

—Alane Adams, award-winning author of
The Legends of Orkney series

"Described in lush, lingering detail, Neverland is all that Peter Pan promises: vibrant, gorgeous, filled with magic and excitement. But it also harbors unexpected dangers . . . perhaps none greater than Peter himself. While she is initially intoxicated by his charisma, Wendy's practical good sense, stubborn loyalty, and newly liberated fire give her the courage to defy Peter . . . only to land, in a stunning cliffhanger, in even worse peril. Dark, even horrific in its graphic bloodshed and psychological menace; but the nuanced portrayals—of a hero frequently excused by his whimsical glamour and a heroine too often dismissed as girlishly insipid—are riveting."

—*Kirkus Reviews*

WENDY
DARLING

WENDY DARLING

Volume Three:
SHADOW

COLLEEN OAKES

SPARKPRESS, A BOOKSPARKS IMPRINT
A DIVISION OF SPARKPOINT STUDIO, LLC

Published by SparkPress, a BookSparks imprint,
A division of SparkPoint Studio, LLC
Tempe, Arizona, USA, 85281
www.gosparkpress.com

Published 2017
Printed in the United States of America
ISBN: 978-1-943006-16-8 (pbk)
ISBN: 978-1-943006-17-5 (e-bk)

Library of Congress Control Number: 2017936257

Cover design © Julie Metz, Ltd./metzdesign.com
Author photo © Erin Burt
Formatting by Kiran Spees

For all Lost Boys and Girls,
may you be found.

"You need not be sorry for her. She was one of the kind that likes to grow up. In the end she grew up of her own free will a day quicker than other girls."

—J. M. Barrie, *Peter and Wendy*

PAN ISLAND

The fairy named Tinkerbell watched from the trees, perched on a tiny sapling branch that quivered underneath her slight frame. Above her head, the leaves were restless with all the unhappiness that had exploded in Neverland. Tink could taste their anger in the air, feel it in her bones.

The plain girl from London was back; she'd been caught by her brother when Captain Hook pushed her off the plank of the *Sudden Night*. Something about that still didn't sit right with Tink, but she kept her thoughts to herself. Tink's eyes narrowed as she studied the girl.

Wendy Darling stood proudly on the platform above Centermost, her gaudy metallic blue floral dress whirling all around her. The Neverland breeze lifted her brown curls and kissed her cool cheeks. The girl raised her chin, and even from where Tink sat tucked back in the trees, the fairy could see that the girl was different now. The Wendybird had changed. Perhaps it was in the way that she stood, or the way her eyes looked steadily ahead, unflinching.

Or perhaps it was in the way that she smiled so coyly at Peter and the way he looked at her in return, with a desire that made Tink's heart throb painfully. Wendy Darling was a girl with a purpose, not remotely the same girl who had fled Pan Island in a flurry of fear. Whatever Hook had done to her on the *Sudden Night* had changed who she was.

Tink lifted her head and gave it a shake, sending tiny cylinders of sparkling fairy dust swirling through the air. Wendy Darling even smelled different. Before, she had carried a starchy chemical smell, mixed with faint chamomile and a sprinkle of lemon, but now she smelled like salt and the stale sweat of men.

Peter, on the other hand, smelled like a flower's first breath. He was so beautiful that sometimes Tink could barely stand to be near him. She loved the red flames that licked through his curly hair, his dark eyelashes against his olive skin, and his emerald green eyes. As he stepped toward Wendy, Tink could see her magic curling off his skin like tendrils of white smoke.

She watched delightedly as Peter berated Wendy in front of the crowd, but it was short-lived, as his tone changed from one of cruelty to one of lust. The immortal boy bound to her in unfathomable ways began to crow about how Wendy had returned because she was in love with him, about how she had returned to be his queen. These same words Tink had so longed to hear spoken to her in whispered, reverent tones. Each syllable tore jagged rips into her heart.

Peter was excited, unable to tear his eyes away from Wendy in that dress. Tink could hear his heart hammering against the walls of his chest as loudly as she could hear every quiet whisper on Pan Island.

Jealousy raced through the fairy, making her magic glow white-hot. She felt as though she were burning in a consuming, delicious fire. Under her skin, white tendrils of magic raced through her veins, lighting up the tips of her fingernails. Wendy stared back at Peter now, the look of hungry desire upon her face so real that it made Tink seethe. The girl—still so plain, even now when she was dressed up like one of the whores from Harlot's Grove—took a step toward Peter, *her* Peter.

Before Tink had a chance to catch her breath, Wendy kissed

him, her lips pressing against the lips Tink loved as the Lost Boys exploded into cheers.

The tree underneath her feet gave a shake at her unhappiness, and Tink felt herself swirling down into that familiar darkness, the safe place.

The place where Peter loved only her. The place where Peter didn't hurt her.

Underneath the ragged shroud Peter made her wear, her wings beat furiously. Tink imagined hurtling toward Wendy; yanking her up by those skinny, pale arms; and throwing her off the nearest cliff. It would be immensely satisfying to see the fear in Wendy Darling's eyes when she saw what a fairy could really do.

And yet . . .

Tink remembered that day when Wendy had washed the wounds that Peter had given her. She remembered how her hands had touched Tink with such tenderness, and the memory of it brought star-filled tears to her eyes.

Perhaps the girl is good. Perhaps it doesn't matter.

Peter pulled back from Wendy's kiss and had the boys bring the prisoner forward—that odd boy from London that John had fetched, the one with messy hair the color of mud and mottled blue eyes. The boy who could never, not in a million years, compare to Peter, and yet, when they shoved him forward and took the bag off his head, Wendy changed. Her face became pained as she struggled to control her emotions. Tink cocked her head to hear Wendy's heart, listening to the way it pulled violently toward the new boy and then back toward Peter.

Tink smiled nastily. It sounded painful. But then, another sound crept underneath Wendy's beating heart. Tink winced as the voices of the stars whispered their cryptic warnings, the ones she had tried her best to ignore. They would not be silenced, not when she was flying or when she was with Peter, not even when she was dreaming.

"Quiet!" she hissed, but it was to no avail. The stars grew loud, louder than Tink's commands, louder than Wendy's heart, louder than every voice in Neverland. Tink covered her ears and began to rock back and forth on the branch, quietly whimpering, her wings shuddering with each word.

A new life is coming, the stars whispered. *And the girl will be the catalyst.*

CHAPTER ONE

Wendy Darling, formerly a resident of Kensington Garden, clutched Peter Pan's hand tightly as they soared above Neverland. Night had long draped its shroud over the island, and now its emerald green peaks were barely visible against the inky black sea. The Bay of Treasures sat far below them, looking to Wendy like a sliver of moon, the pirate ships at her shore tiny dots of white. Stinging wet moisture peppered Wendy's cheeks as she and Peter flew up past the break of the clouds, upward through the gray mist that circled around them. Once, she had found this thrilling. Once, she had wanted nothing more than to fly with Peter for the rest of their days. Now, Peter was a monster pulling her into a hell made of sky. The clouds were left behind as they barreled into the open blackness. A familiar creeping sensation began crawling its way up Wendy's chest as her lungs braced protectively.

"Peter . . ." Wendy struggled to breathe as the air thinned around her. "Not so high!"

But the boy she had once loved looked back at her, a cruel smile dancing across his beautiful, wicked face. "What is it, my love?"

The air was so thin that it cut into her chest like a razor. Her lungs desperately searched for oxygen.

"I can't . . . breathe this high up."

Peter raised his head, taking a deep breath into his strong chest, the wind whipping his red curls around his face. Then he exhaled slowly, blowing his full breath at her face.

"I suppose this is a bit high for a mere mortal like yourself. I'm sorry, Wendy. You know I would never want to cause you distress."

Liar.

Peter squeezed her hand tightly, and the power of flight flowed from his palm into hers. The corners of his mouth twisted up in a crooked smile.

"And I just hate seeing that pretty face turn blue."

Wendy's other hand clutched at her throat as she sucked on the thinning air. Peter did not slow down; instead he gazed back at her, and the green eyes that had once filled her with delight now burned with cruelty. He made no movement to take them lower.

"Wendy, tell me, have you ever seen such beauty?" Peter's smug mask fell away as he turned to stare out at the stars. "They once made a boy from Scotland feel so small."

She raised her eyes to watch his expression, her own messy curls tickling her cheeks. For a moment, he was real, the Peter that she believed still existed somewhere. But then he took a ragged breath and said, "That boy died a long time ago. Now the stars bow to me."

Wendy turned back to the sky, each painful breath ripping through her chest as she struggled to stay calm. Peter was right; the beauty up here was so dazzling that it bordered on painful, and Wendy almost wanted to look away. But she didn't; instead she let the celestial playground splatter across her vision, and she took it all in: the slight pinks nestled against a hazy green, each of the colors glowing from the thousand stars that pulsed within them. They rose out of the sky like giants. Wendy's head was spinning, and so she reached for something hopeful, something good: *These are still the same stars that shimmer over London.*

Damp sweat gathered on her forehead and froze into small drops of ice as soon as they hit the air. As Wendy labored for each breath, Peter began pointing at the stars, tracing the outline of each constellation with Wendy's small fingers curled in his own. She hated the way that her skin pulled toward his, hated the heat that rushed through her body at his slightest touch, hated the way her body betrayed her mind when it came to Peter Pan.

Peter's brow furrowed in concentration as he gestured to the stars. "I call that one The Lasso, that one there with the loop."

He was actually pointing to Pisces, the same constellation that Wendy's father had shown her since childhood. Wendy remembered those magical nights when her smiling Papa had sat her on his lap by their window overlooking Kensington Garden. He had taught his only girl each constellation while they searched for his mysterious star, the one he swore appeared out of nowhere on very clear nights. The star that she now knew was Neverland.

Peter coughed. "Wendy . . . are you listening to me?" His handsome face was tinged with annoyance.

Wendy savored the silent betrayal taking place in her head. *You don't own these stars. You may fancy yourself a God, but I do not.*

Peter saw her small smile and took it to be meant for him, just like he took everything in this world. "I call that one The Snake."

Eridanus.

His hand traced the shape of a diamond with outstretched limbs. "And that one is The Warrior."

Orion.

Wendy silently corrected him as he rattled off more childish names.

"The Knife."

Cancer.

"The Spider."

Perseus.

"See that one? It looks like an antelope."

Monoceros.

Wendy took a painful breath in, happy for this momentary distraction from the panic that was rising in her lungs. Her hand pressed against her heart and clenched as she struggled to stay calm.

"Do you see them now?"

"I see!" She gasped for air. "Peter, please, enough flying."

His hand tightened painfully around hers until her fingers were crushed under his. "There will come a day when I will have your full attention, Wendy Darling. When you will see only me and no one else—not your family or the Lost Boys, not even that pitiful bookseller."

In his burning gaze, Wendy saw the depths of his rage, a jealousy of Booth that fueled his madness, and she quivered with fear.

Finally, Peter's eyes softened as he traced her panicked face with one cold finger. "Oh, fine, we'll head down, but only because I cannot bear to see you suffer, my love."

You cannot bear to see me suffer, and yet you have hunted me, threatened my brothers, and now hold the boy I love captive.

"I also know how you fear heights," he added.

The urge to strike him rose up inside of her. *I am afraid of heights because you dropped me.* His concern for her at the moment was real, but she knew it would be gone in seconds, replaced with the wicked darkness inside of him—*the Shadow.*

Peter spun in the air, his arms circling her waist, his lips slowly tracing up the back of her neck, his breath hot on her spine. And then they were soaring downward, the stars left behind, only a memory for now. As they flew, the air thickened, and Wendy gulped it down hungrily.

Peter stopped in the midst of the gray clouds, and their puffy wetness soaked through Wendy's dress. She shivered in his arms.

"Cold, love?"

Moving ever so carefully so that their hands were never parted,

Peter turned Wendy toward his body and then began slowly peeling off the brown wool coat that was wrapped loosely around him. After lacing his fingers with hers, Peter slid the coat off his shoulders and onto Wendy's narrow ones. With a tender smile, he tucked the collar back, his finger tracing underneath her chin, his touch leaving tendrils of fire everywhere.

Peter leaned forward, and though brushing her lips against his was a thousand ugly betrayals in her heart, Wendy kissed him, tasting trees and earth. Their mouths pressed together, warm and hungry. Desire and disgust mingled inside Wendy's heart, propelling her further into the deception, down into the depths that Hook had once warned her against.

Make him believe you love him, but don't give away something you can't get back, Hook had said.

Wendy had once believed that to be a very crass warning, Hook forgetting himself and his place, but now she understood he hadn't meant it carnally. The captain had meant that she could lose her *soul* to Peter. This redheaded boy could pull her into his fire, just as he had once pulled Hook into friendship, and just as he had once pulled Queen Eryne into desire. It was how he pulled hundreds of worshipful Lost Boys to him—he made them believe he was the father they never had.

"Thank you for the coat. You've been very generous given my earlier . . . rebellion." Wendy shook her head shamefully. "I was so . . . afraid."

Peter tilted his head and inspected her, his emerald eyes filled with an unlikely hope. "Afraid of what?"

"Of you."

He blinked.

Wendy gave another shy smile, lifting her eyes back to the stars. There was no need to lie, not now. "I was frightened by my feelings for you. They're overwhelming. Dangerous. I'm not the girl I was when I left London. Peter, you have changed the very nature of my being."

Peter's body dropped in the air a little—Wendy had always made him do that, an unlikely tell that let her know she was getting under his skin.

"And why did you return?"

They had had versions of this conversation many times over the past few days. Wendy looked at Peter, her eyes lying to him, and did what she always did when it came time to say those three words he wanted to hear—she pretended he was Booth.

"Because I love you."

Peter grinned from ear to ear and pulled her close to him, the wind whipping her dress around them both. Her body shuddered with delight even as her heart recoiled in disgust. *Stupid, stupid body.* Peter looked deep into her hazel eyes.

"I will always take care of you, Wendy. You're mine, and once my great war with Hook is over, Neverland will become a playground—for us, and our children." His eyes lit up happily as he kissed her hair and rested his chin upon her head.

As Wendy raised the coat to wipe her running nose, a familiar smell crept into her nostrils: lye soap, wooden shelves, the dust that lined old book pages. She almost gagged when she realized what it was, but she choked it back, forced it behind the glass smile that threatened to shatter her. *This is Booth's coat. Peter was wearing Booth's coat.*

"Anything wrong, my love?"

Wendy quietly shook her head, a tear forming at the corner of her eye. "Nothing." She blinked the tear back, unwilling to show Peter any sign of weakness, any sign of regret. When Wendy was feeling overwhelmed, she went over the plan in her mind, the plan that she had made with Hook, a plan devised from the information she had gleaned from the mermaids, almost at the cost of her own life.

Get the pipes. Get the fairy. Get out.

Wendy needed the pipes to call the Shadow, just as Peter once had. She needed the fairy, Tink, to tell her the song of her people, long slaughtered by the boy she foolishly loved. And then, finally, Wendy and her family—John and Michael—would get out of Neverland.

John.

Wendy almost growled out loud. She was too angry with him to even think his name. The plan that had seemed so simple had forever been changed with the arrival of one thing: Booth, the boy she truly loved.

Wendy bunched the fabric up in her other fist, feeling the rough texture of the wool, the smooth wooden button on the sleeve. *This is Booth's coat.* Booth, the quiet strength that she had kept bundled up inside of her during her trials in Neverland. Booth, the steady memory of him a source of peace that she wouldn't let anyone touch—not Peter, not Hook, not her brothers.

Wendy had once found comfort in the fact that though the rest of her family was in a constant state of peril, Booth, at least, had been safe. And now he was here, in a cage of Peter's making, perhaps in more danger than all the Darlings combined. Wendy had only seen him a handful of times in the past few days and only in passing, her eyes getting no more than a few seconds to look over him.

From what she could see, he was beaten, hungry, and defeated, wearing a bloody shirt that stuck to his back. At one time, she had known everything about Booth—the way he made quick, short movements when he was angry, the way he ate apples to the core, and the way he lost himself so deeply in books that Wendy would have to flip off his pageboy hat before he even noticed her.

And now, he sat in a cage made of bamboo that dangled under Peter's hut, and the eyes that once loved her now glared at her with simmering betrayal. During those times when she passed by the cage, Wendy barely glanced in his direction because she understood something that Booth did not—that the less Peter thought Booth meant to Wendy, the safer he would be. If she did what Peter wanted, if she cried or begged for his freedom, Booth would be further harmed, perhaps even killed.

And so she broke his heart to keep it beating.

Peter was flying them down now, and through the flutterings of her dress, Wendy could see Neverland laid out beneath them: dark mountain peaks, the water like ink pressing up against Treasure Bay, the golden lights of Port Duette flickering along the shore. Peter leaned east, and so Wendy followed, her life held in the palm of his hand. They veered away from the main island and out across the sea toward Pan Island and the giant tree that pressed itself angrily out of the foaming seas below. As they neared the thatched roof that bore Peter's flag—a yellow moon that snapped in the breeze—Wendy let her fingers trace the side of Peter's face. He turned to look at her, delighted at her interest.

"Wendy, you'll be the last thing I ever love."

I'll be the last thing you ever love because I'm going to defeat you, Peter Pan, one kiss at a time.

CHAPTER TWO

They made their way downward until their feet touched the top of the roof, Wendy's body slowly adjusting to the gravitational shift from flying to walking. Wendy sat down and slid off the side of the circular structure, landing with a thud. When she stood, she found herself with an audience of various Lost Boys, all eagerly staring at Peter, who was busy curling his hands, white tendrils of flight twisting playfully around his fingers.

"What is it, boys?" Peter asked.

"We're ready for you, sir," Zatthu said cautiously.

"Good." Peter brushed his russet hair back behind his ears. "You have everything I asked for?"

"That and more." Abbott stepped out of the shadows, his bright blue eyes flicking momentarily to Wendy.

Abbott wasn't the spy Wendy had once thought he was, but rather, he was one of Peter's generals who had wised up to Peter's true nature. He would betray Peter sooner or later; it was just a matter of when. Or maybe he wouldn't. Abbott remained as mysterious as Neverland itself.

"The boys are gathered in formation."

Peter stretched his hands out before him and reached for the sky, his toes lifting off the ground just a few inches. "Wendy, would you care to join us?"

Wendy shook her head. "Not tonight, Peter. You've left me quite exhausted."

Peter grinned naughtily, winking at Abbott, who made a disgusted face, as if the very idea of girls was repulsive to him. "Return to your bed then, but know that you can't avoid seeing our boys forever. They're proud to show their mother what they've been working on, like any boys would be."

Wendy had been avoiding the Lost Boys since her return, not wanting to see their pained faces, to smell their feral need for love and acceptance. She had left them once and had seen their heartbreak upon her return. It was too much. For many of them she was the only woman they had ever known other than Tink, and she had abandoned them to save Michael's life as well as her own.

He waved his hand dismissively. "Goodnight then, Wendy. I'll come check on you before I head to bed."

Wendy made her way to a wide branch strung with ropes and pulleys—the Lost Boys' method of making their way up and down the tree. The ropes ran from the top of the Nest to the pips' hovel near the base, where water smashed against the tree's roots. It was a badge of honor that she didn't even need the ropes anymore. Wendy Darling, a girl who used to wear petticoats and be discerning about what sort of teacup she used, flung her arms and legs spread-eagle around the tree trunk. She exhaled once and then was flying down the trunk, hair whistling above her in a wild tangle. When she saw the vibrant red hibiscus that marked the level just below Centermost, she leapt off the tree, rolling on the rough boards before leaping to her feet and brushing off her dress.

The night was quiet aside from the pitter-patter of tiny reptilian feet as florescent geckos scattered at Wendy's approach. A thick canopy of leaves danced overhead, offering glimpses of flickering lanterns visible in the breeze. From where she stood, Wendy could faintly hear the Lost Boys chanting their war-rhymes as Peter stoked their fury:

Pirates, pirates in a row,
Waiting for the wind to blow.
As they sit and dream of love,
Death comes from high above.

Wendy closed her eyes at the words. Somewhere, across the turquoise sea, Captain Hook and the *Sudden Night* would be making their own preparations for war—loading the cannons and greasing the gears that turned the weapons built to kill flying boys. Wendy stepped toward the small nest that was now her sleeping area: a ratty hammock enclosed in a tangle of roots, a far cry from the heavenly hut above the trees that Peter had put her in when she had first arrived. She ducked inside and began unbuttoning the coat, her fingers moving lovingly over the worn wool. *Booth's coat.* What a gift Peter had given her. She carefully spread the coat into the hammock and then lay facedown on top of it, breathing in Booth's scent, remembering their first kiss in the attic of Whitfield's. After a moment of girlish indulgence, Wendy rolled over onto her back, the stars barely visible through the web of tree branches above her.

Revolutions are fought with cannons, blood, and ships, she mused. *But perhaps some revolutions are as simple as smelling a coat and whispering prayers into the night sky.* Wendy was technically free, but in reality she was Peter's prisoner. Her shackles weren't made of iron, but of beating hearts—first John's and now Booth's. A guttural growl escaped her lips. *John.* How foolish could her brother be?

The sound of a twig snapping made Wendy sit up in her bed. Her heart pounded as she searched for the ivory-and-sapphire dagger she had hidden under her pillow. It gave her comfort, even though she had never used it.

She hoped never to use it.

The leaves directly behind her head gave a shake as a dark figure stepped out of the shadows.

Wendy grabbed the lantern beside her bed and held it aloft. "Who's there?" Her fear faded into a relieved smile as Oxley stepped forward, his face drawn. "Oh thank God, it's you!"

Oxley's frown slipped into the friendly grin that had been her only light the last few days. "Who did you think it would be, Wendy?" He shook his head. "Of all the things you could be afraid of on this island, a general with acorns in his pocket shouldn't be one of them."

Wendy held her arms out, happy to see her only friend—and ally—on the island. "You're right. I should have given you a hero's welcome. A red carpet and a glass of my finest champagne. Cucumber sandwiches and French macaroons." She patted the hammock next to her.

A wistful smile passed over Oxley's face as he plonked down beside her. It alarmed Wendy. Oxley was a boy of big smiles and unrestrained joy, not minute glances that hid his true feelings. She turned toward him and folded her legs underneath her, taking his mahogany hand in her own, noticing again the hundreds of raised dots on his skin. He was a warrior, as was his father, Voodoo. "Oxley, what's wrong? You look as though you've seen a ghost." Wendy scooted closer to him, and after a moment, she looped her arm around his shoulders.

Oxley swallowed, searching for the words that struggled to come. "I fear we will all be ghosts soon enough, Wendy. I have a note for you from the captain."

"Oh!"

Wendy sat up straighter, and the hammock rocked underneath her. Oxley was Hook's only spy on Pan Island—his father was one of the pirates on the *Sudden Night*, serving out a life debt to Hook. Since Wendy had returned, Hook had been unnervingly quiet. Coupled with the fact that it was very hard for Oxley to communicate with her because Peter was always sniffing around, the result had been a deafening silence from her ally and closest friend in Neverland, the man she trusted above all others—Captain James Hook.

"Wendy . . ." Oxley's long-lashed brown eyes met hers as his voice brought her back to reality, his dark skin glistening in the humid air. He handed her the note with a shaking hand. "It's happening."

Wendy snatched the curled paper out of his hand and held her breath as she read the words written in Captain Hook's angry scrawl.

Maison and the Undertow *are on the move toward Neverland. Status of* Viper's Strike *unknown. The* Vicious Seas *is on its way. Our secret armory was raided a fortnight ago.*

Oxley grinned naughtily and pointed to the last sentence, marked by an angry blot of ink where Hook had stabbed his quill through the paper. "I was there for that raid! It was actually quite fun before Peter went mad. Oy, that boy, he has lost his head. Peter wanted to leave Brock locked in the armory with a gun, with the aim to open fire on as many pirates as he could when they came through the door."

"That's terrible!"

Oxley's face twisted in rage, an emotion Wendy had never seen him express before. "Peter knew Brock would die, and he didn't care. He doesn't care about any of us!"

"But you stopped him?"

"Aye, I was able to convince Peter that we needed Brock for the war to come; otherwise that boy would be dead and buried." He sighed and leaned back, his eyes focused on the leaves about them. "Brock would be one more burning lotus floating in the air with his name on it. Did you know that they all just end up washed back ashore on the north side of Pan Island? I stumble across the flowers constantly, withered and water-soaked. The last breath of boys who die for *nothing.*"

"Oh, Oxley." Wendy rested her palm on his face, feeling the raised bumps on his skin, the tribal markings of a home he left long ago. "How horrible this all must be for you, to always stand between the boys and Peter, to never rest, to play both sides."

Oxley closed his eyes at her touch, his shoulders sagging. "He is the devil. Or the devil is in him; I can't decide which. I once worshipped the ground he walked on. He gave me confidence in myself, gave me strength. He gives it to all the boys, and then he takes. He takes without ceasing, Wendy."

She nodded, understanding more than he knew.

Her friend sighed, his eyes ringed with exhaustion. "I shouldn't be surprised by anything Peter does, but the depths of his madness are coming to the surface." He opened his eyes and looked out at the sliver of ocean visible from the edge of Wendy's hammock. "He's poisoning all of Neverland, one drop at a time." He lay back on her hammock, resting his hands on top of his bald onyx head. "It should be over soon, probably for the worst. Peter has more guns now than he knows what to do with." He shook his large head. "Excuse my language, Wendy, but Peter is quite the prick."

A laugh bubbled out of her. "Oxley—I lived on the *Sudden Night*, remember? There is nothing you could say that could even make me blush."

Wendy focused her attention back on the last lines of Hook's letter.

The captive boy is not worth sacrificing all of Neverland. Get the pipes. Get the fairy. Return to the Sudden Night *as soon as you can. War is imminent.*

His sprawling signature was followed by a small note: *Smith insists that I send his regards.*

Wendy crinkled the letter in her hands, urgency flooding her veins. She leapt up from the hammock, leaving Oxley rocking in her wake. She made her way over to the torch near the door and lit the corner of the paper. There could be no evidence of this; if Peter ever found out, it would be Oxley's death. Wendy watched Captain Hook's note curl into licking flames and crumbling ash. Within seconds, it was gone. She brushed the remaining pieces into the foliage behind her hammock. She turned back to

Oxley, his feet violently shoving the hammock back and forth, its rhythm expounding until it was rocking so violently that it threw shadows over the room.

"War," he whispered.

"I'm sorry?" She blew the last piece of ash off her fingers.

"Real war is coming. Not games, not raids, not fights, but real war. Pirates and boys dying. Cannons. Guns. Fire." He raised his eyes to Wendy. "How can we stop it?"

Wendy took his hand in her own, bothered by the despair that filled Oxley's normally cheery eyes. When *he* lost faith, all was lost indeed.

"We have to stop the Shadow before we can stop Peter Pan; otherwise we have no prayer," Wendy said.

Oxley nodded before leaning his head against Wendy, and her heart broke for this weary soldier, a boy who had been asked to do too much. Hook's note had struck a chord. She had played with Peter long enough, drawing out his affection while keeping Booth safe. Her delays were costing valuable time that could be spent advancing their plan to call the Shadow, one way or another. She had to get the pipes, but much harder than that, she would have to convince a delusional fairy to betray the boy she loved, and she had no idea where to start.

"Oxley, you'd better go before Peter notices your absence." Wendy reached out her hand and helped him up from the hammock. His body bumped into hers. "Oof! You're solid."

"Wendy." Oxley reached out and brushed a strand of hair away from her face. Wendy froze at the intimacy of the movement. "It's not hard to see why everyone on this island is in love with you."

"Oxley?" Her mouth was suddenly full of cotton. This couldn't be happening.

Then Oxley grinned. "Don't worry; I'm not getting in line. I'm just saying that your kind heart is shaping this island just as much as Peter's is bending it to his will. We must believe that good will win."

Tears filled Wendy's eyes as she leaned forward and gave Oxley a soft kiss on the cheek before ushering him toward the door. He took once last glance around their tiny little nest of deceit, his eyes hopeful.

"Wendy? Will you say a little prayer for me and my da? That someday we'll sail on the *Sudden Night* together, free from Peter, free from all of this?"

Wendy nodded. "Of course I will."

Oxley wrinkled his face up with a naughty grin. "Honestly, I'm not sure I believe in any of that nonsense, but I figure it's better to cover myself in every specific area. G'night, Wendy Darling. Sleep like all the world is depending on you!"

Oxley disappeared into the dark folds of Pan Island, leaving Wendy standing alone, her torch flickering in a sea of black.

CHAPTER THREE

The next morning, wearing her widest doe eyes and a spine made of steel, Wendy made her way down to breakfast in the kitchen. She watched with a false smile as Lost Boys ran frantically back and forth, bringing steaming bread spread with berry jam to the generals' alcove, where Peter sat smugly with Abbott, Oxley, and John. As the generals feasted above, the remaining Lost Boys fought over food rations that were already too small.

There were too many boys and too few rolls. Hungry tummies made for flared tempers, and Wendy saw the hollowed eyes watching every bite of food pass by their pained faces. Their bodies were crammed together on narrow benches, a tangle of limbs and sweat as they jostled for food and space. Since Wendy had left the first time, she estimated more than fifty boys had been brought to Pan Island. Peter still controlled the portal—with the help of the Shadow, Hook had guessed—and now he was using it unrelentingly to bring him reinforcements.

These tattered boys had shown up overnight to join Peter's army, but they were naive and unprepared for the realities of Pan Island. There was no time for explanations or the Lost Boys' bonds of friendship; no, these boys were brought here to be soldiers, to be casualties, to be Peter's slaves. And they loved Peter for it, not understanding in their youth that death wasn't some glorious destiny.

It is death, and it is forever.

Wendy watched Peter gleefully shoving a fig into his mouth while he laughed hysterically at something Abbott said. Anger roiled through her veins, making it hard to breathe. She saw Peter's eyes linger on her.

She turned to head to the beach—*anywhere away from here*—when Peter grabbed her up in his arms, his feet lifting off the ground just a little, spinning them in a circle as they rose up in the air, the eyes of the Lost Boys on them. She could feel their accusing stares. *You left us. You left us.* He spun them around, his lips on her neck. Wendy thought she saw a flicker of movement in the tree branches that stretched over the kitchen, the hint of a wing like a dancing light. She froze, her breath caught in her throat.

Tink.

Wendy hadn't seen her since she came back, and though she had searched for her, it had been to no avail.

There was a flutter of wings, and two starry blue eyes peeked fearfully out from the shadows. Tink had made herself known. Wendy carefully untangled herself from Peter, being sure to keep their skin connected so she didn't fall.

"Where are you running off to?" he demanded.

"I was just heading down to the beach to take in some air." Wendy nuzzled her jaw reassuringly against his hard, strong shoulder. Peter returned her to the ground, the Lost Boys watching in obedient silence. Wendy met Tink's eyes and tilted her head toward the shore. *Follow me*, she thought.

"Wendy, watch this." Peter spun around, planting his hands on his hips. "Attention!"

The boys leapt to their feet, falling into formation where they stood.

"March!"

The boys marched in a single line out of the kitchen, some leaving behind uneaten food, something unimaginable. Their eyes were full of adoration as they passed Peter, blind love rendering them into nothing more than worker bees.

"See?"

The pride on Peter's face turned Wendy's stomach. She pasted a smile across her face and then left without saying a word, making her way down to the beach.

As soon as her feet touched the sand, she let out a sigh of relief. Away from the prying eyes of curious little boys she could finally breathe. Here, away from a boy who both repulsed and excited her, she could hear her own thoughts. Since her arrival here, Wendy had not had a single moment to herself. Lost Boys accompanied her everywhere, and she knew that Pan Island hid a hundred eyes at any one time.

Her heart pulled toward the open sky. Wendy knelt in the sand beside the water, careful to not let her toes touch the foamy waves. She had barely made it out of Miath—the mermaid's coral garden—alive, and Queen Eryne had promised Wendy that if she didn't defeat the Shadow that she would come for her payment of Wendy's blood. The thought gave her a headache. *A lifetime is a long time to stay away from the sea, especially when you live on an island.*

As Wendy stared at the crashing waves, she thought she saw a flicker of something underneath the surface—a swirl of hair, perhaps, and the curl of glittering lips. She backed up a step from the waves, telling herself that the minute she heard singing, she would run for her life, but the haunting song that had once pulled her into the deep didn't come. Instead, there was a slight scuffle of sand behind her. Wendy turned, brushing the hair out of her face. When she saw who it was, her body coiled defensively.

John.

Wendy hadn't seen him since he had dropped her at Peter's feet, with mumbled apologies. She had forgiven him then, thinking that John was apologizing for how he had treated her earlier, but as soon as she had seen Booth's face, her forgiveness had curdled inside of her and become a black, hard thing, a true disgust for her brother and what he had done.

He stood before her, hands wringing nervously together, his brown eyes on the pearled sand as the blistering Neverland sun reflected off his glasses. *John Darling.* His name stirred up an anger inside of Wendy that she didn't know existed. Unbridled rage flooded her senses, intoxicating, potent. Wendy's hands curled into claws as she looked at his smug, terrible face. This moment, she knew, had been a long time coming: a sibling rivalry that had been born the moment John came into the world. For so long, their mutual love for Michael had forced them to be civil, but now Michael was gone, and there was nothing holding Wendy back. She was done being polite. At this moment, he looked more like a man than a boy, and any protective feelings for him disappeared like steam from a kettle.

"Wendy." His voice was pleading, pathetic.

"Don't speak to me, John. Don't presume to say my name. Walk back into the trees and disappear, and I'll go on pretending that you're dead."

"Wendy . . . if you could just, for a moment, let me explain."

His voice had returned to the cadence that it possessed in London, that uppity, sniveling sound that drove her mad. Gone was the bravado that seemed to overcome him when he had first gotten here, and it was replaced by something else: self-doubt. She could hear it in him, but she didn't care—there was only what he did, only the agony that he had wrung out of her.

She slammed her hands hard against his chest, sending him stumbling backward.

"Wendy!" John leapt back in surprise. "What's gotten into you?"

She snarled at him, and he stepped back, rightly afraid. She picked up a handful of sand and threw it at him, granules and tiny seashells bouncing off his boyish cheeks. The shock in his face quickly turned into rage, and John returned the favor, grabbing his own handful of sand as well and flinging it at her with a furious scream.

Wendy closed her eyes as it showered over her, and then she lunged at her brother, shocked at her own behavior. His eyes went wide as she flew at him. Gone was the meek girl raised to be proper in a rigid society, the girl who had trusted her brother to put family first. In her place was the true Wendy Darling—and she was furious. She tackled John around the waist and followed him down into the sand. He grunted as he hit the ground, his body crumpling underneath hers as she unleashed every feeling of agony that he had caused her. Her slaps railed at his head, his chest, his ears. Her voice choked out the words as he shuddered underneath her.

"How could you do this to me? To Booth? How could you bring him here? You took him from his home!"

Angry tears were falling now, the salt burning its way down her cheeks, tracing a ribbon of rage.

"He was the only safe place in my mind." She leaned forward. "And in my heart. You took that from me, you selfish prat! You can't let anything be even partly mine—not Booth, not Michael, not Nana!"

John stifled back a sob as Wendy hit him again and again. He made no movement to stop her. Finally, when she saw a trickle of blood appear at the edge of his nostril, she sat back with a frustrated yell. He stayed still, his ribs heaving as she untangled herself from him.

"Look at me," she hissed. "Look at my face and tell me how you could do this to your family. To your sister." Her voice threatened to break. "A sister who prayed for you every damned day on the *Sudden Night*. A sister that bargained with Hook to save your life. A sister who came back to save you and all of Neverland." Her voice faltered on the last sentence, her anger rushing out of her, leaving only sadness behind.

"I'm sorry, Wendy, I swear it—"

She cut his apology off. "I fought for you, John. Even now, I am fighting for your damaged soul." She blinked back tears. "And while I was fighting for you, what did you do? You went and got the one thing that belonged to me alone and gave it to Peter Pan."

She shook her head slowly, the truth of her words piercing her own heart.

"And now I have to choose between the boy I love and every person in Neverland." A jagged breath tore through her. "Damn you, John. Damn you. Our father would be ashamed."

John took a deep breath as she climbed off of him and rolled him away from her. Blood poured from his nose. Wendy could see that he was struggling to hold himself together; while his face was a mask of calmness, his chest was pumping and his hands were shaking. He turned to pick up his glasses in the sand, and all of the sudden Wendy felt as though her chest had been punched through.

"John? Show me your back."

"I'll not have you ordering me about," he proclaimed weakly, his words not matching his defeated tone.

"I said show me."

Slowly, he did what she said, lifting his tattered gray shirt. Nausea rushed through her, and she dropped to her knees, pressing her own dress into her mouth to keep from screaming. The smooth back of her brother was gone, and in its place were hundreds of small raised scars in a crisscrossed pattern that ran all the way from his upper shoulders to the base of his spine. Wide lashes that had dug deep ran next to thin slivers. The skin was mottled, hastily pulled together as it healed.

"John?"

A whimper escaped her lips as she gently ran her fingers over one of the scars. Tears fell from her cheeks as she rolled his shirt back down, unsure of what to say or do. With a grimace, John steadied his shoulders, and Wendy could tell his wounds still ached. He wiped the tears from his eyes with the back of his hand.

"Peter made the generals take turns whipping me, and when they didn't hit me hard enough, he took over. He told me I could be a general again if I brought him to the boy that you loved. He told me . . ." John bowed his head. "I just wanted it to stop."

He let out a sob and then covered his mouth, and Wendy recognized the look on his face. She had seen it growing up, when young John had ended up beside her bed with his blanket in one hand and sucking his thumb; John was deeply afraid. She sat back from him.

"And Peter?"

John looked down at the sand as he sniffed. "Peter is still our leader. You have to listen to him, Wendy. He's going to be our father now." His voice was dead as he spoke the words, and Wendy knew without even asking that he was thinking of George Darling back in London.

"John, how can you still think he's good?"

John's eyes met hers. "I don't. But does that matter? He's going to change things for all of us."

She could tell by the look in his light brown eyes that he didn't believe a single word of what he was saying.

He blinked once before stepping back from her.

"We aren't alone."

Abbott stepped onto the beach just past the trees, his blond hair glinting in the sunlight. He looked them both up and down—the blood on John's face and Wendy's torn knuckles, the sand spread around them. A grin stretched across his face as he gestured toward Wendy's brother.

"John! What are you doing down here, man? We have things to do! You're always yanking about."

John snuck a quiet look at Wendy before wiping his bloody nose on his sleeve.

"Maybe you don't have to choose. Between Booth and Neverland."

Wendy stared at John for a long moment, not sure she heard

his words correctly. Abbott looked over at Wendy, exasperation written across his face. It was the way he always looked at her, like he couldn't believe that she was still here.

"Ugh. This family. You, Darling, you're to dine with Peter tonight. Meet him in the empty hut above Centermost when the dinner bell rings. He says, er, to wear a dress?" The last sentence looked like it pained Abbott to say, a delightfully awkward look crossing his features. Wendy nodded once before turning back to the sea.

Abbott's and John's voices disappeared into the roots of the tree, consumed by Pan Island, like the voices of so many other boys before them.

Wendy let out a long breath, her arms clutching at her sides, at once feeling both ashamed and justified in the way she had treated John. Her breath caught at the thought of the scars on his back and the way that he had let her beat him bloody without fighting back. She had seen doubt in his eyes, true doubt.

Whoever Peter Pan was, it was clear he was no longer the charming friend and savior that John had once thought him. Perhaps her brother had seen Peter's true colors in the red blood that had painted his back. Wendy's eyes traced the lapping waves. Really, the question was whether she trusted John. Or was he playing a game with her as well? Even if John had seen the truth about who Peter really was, that didn't mean it was real. Her brother was smart, even if he was the biggest idiot she had ever known.

Wendy had just settled into her mind when she saw it again—there, in the water, a flash of color, definitely not an animal, and closer than she would have liked. An odd gray mist rose out of that same crush of waves, swirling toward the shore with alarming speed. With a yelp, Wendy scooted backward from the water and shot to her feet, her body poised to run. The air was electric. From the water, short black hair tinted with plum emerged, the ends streaming. Gold eyes with long dark lashes followed; the marbled face of a mermaid was looking hungrily at Wendy. The mermaid rose up only to her shoulders, her enormous tail whipping the saltwater behind her into a small whirlpool that helped boost her height. Wendy stood back on the shore, her heart clutching at the sight of her. It wasn't the mermaid she had been dreading, but this one was dangerous nonetheless.

A porcelain hand with six fingers rose up out of the water, and one finger pointed slowly at Wendy. "I have a message from the queen," the mermaid hissed, her voice lulling like water over rocks. Wendy knew it to be a dangerous lie.

"I remember you," Wendy replied, not wanting to display the fear that this mermaid's very presence caused in her. This same mermaid had pulled her out of the water at Miath and sent her on her way, desperate to save Sybella, the rock and goddess of their people.

"You saved my life," Wendy said softly. "What is your name?"

"Indra." Her name poured out of her lips in a tumble of song. "Don't mistake me for a friend. I may have saved you, but your blood calls to me even from over there." Her words were sung without emotion, chilling in their honesty.

Wendy stepped back a few additional feet from the shore.

"What is your message, Indra?"

The mermaid's posture changed, shoulders curling in, cheeks tightening.

"It stirs," she whispered, and a shiver shot down Wendy's spine. She closed her eyes, feeling the pressure build in her head.

Wendy watched with fascinated horror as Indra's eyes turned from gold into black yawning holes. With a whisper of a song, she slipped silently under the water, leaving not even a ripple in her wake.

The waves rose unnaturally and crashed over Wendy's legs and feet. She took a step forward, her eyes on the sand. As the foamy water pulled back from the shore, it revealed a message carved out in deep groves in the brown sand: *Beware the Shadow.*

As Wendy knelt before the shore, Pan Island rose above her, its impassive pale roots pressing upward. She thought of the small hut at its peak, the one that held a red-haired boy who, like this tree, had pushed himself out of the sea and up into godhood. The message was clear: it was time to move the plan forward. And yet, how could she, with Booth's life at stake?

Ticktock. Ticktock.

She lifted the wet ends of her dress and began making her way back to the tree, back to where she pretended she was Peter's, back to the game.

Ticktock.

CHAPTER FOUR

Evening approached the same way it always did in Neverland, on tiny feet painted an azure blue, followed by streaky lavender trails of clouds. The moon rose above the trees, bathing everything in glowing light before the stars made their appearance. Wendy barely noticed the striking beauty of this place anymore. Everything in Neverland was beautiful—the trees, the stars, the seas, and the boys—but underneath that beauty lay something darker.

She looked into the small mirror that Peter had hung on a tree branch for her. A pink dress had been waiting for her on the hammock when she had returned from the beach. The bodice was made of delicate lace and capped low over her shoulders. At the waist, the soft pink fabric billowed out, stopping at her knees. Wendy ran her hands over it, remembering the girl who would have fallen head over heels for this dress, who would have twirled in front of the nursery window as Liza and her mother clapped in delight. Now all she could think was, *How the hell am I supposed to climb in this?*

She tucked her brown curls up around her head with tiny pearl pins and pinched color into her cheeks before climbing into the dress. She slipped her feet into the same black Mary Janes that had brought her to Neverland. Once shiny and black, they were now scuffed and gray, with mud coating the heels. Wendy had just made her way over to the ropes when a thud sounded behind her.

"Oxley?"

"Unfortunately not. Though I'm sure we would both rather it be him right now." Abbott's sharp clip echoed in her tiny hovel.

"Please tell me you're going to fly me up to dinner, Abbott."

He rolled his eyes at her. "Because it's sooo far to climb."

"Actually, it is, especially in this . . . thing." She gestured to the dress.

Abbott looked confused for a moment and then oddly extended his arm, and Wendy couldn't help but laugh.

"Abbott, are you trying to be a gentleman? How unlike you!"

"Your barrage of insults absolutely makes me want to discontinue acting in this manner. Maybe you can get yourself up there just fine. Have fun humping the tree in that doily."

Wendy gave him a kind smile. "You're right, I'm being snotty. Thank you for flying down to get me."

"Anything for Peter." Their eyes met, and without speaking any words, an understanding passed between them: *We're both in danger.* Abbott put his arm out again.

Wendy put her hand on his, and then they were soaring up through the tree branches of Pan Island, passing the kitchen and the teepee. From above, she could see lines of pips dressed in dark brown leaves, marching up and down the rope walkways to Oxley's militaristic shouts.

"Right! March! Now, turn! Zachary, quit trying to pinch Aja! Jake, leave your pack alone and just walk! Argh! Why are you hanging off the ropes? WHAT ARE YOU DOING?"

Wendy was tempted to smile, but after seeing Abbott's grave face, she refrained. The empty hut above Centermost appeared above her—the one that had been previously used to store the guns—and Abbott deposited her on the bamboo platform that jutted out from the thatched roof.

"Enjoy your dinner," he whispered. "The rest of us will be fighting over one giant pot of chicken bones, thighs, and roots." He went to step off the edge of the roof and then hesitated. With a look of fear, he stepped back and leapt into the air, staying aloft, testing his flight abilities.

"Still have it. Good. One never knows when Peter will decide that it's . . . enough."

With that, he took a clipped step off the platform and soared downward. Wendy turned to the linen curtain that was billowing out of the hut and took a deep breath, filling her lungs with determination and the hint of steel.

Make him believe you love him. Make him weak. Then, steal the pipes.

Wendy squared her shoulders and walked into the hut. A long table had been placed inside and was covered with a feast that made her mouth water: glistening chicken breasts, plump rolls, bowls of berries, and real butter drizzled with honey. Guilt churned up inside her when she thought of the hungry boys below, and she resolved that she would take as much food as she could with her when she went.

In the middle of the table, a beautiful lily sat in a cup of water, its fuchsia bloom spread wide.

"Welcome."

Peter's voice made Wendy jump.

"Peter! Where are you?" Her eyes combed the room, not seeing him.

"Here."

She looked up to the unnerving sight of Peter crouched in one of the upper corners of the ceiling, sitting cross-legged—propped up by nothing but air.

His eyes devoured her. "Wendy. Just when I think I have seen you at your most lovely, you put the stars to shame." Slowly, he began to float down. "I'll tell you the truth: never have I seen such beauty on Pan Island. Not once." He landed softly beside her, taking her waist in between his hands.

Wendy raised her gaze and let her fingers brush across Peter's strong brow. Together they rose up off the ground as Peter aggressively hooked his leg around her, drawing her closer, their hips pressed against each other. Bowing his head, his lips brushed her ear.

"Tell me," he whispered, pressing his hips harder against her. "Tell me why you love me."

Wendy blinked, lies diluted with truth falling from her lips.

"I love the way you fly; it's so powerful. I love the way your smile breaks open like sunlight." She thought for a moment before deciding to confess the truth. "Peter Pan, you make me feel free in a way that no one ever has."

Peter tilted his head toward her, their hearts beating hard against each other.

Don't fall into him, Wendy told herself. *Don't fall. Remember that he murdered an entire race. Remember John's back.* Somehow, it was that thought that broke the spell. Wendy leaned forward, planting the softest of kisses on his nose. "You're also quite handsome, but I believe you know that already."

"I do." Peter pulled her closer, his muscular arms tightening around her. "Or so I've heard. I can also be quite charming."

Wendy laughed at that. "That's an understatement. How else do you think you got me out of the nursery window?"

"Could someone kindly kill me please?"

Wendy's heart felt pierced, as if someone had shot an arrow through it. She knew that voice as she knew her own mind.

Booth.

"Oh!" Peter chuckled, his eyes swirling navy. "Wendy! I was so enamored with you that I neglected to mention that we have another guest for dinner tonight. How rude of me!" He flew them back down to the ground. "Booth! Please come join us at the table."

Wendy watched as the boy that she loved hobbled forward from behind a wooden partition. His wrists were shackled, and a rope was wrapped around his waist and tied to the base of the hut. Her stomach twisted as she took in every inch of him, repulsed by what she had just done in front of him, while simultaneously overjoyed to be close to him. Booth's brown hair was matted and oily, patted down across his forehead. A bloody scratch ran from the top of his forehead down past his right eye. His cheeks were drawn, and underneath his eyes, huge dark bruises sat. Wendy couldn't help herself, and for a moment, she forgot who she was and what she was doing here.

"Booth? What have they done to you?" She started to step toward him but then caught herself. She stepped back, hands at her side, longing to kiss his wounds.

"So you *do* know him," Peter crowed. "And here I was beginning to doubt all of John's stories."

Wendy stared at Booth, but he wouldn't meet her eyes, and Wendy felt everything inside her being shredded like paper.

Peter leaned backward, stretching his arms above his head.

"Both of you, please come sit! A dinner with old friends—what could be better? I've heard practically nothing about your time together in London, and I want to hear . . . every single salacious detail." Peter pulled out a chair for Booth, throwing one arm around his prisoner. "Booth and I have become quite close, Wendy, if you can imagine. Why, did you know that he sleeps just a few feet from me, in the cage that dangles underneath my hut? If I listen hard enough at night, I can hear him breathing, or crying. Depends on the day. Here, Booth. Have a seat, my jolly man! Take a minute. Have some food." Peter produced a silver key from his pocket. "And because you are my guest, I insist that we free you of these shackles. Who put those on you? Oxley? I'll have to speak with him." He gave a hysterical laugh. "Oh, that's right, it was me. Silly, Peter."

The shackles clanked down onto the table while Wendy stood frozen, staring at Booth as Peter helped him into a chair. He sank down dejectedly, still not meeting her eyes.

"Now, Wendy! Your turn. Please sit. Doesn't she look beautiful, Booth?" Peter bent over Booth's shoulder, his face pressed
against the cheek of the boy who had given Wendy her first—and
best—kiss.

"I made her wear that dress just for you," he hissed into Booth's
ear.

Her beloved winced. She could see what Peter was trying
to do; he wanted a reason to kill Booth in front of her, to push
Wendy over the edge into revealing her true reason for returning.
But she refused to play his game; she was smarter than he was.
Instead, she curled her fist, fingernails pressing against her palm
hard enough to draw blood. *I will break his heart to save his life.*
Wendy raised her head and looked Peter square in the face.

"Why would I wear this dress for Booth? That's utter nonsense.
He's a fond acquaintance, nothing more." She sat across the table
from Booth and Peter and reached for a wine goblet. *I'm going to
need this*, she thought, pouring herself a full glass. She recognized
the bottle; it was one that she had helped Peter steal from Hook's
vault a lifetime ago. "Besides, I only wear dresses for you, Peter."

He grinned nastily as Booth looked wounded.

"Pass the chicken, please," Wendy chirped, taking a long sip.
The wine was rich and earthy on her tongue; she swallowed it
with vigor. Peter nodded at Booth, who reached out and fumbled
the roasted bird breast onto a wooden plate.

"Serve my lady, maggot."

Booth's jaw clenched as he smeared butter onto the bread and
sent the plate violently sliding across the table toward her.

"Well, that wasn't very civilized!" laughed Peter, taking on a
fatherly tone. "Booth, we must have the proper respect for those
in authority!" He reached forward and grabbed the goblet of
wine that Wendy had liberally poured for him. "Did you know,
Booth, that our Wendy is going to be the queen of Neverland?
Together we are going to rule this island and change the very
nature of its being."

"How terribly interesting," Booth muttered, his eyes on the food.

"Oh, for God's sake, please eat. Everyone on this island acts like they're starving." Peter tossed a plate down in front of Booth like he was dog. Booth hesitated for a moment. "It's not poison," chuckled Peter. "If I wanted to kill you, I would find a thousand better ways than that. I could drown you in the lagoon. I could splatter your body over the Teeth. I could cut you from belly to tongue and feed your insides to Keel cats. But poison, no . . . how boring."

Booth looked from Peter to Wendy. She gave him a tiny nod, and he dove into his food, swallowing as much as he could as quickly as he could.

"My, my, what horrific manners!" Peter pulled a chicken bone out of his mouth and slurped the marrow loudly. "Now, tell me exactly how you two know each other."

Wendy painfully swallowed her bite of chicken before letting a mask of nonchalance pass over her face.

"Our families are old friends. Booth's father owns Whitfield's Bookstore, which is where my family purchases our books."

Peter rolled his eyes. "Your books, you say? For what possible purpose?"

Booth looked up now, his eyes gleaming with the fire that Wendy knew so well.

"For what purpose?" Booth asked. "Why, reading is the only purpose there is. What kind of culture can exist if its citizens don't read?"

There he is. Wendy could have leapt into the air and screamed with joy, would have kissed Booth unconscious if only she could. She struggled to hide her smile. While keeping Peter from killing Booth was her problem, there was no part of that that didn't include letting Booth humiliate Peter in his own way. Booth took a sip of wine, his confident voice returning.

"Say, Peter, what are some of your favorite novels? I dare say

Robinson Crusoe is quite your speed, what with the tree house and all. Do you have a library on Pan Island? It is said that you can judge a child's education by the size of his library."

Peter was staring at Booth now, a rare glimmer of shame crossing his face.

"I have no desire to speak about books," he snapped. "I only want to hear more about you and Wendy."

Wendy chewed her bread, hoping it would hide the pounding of her heart.

"Honestly, Peter, there isn't much to tell," she said. "He is a friendly acquaintance of mine, but to call him a friend would be stretching it." She let her lashes brush her cheeks and then looked up at Peter with all the intensity she could muster. He sat back in his chair, watching her with curious eyes that said, *Prove it.*

Wendy pushed the creaky chair out from underneath her and slowly made her way around the table. With a coy smile, she seated herself snugly on Peter's lap, drawing his face toward her. Out of the corner of her eye, she watched Booth, who looked as though the food before him had turned to ash. She turned back to Peter, her fingers lovingly tracing his jawline.

"I really don't understand why you brought him here. I thought it would be just us. Alone." She let his hand wander halfway up her thigh. "Take him back to London and then return to me. Consider it a favor to me, and to his father, who I'm sure misses him. He isn't needed here." She let her lips trail his cheek, feeling the blood rush up to meet the surface of his skin as she whispered slowly into his ear, "We don't need anybody else, Peter Pan. Just you . . . and me."

Peter nodded his head, his eyes never leaving her face as he sat back from her.

"Take him home, that's what you would want me to do?"

Wendy nuzzled her cheek against Peter's, feeling the slight stubble of red hair. "Yes. I don't want anything to come between us. Ever again." She pulled back to kiss him firmly on the mouth but stopped, fear rushing through her entire body.

Peter's eyes were navy.

With a snarl he leapt up from the table, and Wendy tumbled to the floor.

"An acquaintance? Do you think I'm an idiot, Wendy? Don't you think I know?" Before she had even hit the ground, Peter had grabbed Booth's hair and slammed his head down onto the table. As Wendy scrambled to her feet, Peter flew up into the air, hauling Booth up with him, holding him aloft with one hand around his neck. Booth's legs were kicking underneath him.

"I may not be as well-read as he is, but I can read *you*, and you're protecting him, even now." Peter flew to the edge of the hut.

"Peter, stop!" Wendy cried out as Peter thrust Booth out over the doorway. Underneath him was an unfathomable drop, thousands of feet separating the top of Pan Island and the hard shore below.

"Tell me the truth or I will drop him. Tell me!" he thundered.

Booth's face was turning blue as Peter squeezed, and a dry croak escaped from his throat as he clawed desperately at Peter's hands. Peter's navy eyes bore into Wendy. "Tell me the truth, or watch him die."

Wendy fell to her knees, her eyes on the ground.

"Stop! Stop! I'll tell you!"

Peter grinned nastily. "Hurry then. I can feel the life escaping from his throat."

"He loves me!" Wendy said quietly. Peter threw Booth to the ground with a satisfied smile, and Booth clawed at his throat as he gasped for air. Wendy glanced over at him, her eyes apologizing for what she was about to say.

"Booth loves me, but the feeling isn't mutual." Wendy blinked back tears, watching Booth prop himself against a wall, the hurt in his eyes searing. "The Whitfields are poor. Early in our childhood, we were friends, but for me it was much like one would pity a stray dog. My parents decided to take the bookstore under their wing, and so weekly I was sent to pick up books. As he grew older and his . . . affections for me grew obvious, I indulged him. Truth be told, I pitied this hungry, lonesome boy with only books for company, and so I let him believe there was a chance. Also . . . ," she paused, the words on her tongue turning her stomach, "I was spoiled and bored. What better way to cure a socialite's boredom than with a handsome distraction? Booth seemed like a rebellion at the time. Haven't you ever felt the thrill of taking something you shouldn't? Doing something naughty?"

Peter smiled cruelly. "You know I have."

"Well, that was Booth Whitfield for me. He was something naughty, something to make my parents mad." She shook her head. "But, to be honest, I regretted it almost immediately." She looked away from Booth's pained face. "What I had thought was a fun distraction became real for him. He became too attached and confessed his love to me in a note that my father found. Honestly, I was grateful to have a chance to end the courtship before it even began. Booth told me to be brave." She swallowed. *Forgive me.* "But I wasn't. Not brave enough to tell him that I didn't love him. Not brave enough to confess that he was nothing more than my entertainment. He's not worthy of my station, not worthy of our single kiss."

Booth was staring at her in shock, his lip curling as sadness passed over his lovely features. Wendy wouldn't meet his eyes, and instead she raised her face to Peter.

"I have only met one person worthy of my kiss."

Peter's green eyes fixed on hers, and a wordless desire passed between them. It had to be enough to save Booth's life. She had to want Peter enough.

"And there is only one person worthy of my bravery."

Wendy leapt to her feet, surprising both of the boys, and sprinted to the edge of the platform. Peter barely had time to yell her name before Wendy plunged off the edge with a wild leap, flinging herself out and over the lip. Cool night air rushed past her face as she arched up and away from the wood, gravity quickly pulling her body away from Peter's hut and hurtling her downward.

Booth's screams echoed above her head, the hut already so far above her that she could barely make it out. Wendy fell—the very fate that haunted her nightmares upon her. The black pitch of sky disappeared into the canopy of trees as she dropped through the open branches, leaves whipping her face, her heart feeling like it would explode in her chest. Air whipped around her and parted beneath her. Wendy saw Centermost pass by her in a blur of voices, heard the cries of some Lost Boys as they saw her falling past them. A branch slammed into her hip and sent her spinning, spiraling downward, falling faster now . . . head over heels, tumbling into the dark.

Perhaps she had misjudged. *Foolish girl.* The ground soared up from below her, approaching more quickly than she ever dreamed. Her mouth opened to scream, but she knew that it would be too late, that the sound would splatter along with her body onto the hard roots below her.

Then his strong arms wrapped around her. She felt the jerk of weightlessness as her fall came to an abrupt and strange stop, the scent of trees and unbridled adventure on the wind. Peter held her gently, his own panicked breath washing over her face. "Wendy! Gods! What were you thinking?"

For once, Wendy could tell she had taken him off guard. Peter's voice was unhinged. *He is scared.*

"You could have died! Why would you do that?" For the first time in a long time, she saw the true Peter, stripped of his evil, stripped of the Shadow. Her surprising act of faith in him had thrown him. Wendy tried to seem calm, though every part of her was shaking from the fall.

"I told you, but you didn't believe me." With a sigh, she rested her head in the small nook of Peter's shoulder, a place she had always fit just right, the cruel irony of it not lost on her. "Peter, you make me brave. Not him. I thought I wanted him once, but now I see that he is nothing more than a shadow of you."

Speaking of the Shadow . . . as Wendy stared at Peter, she saw the navy in his eyes receding. Perhaps it was enough to save Booth, this silly, reckless act. *He believes me. Thank God.* "What will you do with him?"

Peter frowned. "He's not your concern anymore, the poor sap. I'll keep him around for now, as my own little insurance policy." His mouth twisted and his eyes became lost in thought as his voice turned cold. "John lied to me. He told me that you loved Booth."

Wendy tried to quiet the voice inside screaming the truth: *I do, I do.* "As if I would ever tell my brother, the most indiscreet voice in the Darling household, the truth. Booth loved me, and while I did have feelings for him at one time, I always knew he was a temporary distraction. I was waiting for something bigger." Taking Peter's hand, she climbed her way up his body as they floated in the air until her face was level with his. She bit her lip nervously as she wrapped her legs around his waist, feeling his body harden beneath her as he stopped breathing.

"The only future that matters now is ours. And the future of Neverland."

"Hmm . . ." Peter lowered his head to hers hungrily. "I like the way that sounds." Their lips pressed together, and while her unfaithful body rose to his every touch, Wendy's mind lingered somewhere else—on the blue of Booth's eyes, a blue like the sky in London, pale and true. As their lips pulled together and parted like waves and the shore, she stole into the memory of Booth like a retreat, her mind trying to ignore how Peter tasted like salt and tree bark.

CHAPTER FIVE

That evening, after Peter had gone to bed, when it seemed even the stars were exhaling their relief, Wendy lay awake in her bed, her heart clocking every passing minute. *Ticktock.* It was time to talk to the fairy. Wendy had to save them all, and she wasn't sure how long she could maintain this false affection for Peter—a mass murderer, a psychopath. The further she pushed, the further she fell away from herself. She needed to act soon, for the sake of Booth, and John, and Hook; she couldn't wait much longer.

Wrapping a white scarf over her head, she crept out of her hollow, leaving only a quietly rocking hammock behind. Wendy made her way from the bottom of the tree upward to the core of Centermost, a magical open space lit by dangling lanterns that let off a silver pink hue.

Wendy knew that the flickering flames that burned without heat were not of this world; she knew that they were created by a certain possessive fairy every night. If Tink was anywhere, she would be here, as this crossroads was her favorite spot to watch the Lost Boys. Finding her might be easy, but getting her to talk might be a different story. More painful truths had never been uttered, and Wendy cursed everyone on this godforsaken island that she would be the one to deliver them to a half-mad fairy. *This will not go well.*

Silently she made her way over the lashed walkways, stepping lightly to avoid the big holes in the wooden planks, her hands holding tightly to the knotted ropes. The island was unnatural in its quiet stillness, its leaves and flowers curling protectively in, cradling the boys who slumbered in its bosomy breast. Above Wendy's head fireflies danced in blinking figure eights, leaving spots of light flashing in her vision, reminding her of the pop of a lightbulb. She hadn't seen electricity in months, a jarring thought.

When she reached the center of the rope walkway, suspended between the canopy above and the dark chasm of branches below, Wendy picked up one of the lanterns and held it above her head. Tink was close; she could feel her moving through the tree around her, a buzzy white energy that made the hairs on Wendy's arm stand up.

"I know you're there," Wendy whispered. "I need to speak with you."

A thud sounded behind her, and Wendy turned. Tink crept forward as a cylinder of fairy dust swirled around her. She looked just as Wendy remembered her: a small girl, a head shorter than Wendy, slight and narrow. Upon her head, a wild bramble of white blond hair was dotted with plum berries and soft moss. Her pale skin was highlighted by sharp cheekbones, her perfectly symmetrical face drawn above her bitten lips. Tink's vast beauty was swallowed by her unhappiness, her star-flecked blue eyes giving way to a vacant, hopeless stare. All around Wendy, fairy dust fell like tiny glittering mirrors.

"You wish to speak with me? I suppose we could speak . . . either that, or I could kill you where you stand. I haven't decided yet." Tink's voice, while ringing through Centermost like bells, lacked the commitment and malice it once held. The faded brown shroud that Peter made her wear hung on her thinned frame, rippling every few seconds as her wings clipped together, unhappy to be concealed. When Tink moved beside her, the glow from

Wendy's lantern bathed the fairy's face in light, revealing an egg-shaped bruise on her temple.

"Oh, Tink," Wendy whispered. She stepped forward, reaching out to touch her face. Tink closed her eyes at Wendy's touch, and a tear full of bursting stars dripped down her cheek. "What dark things has he done to you now?" Through her hand, Wendy could feel Tink's deep magic pulsing through her skin like electricity.

Her eyes bore into Wendy's. "You know nothing about Peter nor the things he does."

"No, Tink. I think it might actually be you who has been left in the dark all these years."

Tink blinked. "What are you talking about?"

Wendy took a breath. "I'm about to tell you something, and it's going to upset you greatly. But I need you to hear what I have to say. Tink . . ." She paused as Tink's eyes narrowed murderously, and she softened her voice.

"Peter uses you. He hurts you, he manipulates you, and he uses your power to make himself strong. He's a murderer, Tink. You know what he does with Lost Boys who get too old or too smart." Wendy paused, weighing the words on her tongue. "He will never love you the way you want."

Tink's hands began trembling as Wendy's voice continued peeling open the delicate layers of her heart.

"Honestly, Peter can't truly love anyone—not you, not me, not the Lost Boys—because his soul is filled with a void of his own making. This evil grows with power, Tink, *power you gave him.*"

Wendy dropped her voice, looking around to be certain they were alone. "Do you know what the Shadow is?"

"Stop!" Tink curled her body protectively, hands covering her ears. The pressure in the air dropped around them. Everything went silent as Tink's emotions coiled out from her body and steeped into the world around them; even the branches above them trembled. The fairy rose to her feet, buoyed by the power of the natural around her. She stepped toward Wendy with volcanic rage twisting her face.

"Don't talk about Peter that way. You don't know him like I do." The fairy dust around her began violently pulsing out toward Wendy, the glittery pieces compounded by waves of light that burned Wendy's skin in little flashes.

"Yes, I do. I know that his love feels like the best love until it suddenly doesn't." Her feet were being pushed backward by the force of Tink's magic, and she leaned in, flinching when the tiny bursts of it seared her palms and forehead. With her hands trembling and the lantern held above her head, she looked fearlessly at the last fairy in Neverland. The dust was circling hungrily around them both now, creating a vortex of sound and shimmer. Wendy's voice turned sharp.

"Tink! You need to listen to me! Peter . . . he murdered your entire race. He killed the fairies!"

"ENOUGH!"

Tink screamed with a roar that shook the beams beneath Wendy's feet. The fairy leapt backward and pushed her hands out in front of her, trying in vain to defend herself from a truth that she already knew. A thick wave of fairy dust tinged with white heat threw Wendy backward, her feet leaving the ground, her lantern flying over the side of the rope walkways. She landed hard on her back in the middle of the walkway, the fairy dust falling over her in blazing crystal shards. Wendy's spine throbbed dully as she groaned and turned over. Tink rose up into the air above her, denial twisting her face into stone.

"Don't speak to me about my people. If you dare to speak to me about this again, I'll kill you; I swear it. Peter can mourn your broken body, and I'll suffer the consequences." Though her face was deathly serious, Wendy could hear the thread of despair winding through her voice.

Wendy looked up, unafraid, her voice dropping to a whisper.

"Tink, you have to face the truth sometimes. For your dead family, I beg you to see reason."

"Peter is my family. He is the reason for everything in this world. You will never understand what we share."

"If you truly believe that you can love Peter no matter what, then you should be able to hear anything."

Tink snarled before moving her body directly above Wendy, hovering for just a moment before she spit on Wendy's face. Wendy raised her hand, but it was too late; it hit just under Wendy's eye, where it burned through her skin like a spark from a fire. She cried out in shock as she tried frantically to wipe it away. "Tink!"

"Never speak to me about Peter." When Wendy looked up again, Tink was gone, leaving only a streak of fairy dust that arched into the dark leaves. Wendy rested her hand against her cheek, her fingers gingerly pressing the spot under her eye, where the fairy's spit was still warm. She looked down. The hairs on her arms were singed.

She had been right. *That didn't go well.*

The next morning, Wendy awoke to the thudding of a hundred dirty feet around her and the unwelcome feeling of hands all over her body, lifting her out of the hammock. She was discombobulated, barely awake enough to register the Lost Boys' grubby limbs, their sweet, smelly breath. She struggled against their hands. "What the devil? What is happening?"

She opened her eyes and saw their faces peering at her, toothy grins with missing teeth, tangled hair, vulnerable eyes. Their hands held down her body.

"What are you doing? Get off me, boys!"

"Can't! Peter's orders!" Patel yelled, one grubby hand pushing down her shoulder.

Brock was giggling madly as he leaned over her, the sickly smell of fruit washing over her face.

"Morning, Wendy! We missed ya!"

Wendy twisted her body left and right, but it was to no avail. There were too many of them, a horde of smiling, laughing little boys. Brock raised a feather above his head, signaling everyone to listen to him, but no one did.

"Pick her up on three! One, two—"

The front of her legs came up first, and then her arms followed in an awkward tangle, because the only people the Lost Boys listened to were Peter and the generals, none of which was here. Wendy's body was then hoisted above their heads, their hands pressing up against her back, her shoulders, and, to her shame, her bottom.

"Put me down! This instant! Boys! I'm ordering you!"

They giggled as if she had told them something ridiculous.

"Can't disobey Peter. Sorry!" crowed Zatthu, who had a firm hold on her ankle. "But we'll get you safely there, Wendy! Stop wiggling and just lie still!"

With a sigh, Wendy surrendered and let the boys carry her through Pan Island, over walkways and overhanging branches, silently praying that no one tripped and sent her flying over the edge. While part of her hated this intrusion and wondered what strange morning these boys had in store for her, the other part relished their closeness. *They don't hate me after all, even after I left them.* A familiar voice shouted directions at the other boys.

Wendy lifted her head. "Thomas!"

"Hiya, Wendy!"

"Where are we going?"

The boys bounced past the teepee and down the north side of Centermost, weaving their way up and down tree branches with ease, Wendy's body swaying from side to side.

"Not sure, but Peter said to bring you to the Red Flower Lookout and to make sure your feet didn't touch the ground."

Wendy smiled. "He didn't mean that literally, Thomas. Ow! Patel! Watch where your hands go!"

"Lit-er-rally." As Thomas puzzled over the word, Wendy noticed that his blond ringlets were starting to turn a light brown. Thomas was growing up, which meant that Michael was too.

Michael.

The mere thought of his name brought unwelcome tears to her eyes. Her little brother was out there somewhere, protected by Lomasi and the hidden Pilvinuvo tribe, the safest place for him to be. Her logical mind knew this to be true, and yet every morning she woke up longing to tousle his blond hair, to kiss his chubby hands. There were only two other Darlings on this island, and one of them she wanted to kill, so it had always seemed like Michael and her against the world—a world that she would give to hold him for just a few minutes.

"Wendy!" yelled one of the boys. "Tell us a story!"

"Yes, yes!"

Above her the world bounced, and her stomach turned, but Wendy closed her eyes, recalling an old Irish folktale of Liza's. "Only if you put me down."

When they did, Wendy brushed off her dress and began walking beside them, her voice steady as she began her tale.

"There was once a very poor man who lived with his large family and many dogs."

"I wish I had a dog!" burst out an alarmingly young Lost Boy.

"*Listen!*" Wendy said sternly, remembering Liza's soothing voice. If she closed her eyes, she could almost taste the sharp tang of her Earl Grey tea. "There was once a very poor man with a large family that he could not afford. Because he was so poor and low of status, he could find no one to be godfather for his newborn son. Without a godfather to pay his way, the man knew his son would soon starve and die. Desperate, the poor man finally called for the men of the village to appear so he could choose a godfather at random. One of these men was

Death in disguise. When Death stepped forward in an expensive coat, the poor man chose him, rejoicing that his son would not only live but also have a rich godfather for all his life. When they had finished making the deal, Death said to the man, 'You make no distinction between high and low.' The poor man didn't understand what he was saying but continued feasting late into the night, intoxicated by the idea of the man's wealth. The son was raised up in Death's household, cared for and educated as Death's own child, never knowing that Death was his godfather. Years passed, and it was time for the young man to get married. On his wedding night, Death, dressed in his fine coat once again, called the young man from his bride's arms and took him down into a cave by the seashore. Inside the cave, countless candles burned, and all of them blazed strongly except for one—a black candle with a weak flame burning down to the quick. 'Whose light is that?' asked the godson. 'Your own,' answered the god-father cruelly. He pulled off his coat and revealed himself to be hideous Death. The godson pleaded and begged with Death to put a new candle in his holder, but his godfather did not answer. The young man watched as the light flickered and went out, and then he fell down dead."

The boys stopped walking and were all staring at Wendy with horrified looks.

"What kind of bloody story was *that*?" Patel wailed as poor Thomas sniffled. "Wendy, I didn't like that story."

Wendy nodded slowly. "Boys, do you know what that story is about?" Some shook their heads. Others burst out with random answers:

"Always have an extra candle!"

"Don't go into caves!"

"Always be rich!"

"No." Just ahead of her, Wendy could see the faint outline of Peter Pan, waiting for her. Their eyes met as Wendy lowered her voice.

"The lesson of the story is that you can neither cheat nor persuade death."

She stepped forward, brushing off her dress, which was now covered in a dozen dirty handprints. "Boys, next time, I would prefer to walk myself."

One of the boys gave a shrug and ran away giggling. There was such a desperate sweetness to these boys, all of them lonesome for a mother, longing for any scrap of attention that Peter would give them. His was the last face she wanted to see this morning, but instead of slapping him the way he deserved, she plastered a girlish smile across her cheeks and ducked under the overhanging vines to see what the fuss was about.

Red Flower Lookout lived up to its very literal name. Gnarled oak roots twisted into a loose circle around a view of the sea. Overhead, huge red hibiscus flowers blew open and shut with the wind, their paper-thin petals fluttering in the breeze, stamens pointed at the sky.

Peter stood in the middle of the circle, and for a moment, Wendy watched him just being a boy. One hand clutched the branch above his head while he leaned out over the gap. The breeze ruffled his red curls, the light catching them like a flame. His long tan legs were flexed, and Wendy could see the outline of his muscular chest through his tight maroon tunic. A crown of bronzed leaves encircled his brow, and someone—probably Oxley—had drawn tribal markings up his arm. Without turning back, he reached out a hand for her.

"I can hear your breathing, Wendy. Come and see." She took his warm hand in hers, letting his fingers lace her own, and she stepped out onto the small circle of dirt in the midst of the flowers. She inhaled sharply.

There, on the horizon, sat a pirate ship.

Chapter Six

Peter rubbed his chin as he looked down at the water, one hand reaching out for Wendy's waist, the other resting on his sword. "That's the *Vicious Sea*, the head of Jaali Oba's prized fleet. I've never seen it this close to shore; normally it's on the outer boundary waters searching for treasure."

Wendy tried to keep the surprise off her face. Oba was loyal to Hook, and yet . . . here was his ship, sitting off the shore, ripe for the taking.

Peter's eyes lit up. "The gold that decorates the ship itself is said to be worth a fortune. What do you suppose, Wendy?"

She shook her head once and rested her hand upon his arm. Peter was testing her loyalty. She tilted her head as if she were thinking, rather than taking in the ship's dark wood accented with gold paint and the shimmering sun painted upon its sails. She felt soothed as it rocked on the waves maybe two miles from the shore. "It's a trap," she whispered. "A poisoned gem for you to try to pocket."

"Yes," murmured Peter. "I do believe you are right."

It was strange to see a ship from above; her view of a pirate ship had mostly been limited to her place onboard—the towering masts, Hook at the wheel, Michael scampering across the decks while Smith screamed at him. Looking at the foreign ship now,

Wendy was filled with a longing for Hook's solid, unshakeable presence.

She knew of his sacrifices, of what he was fighting for. What they were fighting for. Wendy's breath caught. She knew why this ship was here. *It's a distraction.* First Hook's note, and now the arrival of the *Vicious Seas*—its captain an ally of Hook's—could mean only one thing: Hook meant to give her *time.* Wendy let her eyes run over Peter's body, lingering around his waist, where the pipes would normally be. They weren't there. Peter caught her looking.

"Is something interesting you down there?" She felt a blush rise up her cheeks, and she turned away.

"Sorry, no, I, er, ummm . . ."

Peter looked at her with one eyebrow raised. "You can take all the time you need later, but right now . . . I have some pirates to kill."

Please don't kill them, Wendy thought. *Please don't kill anyone.* "Maybe it's not anything; maybe they are just sailing off the shore—"

Wendy's sentence was interrupted by a cannon blast, and then another. There was a loud explosion at the base of the tree, and a shower of wood shards rose up to meet them. Black smoke billowed out from water below. Peter's eyes swirled quickly into navy.

"They're blowing up the docks! Move, Wendy!" He shoved her roughly as he pushed past her, screaming frantic orders at the Lost Boys who surged toward them.

"Line up! Line up! Here in a cluster! We have to fight back! Dammit!"

The Lost Boys circled around Peter, their faces either terrified or elated. Somewhere above them, the alarm bell started ringing.

"Gather up!" Peter shot up into the air. The Lost Boys began reaching out their hands to him, worshipping him, desperate for the gift he was about to give. Tendrils of light swirled around him, funneling down from his head to the tips of his fingers.

"It's time to fight!" he commanded the boys.

"Is this the war?" someone yelled.

Peter shook his head. "No, but it's an act of aggression, and we will treat it as such and answer in kind!"

The cheers of the boys rose to a deafening chant as the generals joined the back of the line—Abbott's face was masked with annoyance; John looked unsure, purposefully setting himself out of Wendy's line of sight; and Oxley stared at Wendy with wide eyes.

Moving quietly, Wendy made her way up to her ally, brushing his arm lightly with her fingertips. "Now?" she whispered. He gave a single nod and then turned back to Peter with a loud whoop.

"Flight!"

The other boys joined in the chant.

"Flight! Flight! Flight!"

Peter rose up higher in the air, silver dust running up and down his arms, which were throbbing with each heave of his lungs. He glowed with a pale light that rang up and down his veins, cracking through the pores of his skin. Wendy watched him with awe, the boy made of light made dark. The chants of the Lost Boys rang throughout the trees as Peter's hands opened and clapped above his head.

A loud crack echoed outward, and white light shot out through Peter's hands and filled the room, rushing over every Lost Boy and even Wendy, who stepped out into the wave of light at the last moment. The power washed over her, filling her with light—the mark that made her body feel weightless and free. Everyone was launching off the ground now, including John, who was zooming from branch to branch as if he were born to fly. *The prat.* Wendy stayed grounded, not wanting Peter to see that she had flight.

"Boys! Grab every weapon you can, and head to the docks.

Abbott, grab the iron chest. Oxley, get as many guns as you can carry. And John, carry my sword!" Peter rose up and planted his hands on his hips, letting out a loud crow. The boys answered in return before surging into the air like a flock of sparrows, circling around him. "Now, fly!" Peter screamed.

"You'd better be here when I get back," he said softly, hopefully, to Wendy.

Wendy bit the inside of her cheek. "Where would I go, Peter?"

He wagged his finger back and forth at her, as if he knew her lie. "Say a little prayer for me, Wendy."

"I pray for you every night, Peter," she softly replied, playing their game.

I pray that you'll be defeated and that soon I'll be free of you.

Peter flew down quickly and pulled her hard against his side, his mouth pressing cruelly against her own, and when he pulled back, there was a lick of flame on her tongue.

"When I come back, I'll bring you Jaali's head."

Wendy swallowed nervously. "That seems . . . extreme."

"Not for one of my strongest enemies, Wendy." A dramatic sigh fell from his lips as if he were explaining something to a child. "That seems merciful."

Without another word, Peter launched upward, moving so fast that he was a blur, and then he was gone. Another explosion rocked far beneath Wendy, and another pillar of black smoke curled up over the tree branches. As it blew out to sea, Wendy looked up to the top of Centermost, where Peter's hut lay nestled in the thick green branches.

It's time to get the pipes.

Queen Eryne had said that Peter had sung the song, but in all her time here, Wendy had never heard Peter sing. What she had seen was Peter play his pipes, an extraordinary gift, one that filled him with pride and filled everyone who heard it with peace. If music was made, Peter would have used his pipes. With a deep breath, she pushed off of the ground and was soaring quickly upward, intoxicated at the feeling of flying without Peter's hand crushing her own.

Up and up she flew, trying her best to block out the sounds of a raging battle below; more cannons joined with gunshots and occasional screams. Even though he didn't always deserve it, she offered up a quick prayer for her brother: *Keep John safe.*

Wendy was almost to the top of Centermost now, and she could see the bottom of Peter's hut . . . and the cage swinging underneath it in the breeze. A shadow in the corner moved closer to the bars, and unexpectedly Wendy found herself staring into the hollowed eyes of the boy whose heart she had willingly shredded the night before. She moved closer, reaching out her hands to grasp the cage.

"Booth?"

The shadow of the crisscrossed bars divided his face into small perfect squares: his lips here, an eye there, the mad tumble of his hair.

"Wendy?" He looked confused, staring at her for a moment as he pieced together what was happening. "Are you flying?"

"Yes."

He blinked once, as if waking up, and then lunged forward, his hands covering hers over the bars of the cage. "It figures that you would become just like him, as if soaring through the air like a damned pigeon grants you some sort of elusive mortal superiority."

At the brush of his fingers, Wendy felt joy being released in her veins, his touch like electricity. For some reason, it made her want to weep. Even though his words were harsh, she could see in his eyes that he was happy to see her.

"Booth, listen. I can't stay; there is something I have to get from Peter's hut, and I have to get it now." Somewhere below, a cannon boomed, and the tree groaned again.

Booth's eyes went wide. "What is happening down there? It sounds like . . ."

"A battle. Captain Jaali Oba and the *Vicious Sea* are here."

"That means nothing to me. In fact, all of this translates into a very specific madness. I thought I understood the fabric of my own reality, and the reality of us." His face clouded. "Now I am not sure of any it, and worry that I may be trapped in a terrible dream."

Wendy nodded, remembering feeling like that.

"I know it does, and I don't have time to explain any of it to you right now. But, Booth, I'm begging you to listen to me. I am going to do everything I possibly can to free you when the time is right."

"Free me now!" he hissed. "You're here, and I'm in a godforsaken cage!"

Wendy shook her head. "I can't; not until the time is right. Do you trust me?"

Booth stared at her for a long time, his blue eyes betraying the ways she had wounded him. "Wendy, if I may be honest, I am inclined at the moment to say no. My very heart breaks at the words . . . but . . . no."

His words pierced her, though they were well deserved. She swallowed nervously and then ran her fingers lightly over his, watching a ripple of recognition pass over his face. His heart might not recognize her at the moment, but his skin surely did.

"Booth, nothing I say in front of Peter Pan means anything. I need him to believe I love him; otherwise he will kill you, my brothers, and possibly everyone in Neverland. There is evil that you can't imagine at play here."

His face moved from anger to disbelief.

"Just the good news I wanted to hear."

"I can't explain it now because I have to go find Peter's pipes while Jaali distracts, but what I need you to know . . ." Her mind ran through the thousand things she longed to tell him—all the promises made and broken, all the horrible and beautiful things she had seen on this island—and yet, there was only one thing he needed to know. She pressed her body up against the cage and took his hand boldly in her own, kissing his palm as he had once kissed hers and then laying it over her heart.

He stopped breathing.

"You are still here," she told him. "Don't forget it—no matter what you see, no matter what you hear. The thought of us has kept me going through many dark nights here."

Booth looked incredulous, but his words were strong. "I believe in you, Wendy." He reached out a hand, and with a sigh, Wendy let him cradle her cheek against it. "I always have."

From below, Wendy heard Peter's screaming commands carrying through Centermost.

Leaving him was the last thing she wanted to do, but instead, she pushed off the cage, leaving it swinging in her wake. She landed by Peter's hut with a thud and stepped inside, then uttered a phrase she had heard her father say only once:

"What in the blazing hell?"

CHAPTER SEVEN

Wendy stepped forward, convinced she was in an actual nightmare. Peter's hut was an overflowing mess of trinkets and treasures and useless junk. Every surface was bursting at the seams. On one side of the room, a tangled mess of branches thrust up through the floor, their arms supporting Peter's thatched roof, where dozens of wind chimes whispered in the breeze.

Tied with a sailor's knot to where the branches met the wider trunk, Peter's white silken hammock swayed back and forth, the only bare surface visible to the eye. Wendy felt as if the room itself were swallowing her, a reflection of Peter's mind—chaos and beauty intertwined. On the east wall, a decaying hand-drawn map of Neverland stretched out over a window, flapping every so often in the passing wind.

Wendy stalked over to it. Her fingers traced down the paper, which was soft, like old skin. There, messily scrawled at the bottom, were two names: Peter Pan and James T. Hook. Wendy sighed, her heart aching for these two boys, once friends and now bitter enemies. They had once laughed together, and now . . .

She quickly examined the rest of the map, her eyes combing over messy drawings of ships, caves, and mountains. She found Port Duette and followed the line of the waterfall north, curving through vast jungles with hastily drawn Keel cats until her breath caught in her throat.

She pulled her trembling fingers back. There, underneath sloppily drawn mountain peaks, a terrifying shape emerged. Violently slashed black lines of charcoal created the outline of a figure, tall and slender, arms topped with jagged claws. Its face was open in a perpetual howl, and it was falling forward, as if it were lunging for something. Stamped over the figure was a bloody handprint.

Wendy raised her own hand next to it and knew it immediately; it was the same hand that she had once loved. The hand of Peter Pan. Here it was, proof of the Shadow, something only whispered about between her and Hook, a monster that both inhabited and was controlled by Peter. She took a deep breath, feeling her heart quicken as she looked at the picture, which was drawn with so much pain.

Does Peter mourn his connection with the Shadow, or does he relish its power? Does he even remember who he was without it?

Wendy began frantically searching through the endless piles of trinkets, each mound bigger than the next—pearl strands and gemstones the size of her thumb, pirate daggers, macabre fairy money, carved wooden creatures, scrolls of documents and medallions marked with skulls. It was all very expensive and all very useless.

Pipes, pipes, pipes.

Careful to leave everything the way it was, Wendy ran her hands underneath shelves and delved into treasure chests, lifting branches and leaves, searching every possible strange spot. Minutes passed as beads of sweat began dropping down her face and making their way down her collarbone. *I have to find them. Where are they?* The floorboards were stuck down hard, and the walls revealed no secret compartments.

You know who would be good at this? John. Always so good at puzzles.

The last chest was opened and searched before she leaned back in defeat. Wendy lightly tapped her finger against her teeth, a bad habit that she had learned from Mr. Darling once upon a time, but it helped her focus. She stood, taking in the room.

Tap, tap, tap.

If I were Peter Pan, where would I keep my pipes?

Wendy closed her eyes.

I would keep them somewhere safe. Somewhere only I could get them. Her eyes popped open. *Somewhere high.*

Wendy stood up and bent her knees, leaping into the air like she had seen Abbott do, testing that she still had flight. She did, and the weightless feeling of her body never ceased to amaze her. Wendy ran to the edge of the platform and pushed off with her legs, her body following, soaring straight upward as the air parted before her. As she flew, she heard Booth's voice below her, his very British cadence so foreign and familiar in the jungle canopy.

"Wendy, whatever you are doing, I think the battle is ending! Get out of here!"

She flew up above Peter's hut, desperately searching the roof for something, anything—and then, *yes.* There, on top of Peter's hut, was an unassuming woven basket, tied securely to the roof with a piece of burlap twine. Wendy soared forward, landing next to it, falling to her knees as the wind whipped branches violently around her. Her hands gave a tremble as she reached for the lid.

"Calm down," she whispered to herself. "Just calm down."

She reached down and pulled the lid from the basket. Just as it came open, the bells on Pan Island began ringing, their exacting sound bouncing through her. One ring for pirates, two rings for fire . . . three rings for victory.

Clang. Clang.

Wendy paused with her hand over the basket.

Clang.

The fight was over. Peter would be returning soon, and if he saw her, he would know that she betrayed him . . . and he would know that she knew about the Shadow. Everything would fall; they would be undone. Wendy shoved her hand into the basket, grabbing the pipes, which were golden and surprisingly heavy. She barely looked at them before tucking them into her blouse so that they lay flat against her chest. With a strong kick, she sent the basket rolling off the rooftop, hoping that Peter would think the wind had blown it off. As she turned to go, the voices of Lost Boys began echoing up through the trees, jubilant and proud and rising in song:

> Heave ho, heave ho, down to the depths they go!
> In the water, on the sand, pirates die when Peter lands!
> Heave ho, heave ho, murderers, drunkards, pirates, liars,
> All will burn with Lost Boys fire!

The song was followed with frenzied chants of Peter's name. They rang up through the trees, and from below her came the sound of boys landing inside Peter's hut. Running, Wendy made her way to the other side of the roof, the furthest she could get from the charming voice that rose up to greet her, its tenor like terror licking up her spine.

"Wine? Food? How shall we celebrate? Oxley, open the grain stores."

Oxley's anxious voice answered back: "Peter, oy, I'm not sure that's the best idea . . . we are low on food as it is. Too many boys."

Then Peter's voice sounded again, this time tinged with annoyance.

"Oxley, do you fancy yourself the Pan now? Do you not think I care about my boys? Do you not think that I would starve myself so that they may eat?"

"No, sir." Oxley's voice was tinged with disbelief.

"Good. Let's have a feast then! I'll go get Wendy—she'll want to hear all about our little fight—and then we can meet in the kitchen to celebrate! Ring the bell for the pips and have them bring the casket of wine from the vault raid. With two pirates dead and no Lost Boys down, we have reason to celebrate."

Wendy couldn't wait a second longer. She leapt off the edge of the hut, soaring with her arms out behind her as she had seen Peter do so many times to gain speed. Her body plunged straight down as she flew faster than she ever had, sharp leaves whipping her face while she did her best to weave her way through thick tangles of branches, the cost of keeping herself away from Centermost.

The pipes slipped forward, and Wendy was forced to press her hand up against them, but the wind reacted to her change in position, and it swiveled her form and sent her hips bouncing off branches. Wendy wasn't breathing as she fell, and she was sure that her heart was pounding loud enough for all of Pan Island to hear as she neared the roots of the tree. She was on the back of the island, looking for the unassuming entrance to the pips' hovel.

It was isolated, and because it was where the pips disposed of their waste, everyone had a good reason to avoid this side of the island. Even Peter, who was coming for her now. She soared lower, finally letting out a long breath when she saw the entrance open up below her and the putrid smell hit her nostrils.

She slowed her momentum, righting her body so that she would land feet first. *Almost there; almost there.* Her toes had barely touched the edge of the cliffside when the flight disappeared. She felt it leave her body, felt the warmth and the power seeping out of her skin. A scream escaped her as her feet disappeared beneath her and her body dropped like a stone. She threw her hands out, catching a handful of white roots that ripped into her palms with tiny thorns that cut like glass.

Wendy braced her body as it hurtled against the cliff side, her feet dangling into the air. Below her, waves crashed against a rocky shore. She turned her head and winced as her hands screamed in pain.

"Pull!" she whispered to herself, willing her hands to listen as blood dripped down the roots. "Pull!"

Finally, they moved, one painful hand climbing over the other, her feet slipping against the waste-splattered wall. With a groan, she heaved herself up and over the embankment, pulling until she was fully on the ground. She rolled over and faced the sky, her bloody hands clutching at her chest, making sure the pipes were still there.

Wendy wanted to lie there forever, to let her body rest until blood from her hands wasn't peppering the ground, but she couldn't.

Instead, she ran, her feet stumbling as she wove her way through the dark maze that was the pips' hovel, making her way to her little nook. She had just made it to the entrance of her room when she heard the thud of no more than a dozen feet behind her. She looked back, distracted, and her foot caught on a low-lying branch, that same damned branch that tripped her almost every morning. Wendy hit the ground hard, and the pipes went skittering across the ground, coming to rest in the middle of the room, emitting a dusty golden light. She sprung forward as Peter's steps came around the corner.

"Wendy! I have so much to tell you, you must . . . Wendy?"

In a panic, Wendy sank to her knees, her dress swallowing the pipes underneath it. She clasped her bloody hands together and turned away from Peter so that her back faced the entryway.

"Wendy, why are you on the floor?"

Wendy kept her head bowed, using every ounce of energy she had left to keep from trembling as she clasped her hands together.

"I'm praying, Peter," she said calmly, struggling not to take the deep breath she needed. "I told you that I would pray for your safe return."

Peter's voice was deeply moved when he spoke again.

"What else did you pray for?"

Wendy picked the answer she knew he would like best in order to keep him satisfied and uncurious about what she could possibly be hiding. "That you would kill Captain Hook, and that our future children would dance on his grave."

Peter laughed, delighted. "Why, Wendy Darling! That surprises me, coming out of a proper girl such as yourself." Suddenly, he was beside her, his fingers tracing underneath her chin and up over her lips.

"I can't decide which I love more, this perfect, innocent petal of a mouth or the thought of tasting it." Then he kissed her long and deep, his hands running up and down her neck and over her collarbones, where the pipes had been just moments before. Wendy could feel the pipes pressing against her knees as her legs shook underneath her.

"Peter!" She pulled back with a gasp. "I'm praying." She blinked demurely. "This time is sacred."

"Oh! Sorry!" He leapt back, unnerved by a faith he didn't understand, a faith in something other than him. "When you are done, uh, communing, will you meet me in the kitchen? We are celebrating our victory with a grand feast!"

"A victory?" Wendy tilted her head. "Did you destroy the *Vicious Seas*?"

"We didn't destroy it, but I dare say that ship will be crippled for quite some time. It limped out to sea in defeat after we burned the mainsail."

Peter laughed and ran his hand backward through his hair, and Wendy noticed for the first time that he was splattered with a bit of blood. "My goodness, Peter—are you hurt?"

"No, but two pirates are dead—one shot straight through the head and the other dropped onto the deck." Peter made a squelching sound and splayed his hands apart. "Not much left after that. I'll leave you to your holy prayers. Take the pulleys up to the kitchen when you're done. I'll save you a bottle of wine from Hook's private stash." He let his hand run down her cheek, his pinky finger tracing her jaw, his finger sticking a curl back behind her ear. "And, Wendy?"

"Yes, Peter?" she whispered, not bothering to open her eyes.

"Perhaps take a bath before you come. You're smelling a bit . . . ripe."

He stood up and flexed his arms above his head, and then he was off, soaring upward through the tree, leaving her to catch her breath. Wendy pulled the pipes out from beneath her dress and wrapped them quickly in the dirty cloth she used to wash her face. There was no way she could hide them in the room—it would be the first place Peter would look when he found out they were gone.

Instead, Wendy ran out into the pips' hovel, ducking underneath the dozens of empty hammocks. On the side of the room, a barrel taller than she was brimmed with water that had been strained from the tree leaves above it, a funnel system John had designed to get the Lost Boys clean drinking water. Wendy climbed up a few branches until she could look down into it. She exhaled as she dropped the heavy golden pipes into the barrel, and it wasn't until they disappeared into the dark water that she let herself breathe.

With a sigh of relief, Wendy hopped down and began making her way to the bubbling natural spring on the other side of the pips' hovel. It may have been the only good advice Peter Pan had ever given her, but he was right: she needed a bath before the feast.

She had the pipes. Now she just needed to speak to Tink before Peter tore this place apart.

CHAPTER EIGHT

The feast went late into the night, with pounds of food disappearing into the hungry maws of the Lost Boys. The wine never stopped pouring, and even in her heightened state of awareness about the pipes, Wendy found herself laughing at the Lost Boys' antics, though she silently listened to Peter's tales as he floated above the tables, recounting pirate battles where he had saved everyone with his bravery. It was incredible the sins that his dazzling smile could cover.

She watched the eyes of the Lost Boys as he spoke, their raw hunger for his affection so thick she could almost taste it in the air. Only three boys looked unimpressed—the generals—each carrying secrets of his own: Oxley, a traitor; Abbott, perpetually torn; and John, who looked at Peter with hollowed eyes, his mind somewhere else entirely.

Peter's hands found Wendy all night long, and Wendy whispered promises to him that she would never keep, her comments both seductive and aloof. The boy who could fly had been drinking too much, and it made him both sloppy and volatile. As Wendy reached for a ripe grape, he roughly grabbed her bandaged palms.

"What happened to your hands, Wendy?"

She gave a giggle and shrugged. "I was looking for berries for the boys." She held them up. "Then, Peter, honest truth, I tripped and fell into the bramble! I'm lucky that I didn't end up blinded."

Peter pushed out his bottom lip, so red it was glistening. Wendy had to look away.

"Silly girl!" he crowed. He bent his head and kissed her bandages, a rush of heat transferring from his lips to her knees. "Next time, I'll just have some pips bring you the berries. No need to pick them yourself."

She smiled shyly. "That would be lovely, Peter."

In her mind, words played on a loop: *Tink. Tink. Tink.*

"OY!" Oxley's voice boomed over the crowd. "Look what just came in from the mainland! The shipment from Madam Larouche!"

Oxley was immediately swarmed with Lost Boys, save John and Abbott, who sat above them in the general's loft, looking bored. "Oy, back up, you boors! You'll all get some cheese, I promise."

Once a month, Madam Larouche sent a large crate to Peter via a rowboat from the mainland, all for the cost of keeping Peter happy; for it was he who warned her of incoming ships bringing goods from other islands, goods that she could then greedily buy up herself and sell for a high profit. The boys all reached forward for it now, each clamoring for a treat: rare delicacies like sugared figs, crusted bread, melon cheese, three-seed crackers, and rich berry jellies. To these hungry boys, the treasure inside was worth more than gold.

Oxley threw the crate down onto the ground, wrenching off the wooden lid and pushing back crumpled bundles of hay.

"Oy! What've we got here, lads? Looks like smoked fish, dried salami, cashews, raspberry galettes . . ." The boys swarmed him once again, and he stomped his foot. "Oy! Everyone back up!"

"Listen to your general!" Peter called lazily as he pulled Wendy toward him. "Back up, boys."

Oxley growled at a Lost Boy who was reaching into the box. "Junji! Back up! Peter gets first pick; you know that!"

The circle of boys backed up, looking dejected as they fanned out toward the kitchen.

"How is it, Ox?" called Peter, one hand tracing across the small of Wendy's back as she wriggled away.

Oxley's white teeth grinned at them. "It's good, Peter, maybe the best we've ever gotten! I even see some tins of salted butter at the bottom here. And what's this?" Oxley bent over the crate, his legs kicking out behind him, before he emerged triumphantly with a large white box in his hands, wrapped delicately with an expensive pink ribbon. Oxley turned it over in his hands. "I'm guessing this is for Peter from the madam."

"Maybe it's a cake!" shouted Zatthu. "I would so love a cake." A dreamy look passed over his sweet features. "I feel like my mother made cakes."

Everyone stopped and look at him for a minute, their eyes boring into his small chest. Peter stepped forward, his eyes flashing a curl of navy.

"Mothers." His voice dripped with menace. "The only mother you need is Wendy; is that clear?"

Zatthu's eyes filled with tears. "Yes, Peter."

"I could make you a cake if I wanted to, but I don't, because that's not what leaders do." Silence penetrated the kitchen. "And do you follow me, your leader?"

The Lost Boys answered in sharp unison: "We follow the leader wherever he may go."

Oxley raised his eyebrows as he handed the gift to Peter. "Why don't we just see what's in it first before we all get upset, shall we?"

Peter grinned as he took the box.

"Well, if it is a cake, I'll not be sharing it with you lot. Wendy, come here!"

Wendy stepped forward.

"Why don't you help me open it? Then we can share whatever . . . ," he pressed his lips against her ear, "delicious gifts are inside."

Wendy bit the inside of her cheek.

"I'll let you open it, Peter. Perhaps there will be more than enough to go around. The best leaders are generous with their gifts, the kind of leader I know you are."

She saw his lip twitch.

Oxley sighed and said, "All right, let's get on with this already. It's probably just spiced coconut that we're all making a fuss over. Besides, this is an extra crate this month." Oxley paused. "Peter, wait . . ."

His warning was too late. Peter was already pulling on the pink ribbon, which unraveled gracefully over the sides of the box. The box popped open, and inside was a ticking golden clock, wired to . . .

Wendy opened her mouth to scream the word, but it was too late, she couldn't find it, and then everything was swirling all around her.

Dynamite. That's what the word was. *Dynamite.*

The air was still.

Wendy heard a high-pitched voice screaming Peter's name, and there was a flash of white heat, followed by a burst of glittering dust.

Boom.

The sound shook through Wendy, and it felt as though her heart was being pushed out of her body. Blistering heat shoved her backward off her feet, and a wave of pressured air passed through her, shaking her ribs, curling her spine. Her neck snapped backward. Peter's arms wrapped around her waist, and then a wave of white heat covered her.

Above Wendy's head, glitter and smoke and blood mingled together, raining down all around them. There was a dull ringing sound, and she blinked, struggling to stay conscious. She could hear raised voices, muffled as though they were very far away. Wendy covered her ears and opened her mouth, forcing herself to breath in, the air tasting like ash. And then, sounds. Light. Life.

Wendy lifted up her hands. They were covered with mirrored dust. She looked up and saw the fairy's body that had saved her life. Tink floated over her and Peter, her luminescent wings stretched wide over all three of them in a translucent protective shell. Her face was pale and shaking. A line of blood ran down from her hairline to the edge of her chin. Her once-beautiful wings were riddled with holes, translucent veins now hanging like ripped curtains.

Tink's weak voice broke the silence. "Peter? Are you all right?"

Peter raised his head slowly at the fairy to look up at her, his arms still wrapped around Wendy.

"Yes, I think so, Tink. You?"

For a moment, there was only the two of them, and Wendy was on the outside of a world only they understood. Then Tink's eyes rolled back in her head and she pitched forward, her wings folding behind her as she fell toward them. Wendy caught Tink before she hit the ground, cradling the small girl against her chest. Once the shell of the fairy's wings collapsed, a wall of terrible sound rushed in: the screaming of boys; John's and Abbott's voices rising above the fray, shouting commands; the hideous crackling of flames. Wendy brushed Tink's hair out of her face before pressing her hand against the bleeding wound on her head, Tink's blood sparkling like stars.

Peter leapt to his feet, black smoke curdling out from his skin, his eyes darkest navy.

"Peter . . ."

Don't call the Shadow. Don't call the Shadow. Wendy's hand snaked out and grabbed his arm. He whirled on her with a hand raised, but he stopped when he saw her holding Tink in her arms.

"Take care of the boys. They need their leader right now." Wendy's voice was careful, stern. Peter blinked. For once, he was listening.

"You're right. No, you're right."

Wendy looked back down at Tink. She was breathing, but she

was unconscious, so very small in Wendy's arms, just a slip of a girl—a girl who had saved their lives. Blood from her back was soaking into Wendy's blue dress. Wendy laid her down gently and pushed past Peter, who stood frozen in terror, his eyes unable to take in the carnage before him. Wendy let out a cry and ran forward.

Zatthu, the beautiful boy whose mother had made cakes, was crumpled up against a table, surrounded by a wide pool of blood. Parts of him were missing. Two other boys lay nearby, breathing but bleeding heavily as Abbott and John frantically tended to them.

"John!"

Wendy let out a cry of relief when she saw her brother. He looked up at her with tear-filled eyes, his hands a tourniquet on Brock's leg. The boy cried out for his papa, and John whispered to him to stay strong, that he would be okay, his voice calm and reassuring. A sob caught in Wendy's throat as she looked around the room for the face she wanted to see more than any in the world right now.

"Where's Oxley? John?"

Her brother looked at her for a long moment before shaking his head sadly.

"John?" Her voice rose. "Where is he? Oxley? Someone, please . . ."

Then she saw it, a white tablecloth in the corner covering a large mass, the fabric blood soaked, one shoeless brown foot poking out from under the shroud.

"Oxley!"

She was unaware of herself as she began moving toward the sheet, pushing her way through a fog of boys crying hysterically.

"No, Wendy!" Someone was screaming her name as she reached out for the sheet, her fingers brushing the place where his head would be.

"Stop!" Abbott's arms wrapped around her waist and she was being lifted up, yanked backward, away from him.

She struggled against him. "No! Oxley, NO! I need to see him. Abbott, please . . ."

"You can't help him! He's gone, and seeing his body will only cause these boys more trauma." The general set her down hard. "You can't help him, but there are others that you can help. Breathe, Wendy." She bent at the waist over his arms, a sob escaping her throat.

"I just wanted to say goodbye."

Abbott's voice was broken. "We will. Just not now. He's gone, Wendy. He's gone."

She wrapped her arms around his neck, giving him the strongest hug she could offer. Some of the Lost Boys had begun gathering around Oxley's still form, a few of them sucking their thumbs, others crying, their tears smearing the soot on their faces.

"Maybe if we clap, he'll come back. I heard that somewhere," whispered Thomas frantically. "If we clap loud enough, the angels will bring him back! It has to work, right? Oxley can't be dead." His small tear-stained face looked down at the body. "He was my favorite." He began clapping frantically. "Clap! Clap! He can't hear us if we don't all clap!"

The Lost Boys began clapping through their tears. "Come back, Oxley! Come back!" Their claps grew louder as more Lost Boys joined in, clapping desperately between their sobs.

"Stop!" It was Wendy who uttered the words. "Just stop." The boys looked at her, hungry for hope that she could not give. "It won't bring him back. He's gone." Wendy saw a flash of her own mother as she wiped the tears from her eyes. There were bigger things happening here than her own loss.

"We have to say goodbye, boys." She stepped forward and opened her arms. The boys rushed at her, and she held them all as they clawed at her dress, her hips. "We will never forget Oxley, not ever." Inside, fresh grief tore through her like a physical wound. She could feel her heart scarring. "He will be in our hearts forever, and that is something no one can take away."

Izem looked up at her, tears flooding down his face. "Will we see him again?"

Wendy closed her eyes. "Yes, I believe we will." An old bible verse played in her head, a token from endless rounds of Sunday school memorization, and she spoke it to the boys:

"He will wipe every tear from their eyes. There will be no more death or mourning or crying or pain, for the old order of things has passed away."

Wendy felt as though she were coming apart, and yet she stayed on her feet, holding these boys as they cried. *Oxley, my friend, my ally. Hook's spy. Voodoo's son.* She thought of the way he cared for the Lost Boys, the way he patted their heads, held their hands. The way he made her laugh when all had seemed lost. A wave of despair passed over her, and her knees trembled. *He can't be gone. He can't be.* Peter appeared through the smoke like an apparition, blood smeared across his devastated face, a terrifying expression masking his beauty.

The boys melted away into the smoke, leaving Wendy's dress soaked through with their salty tears.

"Hook will pay for this." In his hands was a crumpled piece of paper that he pressed into Wendy's bloodstained palm. She unwrapped it, pressing her sleeve over her mouth to avoid choking on the smoke as she looked at the note.

Death chases all of us. — Captain Hook

Peter growled. "Oxley was not his to take. The Lost Boys belong to me and me alone." Beneath the surface, Wendy heard the implication: *Only I decide when Lost Boys die.* He narrowed his eyes. "I will skin Hook and every one of his pirates alive for this."

Wendy handed him back the singed piece of paper, her mind spinning. "Are you sure it was Hook?"

Peter grabbed her shoulder roughly.

"Wendy, are you blind? Did you read the note?" He gave her a hard look. "You must be in shock."

Wendy blinked. Gods, she had almost implicated herself. "I am . . . Oxley . . ."

An actual, real tear fell out of Peter's eye. It passed through Wendy like the bomb had, damaging and shocking every part of her. He stood rooted in place. Shaken.

"Peter?" He blinked. Wendy took his hand in hers. "Be with your boys right now."

"Sure." He looked down at his maroon tunic. "This isn't my blood, Wendy."

"I know."

He straightened his spine, and Wendy felt a tinge of fear. *Don't call the Shadow.* She leaned toward him, her voice quiet. "Now is the time to plan revenge. Carefully, and slowly, so that we may not fail. So that when the time comes, Hook will feel your pain."

He nodded his head once in agreement. "You're right, Wendy."

Wendy turned from him, unable to bear his face for one second longer and unable to trust herself to not betray what she knew: *That was not Hook's handwriting.* Not only that, but Hook would never do this, not while Wendy was here on the island.

"You're right. They will burn, but not tonight." He sighed. "Go tend to the fairy. Make sure she lives."

The fairy. He said it with such carelessness, as if he weren't Tink's whole life, as if she weren't the reason they had survived the bomb.

"I'll take Oxley's body to the sea."

Wendy winced as a cry made its way up her throat. "Peter, mark the place with seashells. That way the boys can visit him when they want to."

Peter tilted his head. "Why would they want to do that?"

But Wendy was already turning away, making her way back through the chaos to Tink, who was still lying on her side in a pool of fairy dust, her torn wings folded protectively around her like a blanket.

Tink's eyes fluttered. "Wendy?"

"Up you go." She lifted the fairy in her arms easily, cradling her gently against her chest. There was a time to get answers, and while Oxley's blood was still wet on her dress, by God she would get them.

CHAPTER NINE

Wendy carried the fairy away from the kitchen, and Tink's head rested against Wendy's breast as she made her way deep into the folds of Pan Island, where she knew the sparse medical supplies were kept. Though Tink was light in her arms, each step was heavy, laden with the flashing memories of Oxley's body and the boys' distressed faces as they looked to her for comfort. Finally they arrived at a small shaded alcove where several hammocks lay empty.

Wendy left Tink in one of them and went over to the rickety wood dresser with three cockeyed drawers. As she reached for the drawers, geckos scattered from inside the dresser, their home disturbed. Wendy brushed the nest of leaves off the top with a shake of her head, her words clogged with frustrated tears.

"Does no one tidy up? You would think at least the medical supplies could be kept clean."

For a moment her words dissolved into tears, but she forced herself to take a deep breath, focusing on the task at hand. She jerked open the second drawer, finding nothing but a moldy piece of bread and a few linen wraps. She pulled the wraps out of the dresser, blowing the dust off them.

"I heard it." The fairy whispered as Wendy jerked around.

"Tink?" She rushed to her side, touching the fairy's face, turning it toward her. "Tink? It's Wendy."

The fairy's eyes fluttered. "I could hear it. The bomb. It was so loud. Ticktock, ticktock, all the way from the other side of the island. But I still didn't make it in time, I still didn't stop it."

Wendy leaned forward, her eyes meeting Tink's.

"This isn't your fault. And you did make it in time. You saved me."

Tink took a labored breath. "And Peter. Peter is all right?"

"Yes, Peter is fine." Wendy closed her eyes. "We lost Oxley though, and Zatthu."

Tink let out an inhuman cry.

"Oxley? No!" She shook her head back and forth hysterically. "No more. No more boys. First Kitoko and now Oxley. It's that bastard, Hook."

"Hook didn't do this," whispered Wendy. "This isn't Hook's style."

"Whoever it was will pay with Peter's wrath." Tink smiled painfully.

"Yes, and then whoever feels Peter's wrath will take revenge against him, and then Peter will retaliate, and it will go on forever and ever, this cycle of violence and pain and dead boys." Wendy stretched out the linen wrappings. "Here, sit up."

"No." Tink closed her eyes. "No wrappings. I'll bear these wounds."

Wendy held up the wrappings. "They'll become infected."

Tink's eyes popped open, and she gave Wendy an annoyed look. "My people carved this island with their magic. I'm not going to get an infection."

With one hand, she pushed Wendy backward, her strength staggering, even in this state. Wendy looked around, making sure that there was no one near them.

"You can stop this, Tink," she hissed. "And if you refuse to listen to me, Oxley's blood will be on your hands too."

Maybe it was the bomb that had shaken the fairy to her core, or the fact that her consciousness was spotty, but this time, when

Tink opened her mouth to protest, no sounds emerged. Bells of mourning began to ring out through Pan Island, and Wendy imagined Peter lowering Oxley's body into the sea. *I will have to tell his father*, Wendy thought with a shock. When she turned back, Tink was standing beside her, and the fairy spoke in a voice just above a whisper.

"I know what you seek. But you think I have answers I do not." Tink moaned as she pressed her hand onto her wounded side. "You think that I'm a naive little girl who can't see her own truth, someone like the person you were when you first came to this island, but I'm not." The fairy closed her eyes, wincing as she stretched one bloodied knee over the other. "You would ask me to betray Peter, and think that I would help you destroy the boy I love simply because of his dark secret."

Wendy gasped, half out of shock and half out of anger.

"You know about the Shadow."

Tink nodded. "Of course. I hear all things, Wendy. The whispers of the trees, the yearnings of waves. I know that Peter sent his monster to kill my people and the pirates on the Sunned Shore. He hides the truth because he knows it will hurt me."

Wendy shook her head and let out a murmur of disgust.

"Tink, no. He doesn't tell you because he's afraid you will take your powers away from him. It's not to save your feelings. Peter cares nothing of your feelings."

"You don't know that!"

Wendy put a hand on her shoulder. "Take a breath."

A cruel smile crossed Tink's face. "I know more than you could ever fathom with your limited human mind." She reached out a thin finger and traced it down the collar of Wendy's bloodied dress. "I know that even though you loathe Peter, you still desire him. I know that you have many more feelings for Booth than you let on. In fact, your heart pulls to him even now."

Wendy blinked, struggling to control the anger rising up inside of her. Tink let her fingers crawl up to Wendy's face. "And

I know that you aren't really on our side, no matter what you say, no matter how often you spread these . . ." Her fingers were on Wendy's mouth now, pressing against her peach lips. Wendy sat back with disgust, wiping her mouth. "You betray Booth with your body, and you betray Peter with your mind."

"You're delusional," Wendy spit out. "All of that may be true, but this isn't about me, Tink. The question is, how can you overlook a genocide?"

Tink's arms began trembling at the word. Finally, Wendy had hit the right spot.

"Here." Wendy helped her lie back down in the hammock. "Don't injure yourself further." Tink's eyes filled with star-streaked tears, and her voice was pained.

"The only thing that keeps Peter from calling the Shadow is that he thinks I don't know about it. That's what needs to continue. To keep everyone safe."

"But if you know, how could you possibly . . ."

"Love him?" Tink tilted her head. "Because I know no other way. Love finds us. It twists us; it bears our sins, our shame. I bear that because I love Peter. He's not perfect . . ."

"He's a murderer," Wendy snapped, hearing her own words pull at a deep understanding within her. "You're speaking as though he forgot to send a love letter. What you have for him is not love," she snarled, her patience for Tink's nonsense worn thin. "It's delusion. You're in love with your own delusions."

Tink stared hard into Wendy's eyes before softly answering her. "Even if that is true . . . it is the only love I have. And I will take him, Shadow and all."

With a sad sigh, Tink turned away from Wendy, curling her wings protectively around her body.

"I will not help you defeat Peter, not even for my own people. I would rip out my own heart to save his. You must understand." The fairy's voice quivered.

"No, I don't understand. You will sit idly by while Peter kills innocent people; you have watched him destroy races. The Lost Boys will die in this war, Tink; you know that." Tink's body remained turned away from her, as still as stone. Wendy turned to go, her heart simmering with an anger, but then she glanced her feet—her bare feet. Her shoes had been blown off by the blast, and now she was looking at her toes, which were spotted with Lost Boy blood.

"NO."

She furiously spun around and shoved the hammock violently, rocking the fairy's body. Then she crouched over Tink's face, her anger washing over both of them. "Tink, you may be the most powerful being in Neverland, but you're the most pathetic coward I've ever known. You're worse than Peter, because he acknowledges his evil. You let yours rule your heart with complicity, a lazy evil that is somehow worse than Peter's."

She lowered herself to the level of Tink's face, which was hidden behind her faintly glimmering wing. Wendy lowered her voice until it was a gentle, unbearable tone.

"Tink, I pity you, and I will until the moment Peter kills me or the Shadow rips me apart."

Under her wing, Tink murmured something.

"What did you say?" Wendy snapped.

Tink slowly uncurled her wings, revealing a face streaked with tears. "I don't know the song. That's what you want, isn't it? The song that calls the Shadow."

Wendy blinked in shock. "Yes. I need to know the song so that I can call it out of Peter, and then we have to destroy it somehow. Tink if you know anything, you need to tell me. God, please." She grabbed Tink's ripped-up hands and pressed her lips to them. "I am not above begging."

The fairy wouldn't look at her. "I don't know the song, I swear, but even if I did, I wouldn't tell you. I won't betray Peter. I . . . can't."

Wendy ground her teeth together. "Then why are you telling me this?"

Tink took a deep breath and repeated the words that Wendy had heard only once, from the mouth of the mermaid queen. "The one who bears it and the one who fears it."

Wendy froze. "What are you saying? What does that mean?"

"Come closer."

Wendy leaned forward, bending over Tink's crippled form, her ear pressed against Tink's bruised lips.

"It means I am not the only fairy left in Neverland. The one who fears it has been left behind."

Wendy sat back in amazement as Tink reached out and grabbed her hand roughly. She gasped as Tink poured the power of flight into her, stronger and purer than Peter's had ever been. White light circled out from her palm into Wendy's, glittering tendrils that crept up her arm and soaked into her body.

"The fairy—he waits forever in fear in the Forsaken Garden, waiting for a death that will never come, a mere shadow of the king he once was."

Wendy's memory flashed to the immaculate wooden carving of the fairy king that graced the door to Captain Hook's chambers.

"Qaralius?"

Tink gave the slightest of nods. "He knows the song."

"How do you know he's alive?"

Tink turned her head. "I hear him crying in the night, pitiful cries of such regret and sadness that I cannot stomach them." She grasped Wendy's hand for a moment before turning over. "Go to the Forsaken Garden. Tread lightly, but hurry." The fairy's lips trembled. "The fairy king and I both live in a prison of our own making—his of silver, mine of love. I've come to believe that pain is our race's destiny."

She waved her hand, and Wendy's feet moved backward as the heat of Tink's magic pushed her away.

"Leave me. This is the second time you have tended to my wounds, and each time it hurts all the more."

Wendy sputtered, her brain wheeling with this new

information. "Tink, you can't just tell me that and then turn me away. Please!"

Tink's wings beat back and forth, thrumming quarter notes through the trees. "Wendy, the war isn't coming—it's here. It came wrapped in ribbons. You must go now. Any minute, Peter will discover that you've taken the pipes, and his anger will consume us all."

Tink tilted her ear toward the sea.

"They are giving Oxley to the sea now, so you have some time. You must go now."

Wendy closed her eyes, reaching for her strength in the face of this shattering news. There was a numbness that threatened to overtake her emotions, and somewhere past that was the will to move, past her shocking grief over Oxley, past the anger she felt toward Peter, past the disgust at whoever had sent a bomb into a nest full of children. A light flickered in her mind, a tiny flare of hope, and she thought of Michael's face . . . and all she had to lose. Wendy grabbed on to it and buried it in her heart before crouching to go—for she had much to do and little time to do it.

"Wendy?"

She looked back at Tink. "Yes?"

"Whatever you do, don't go alone."

Wendy stood silently, letting the breath of Neverland wash over in her in all its sweetness before she answered: "When you have known real love, you are never truly alone. I hope that one day you understand that."

Then Wendy soared up into the air, flying quicker than she had ever dared before, freed by the fact that her flight had not come from Peter. As she soared upward, she spared a small prayer for Tink, for a girl driven mad by desire. Her thoughts turned to Hook, and how she couldn't wait to tell him that changing the fate of Neverland might be easier than changing a damaged heart. Her own, on the other hand, was beating quite strong.

CHAPTER TEN

Wendy flew upward, the branches of Centermost flying by in a blur. She soared past the kitchen—where splatters of blood stained the floor—and past the teepee, where Peter had once told stories of bravery that wooed a starry-eyed Wendy. She flew up through the trees to the armory, where Peter had arranged for all the newest weapons to be kept. Wendy landed hard on a long wood platform and ran forward, toward the pile of weapons covered with rain-splattered tarps the color of a gray sky. Moving quickly, she began throwing back the coverings one by one, looking for what she needed, pausing to grab a fancy silver sword before she found what she was really looking for: an ax.

She tucked the sword into the belt of her dress and held the ax firmly in both hands as she leapt up, her body catching the air like a plume of steam, moving ever upward. Wendy's heart was pounding nervously, and for just a moment, as the sky opened up above her, she longed for a time when she wouldn't be scared all the time, when life would just . . . be. Someday a time would come when the lives of her family wouldn't hang in the balance with every passing hour. Someday she would once again sit and read a book only to lose herself in its pages.

Unfortunately, that day would not be today, as evidenced by the large wooden structure that hung in front of her, its body

84

tossed back and forth mercilessly by the wind like a cheap toy. Her voice rose nervously as she quietly called out his name.

"Booth?"

"Wendy?"

She stopped herself in front of the cage, breathing hard, her dress blowing around her.

"Booth, move back from the door."

He lunged forward, pressing his narrow face between the bars, his eyes red with grief. "Wendy . . . thank God you're alive! I heard an explosion and feared the worst! What fresh hells are happening on this island? Visions of you strewn about had me fearing that I would never get to tell you all that lies in my heart, and so I must confess to you now that—" Booth blinked, interrupting his own stream of everything she wanted to hear.

"Wendy, by God, are you holding an ax?"

Wendy took the weapon in both hands, gripping the splintered handle as hard as she could.

"We don't have time for a conversation right now. Move back from the door, Booth."

Booth's blue eyes widened, and he swiftly moved back from the door, pressing himself against the far end of the cage, his face held in glowing awe of her. With a grunt, Wendy brought the ax down on the bamboo cage. It stuck in the wood, and she almost lost the ax, her hand jerking back in surprise before catching the handle.

"Dammit!"

As she swore, she heard Booth give a deep chuckle. "Wendy Darling of Kensington, what would your parents say to hear you use that sort of language?"

Thwack.

The ax stuck again in the door. Again. A bead of sweat dripped down Wendy's face and down between her breasts. Booth spoke out of the corner of the cage. "Try swinging it downward, not sideways—"

"I know how to use an ax, Booth." Wendy snapped, her annoyance triggering her to swing harder, faster.

"Well, then," Booth nodded. "I shall be silent in my corner and say no more."

"Good."

On the next blow, the cage began coming apart. Each strike of the ax ricocheted up Wendy's arms and into her jaw, the sound so loud that she swore the entire island could probably hear it—from the treetops all the way down to the seashore, where Oxley's body was floating out to sea. *Oxley.*

Crack.

Crack.

For him, she would beat Peter. For him, she would make all right again.

She brought the ax down, and the bottom of the cage began to splinter open. "Hold on to the side bars," she ordered Booth as she raised the ax up above her head, thinking that it was surprisingly hard to get leverage when you were suspended in the air. Wendy took a deep breath as Booth wrapped his hands around one of the bars, and she imagined Peter's face as she brought it down one last time.

CRACK.

The bottom of Booth's cage split and fell open, the plank dangling from one last wicker tie. Booth's legs shot out from under him, and suddenly he was hanging above Pan Island, the ground thousands of feet below him. Wendy hooked the ax on a branch before slowly reaching out to Booth with one hand, taking his elbow softly, her lungs catching when her fingers brushed his skin. Here they were, with no barriers between them for the first time since she had kissed him in his attic so long ago. Wendy suddenly felt shy, here with him so close.

What if he doesn't want me anymore? What if . . . Then he turned, and their eyes met, and he pulled her into his arms, wrapping her up in himself, and Wendy gasped out loud at the relief she felt. It was as if by holding her he was taking a weight off her shoulders and onto himself.

"Wendy," he breathed. "If you would be so kind . . ."

He looked desperate then, all pretense falling away as his eyes fell gracefully over her. The next sentence looked as though it pained him.

"May I hold you?" Booth asked. "For just a second. I know we're in quite the rush, but . . ."

"In London, I thought you were dead," he whispered into her hair. "I thought they would find your body floating in the Thames." His lips pressed ever so softly against the side of her neck, his gentle touch roaring through her like a stampede.

"How did you get here?" she asked, longing instead to ask him other, more abstract questions: *Do you still love me? Has Peter ruined me for you?*

Booth pulled back and frowned.

"In the early morning, John appeared outside of my attic window. He said that you had been kidnapped and that he needed help saving you. I didn't hesitate for a second. I never wondered why he came to me instead of the police, or how he had gotten on top of our roof." Booth sighed. "I followed him blindly, over the rooftops and into an alley. Before I knew it, he had grabbed my hand, and we were flying over London as I screamed. He wouldn't speak to me, except to tell me repeatedly not to let go of his hand."

Wendy shook her head, disgusted.

Booth continued. "When we rose above the clouds, Peter was there, waiting for me . . . with a black bag." He cringed. "The last thing I saw was Peter bringing down a giant stick . . . and then I woke up just in time to see you declare your love for him."

Wendy squeezed him for just a moment, hoping to reassure him that what he had seen between Peter and her was nothing more than a lie, but she suspected Booth might have discerned a kernel of truth: that even though she hated him, her attraction to Peter was apparent.

"We have to go," Wendy whispered, wishing that they could stay tangled up in each other forever, floating above the all the world's problems. "Don't let go, whatever you do. You'll fall."

Booth nodded as he kicked his legs underneath him. "I remember that little fact from my delightful trip from London with John." He paused for a moment, letting himself rise up in the air, his fingers tangled with Wendy's. "I may be off my trolley, but it's somewhat remarkable, is it not? This feeling of flying? There is nothing quite like it, not in all the world."

Wendy sighed her agreement as they plunged away from the broken cage.

"Speaking of your trip here . . ." Booth turned his head, an unhappy expression marring his so-welcomed face.

Wendy shook her head. "You're not going to like this, but there are two more things we have to get before we can leave."

They flew down to the familiar stench of the pips' hovel.

Floating above Booth's shoulders, Wendy peered into the water barrel. A baby black-and-yellow snake slithered across the surface, and Wendy yelped when it bit at her. With a frown, she plunged her hand inside, grabbing the snake swiftly behind the head before flinging it out of the barrel and into the trees. When she looked down at Booth, he was staring at her with utter amazement.

"Wendy, what kind of delightful jungle woman have you become out here?" He smiled. "You're so fetching in this strange place." His smile faded as she took a breath. "You know, I could certainly go into the barrel instead of you. A lady of society going in doesn't seem quite right."

Wendy rolled her eyes before turning back to the water barrel.

"Things are different here in Neverland, Booth. You had better get used to it."

"I guess I must then."

Wendy glanced again into the barrel. She could see the faint gold glimmer of the pipes dancing underneath the water, their glow throwing light onto the sides of the wood. She hovered momentarily above the barrel before slowly letting herself sink below the surface, the dark water swallowing her head. It was black and deep, the worn wood of the sides rotted. She sunk lower, her feet brushing the rough bottom of the barrel. She bent her knees and reached down, her hands flailing in the water as she struggled to find the pipes. Finally, the tip of her fingers brushed metal, and her hands wrapped around the instrument.

She closed her eyes as she pushed herself off the wood, her body rising, half flying, half floating back toward the light, where Booth was waiting for her. Her head broke the surface and she took a deep, gasping breath, and Booth let out of a sigh of relief, offering a hand as she landed beside him.

He smiled, and she was struck at how changed they both were; they weren't children in his father's bookstore; they were different people and yet still the same. Booth was still the child that had stolen her apples and the man who had slowly, seductively pulled a glove from her hand to kiss her palm. She caught his eyes tracing down her wet form before he caught himself and looked flustered, and he glanced to the ground and then the ceiling, a blush climbing up his cheeks.

"Did you get them?"

Wendy tucked the golden pipes inside her blouse as she shivered. "That was the easy part." She shook the water off her body. "Now, let's go get John."

Booth groaned.

"I hate that little bugger. He's even worse here than he was in London, the prat. Are you sure it's not Michael that we can bring instead?"

At Michael's name, Wendy's breath caught under her rib. She tried not to think of him often, her Michael, because nothing but pain followed. She missed him so much—the way his head curled just under her chin, his petal-soft cheeks, the way he said her name with a hint of a question: *Wendy?*

"Michael is somewhere safe, thank God, but John is not. I can't leave him here with Peter once again. Not only did Peter whip him last time, but the guilt of leaving him behind almost killed me."

She expected Booth to berate her weak heart as Peter would have done, but instead, he took her face gently in his hands. "You are the best sister that anyone has ever known. Your parents, wherever they may be at this very moment, would be so proud."

"Thank you, Booth."

He stared at her for a long moment before stepping backward; they both heard the voices of Lost Boys rising up from the beach. Booth snatched a tattered piece of maroon fabric from one of the Lost Boys' hammocks and tied it around his head. He tucked the fancy long sword that Wendy had grabbed into the waistband of his pants. His eyes met hers.

"Do you need a weapon as well?"

Wendy smiled back at him. "I'm fine." For some reason, she didn't tell him about the gemstone dagger that was always tucked securely against her back, the weight of it uniquely comforting. The dagger felt like her secret, a little bit of fairy magic that was hers alone. Wendy turned, her hand reaching out instinctively for Booth. His fingers wrapped around hers and they both rose into the air. Wendy pulled Booth behind her as they made their way down to the shore.

Through a swatch of blue-veined leaves, Booth and Wendy watched the Lost Boys morosely make their way up the beach. She watched in silence as they marched past her hiding spot, their sniffles yanking painfully at her heart, the devastation on their faces profound for ones so young. Though Peter fancied himself their father, the truth was in their eyes: Oxley had been the closest thing any of them had known to real family. She wanted to pull them close, to whisper away their demons, but she couldn't.

The Lost Boys would burn with anger until pushed into a war they weren't ready for. And to stop the war, she had to stop Peter. And the Shadow.

Only Peter and the generals remained on the beach now, the three of them watching the rolling waves murmur against the shore. After a moment, Peter reached out and pulled the two remaining generals into a forced embrace. John leaned in too much, hungry for Peter's affection, whereas Abbott pulled back, his body going rigid at Peter's touch. Peter touched their faces for a moment and then launched off the ground without a word.

"Don't move," whispered Wendy, her body freezing up in fear. Peter passed about twenty feet over their heads flying straight for his hut, where he would soon notice that the prisoner that usually dangled below it was missing. Also, his pipes. And the girl he wanted.

Abbott turned away from John, his shoulders heaving. Wendy's heart twisted painfully at Abbott's grief, for this general who had lost all his friends. She longed to take him with them, but Abbott was needed here more than ever. She squeezed Booth's hands, now wrapped slightly around her waist, and she was aware of his warmth.

"It's time."

"But the general is still there!"

"He's fine. He hates Peter."

"That doesn't mean he won't betray us to him."

"No, it doesn't." Wendy watched Abbott cry, her heart pulling out of her chest at his unfathomable loss. She stood. "Peter will know everything very soon anyway." Her heart pounded as she pulled Booth forward out of their hiding spot, aware that this would probably be the last time that her feet touched the soft sand of Pan Island. Together they sprinted onto the beach, approaching the boys from behind. When they were almost upon him, John spun suddenly, his eyes going wide.

"Wendy? What are you—" He didn't have time to finish as

Booth tackled John with such force that it knocked him back several feet into the sand.

Abbott stepped back and raised his hands, and his voice betrayed his confusion as he looked down at the boys scuffling in the sand. "What are you doing out of your cage?"

Booth didn't even look up as he wrestled John into submission.

"As it turns out, Abbott, I am a man who can walk upright, not an animal. I'm Booth."

He pushed John's face down in the sand while he reached out a hand to shake. After a second, Abbott awkwardly took it.

"We're here for him," Booth added.

John looked up at his sister. "Wendy! Booth! I'm sorry! I had to, Peter—"

He didn't have time to finish. Booth's fist met the side of John's cheek with a crack, and he slumped sadly onto the beach. Booth flexed his hand happily. "That's for shoving me into a black bag with Peter. Sorry, Wendy, but I must be honest—I've always wanted to punch your utterly terrible brother."

Abbott's eyes lit up as he stared at Booth. "I like you," he announced, and Booth grinned. Then Abbott's smile faded. "Peter's not going to like this."

Wendy looked at him. "I'm sorry to leave you with this, Abbott, but that's why you should go . . . now. So that you can claim ignorance. We are taking John, and we won't be coming back."

John struggled on the ground, but Booth pushed his knee against his spine. "Be still, John, and it won't hurt."

Abbott's blue eyes, sharp like a cold sea, watched her face. "It's here, isn't it?" Wendy nodded before reaching out and taking the general's hand.

"We're going to end this, Abbott. Peter's reign must end."

Abbott shook his head sadly. "Peter will have us fight. You know that. It will come to blood."

"Yes, and I need you to do everything you can from the inside to derail his plans."

Abbott looked up at the sky, his voice choked. "I'm going to die, aren't I? Just like Oxley."

Wendy grabbed his wrist. "Not if I have anything to do with it."

Abbott stepped away from her and began making his way toward the giant roots that held up Pan Island. "I didn't see anything here. In fact, I am probably just hearing the whispers of ghosts, nothing more." Just before he stepped back into the thick trees, he looked at Wendy. "I was wrong about one ghost though. She's more solid than mist."

Wendy smiled at him, and then he was gone, mysterious Abbott, the general who had always held his cards close to his chest. Wendy turned back to Booth, who was hauling John to his feet, blood gushing out of his nose. She had just opened her mouth to ask if they were ready when a huge gust of wind passed over them, bursting through the trees. A scream of rage echoed down from the top of the island, filling Wendy's chest with fear.

Booth's eyes grew wide. "He knows."

Without waiting for their consent, Wendy grabbed John and Booth by the hand before shooting out over the ocean, her face determined as she aimed toward the mainland.

CHAPTER ELEVEN

With Booth clutching one hand and John the other, Wendy soared low over the water, flying as fast as her body would allow. Tink's flight was so clean it pulsed through Wendy's bloodstream, a white heat whispering through her body like a lover. *Fly, fly, fly . . .*

"Why are we flying so low?" yelled Booth over the wind.

"Peter!" Wendy answered. "Peter always flies high up. He doesn't know I have flight, so he'll be looking for boats near the shore, at first anyway. We just have to make it to the mainland, and then we can hide."

Underneath them, waves gently rose and sank, the deep blue peppered with foaming white caps. John was struggling, attempting to twist his wrist away from her hand, and Wendy gave a yelp as he yanked—hard. She leaned into him as they flew, hissing in his ear. "If you want me to drop you in the middle of the ocean, so help me God, I will. I doubt even Peter could find you in the middle of Neverland Sea."

John continued trying to pull his wrist free from Wendy's grip, causing her to tilt.

"Dammit, John! Stop it!"

"You're taking me against my will!"

"I won't leave you behind again!"

Their argument began growing, at once overtaking Wendy's

assurance that this was the right idea as she struggled to keep the boys aloft. "John! STOP!" John continued turning his wrist until Booth's light voice cut over them both.

"John, do tell me: have you read *The Great Ocean Adventure* by Sir Thomas R. Taylor?" John shot Booth an annoyed look, but he continued speaking in a calm voice as they soared across the water. "It appears you have not. Well, in *The Great Ocean Adventure*, William is lost at sea, with only his faithful German shepherd to help him. It's really a commentary on how society leaves orphans to fend on their own with no resources to aid them, but anyway, adrift on the ocean, William's dog helps him navigate toward a deserted island using only his sense of smell. There, William finds food and a compass that will eventually lead him home."

"Why are you telling me this?" yelled John. "I don't know how many times I have to tell you, but I don't care about your bloody books!"

Booth looked over at Wendy with such a magnanimous smile that her heart tipped inside of her and she almost lost their forward momentum.

Just fly. Just fly.

Booth continued speaking, his voice lulling, calming to her rising panic. "Well, William makes it to the island, but his dog does not."

"And why is that?" snapped John. "Was William forced to eat him?"

"No. His dog was snatched out of the boat by a tiger shark as William pulled the vessel into the shallows. By the time our hero got around the boat, all that was left of his dog was some floating fur, and the water was the color of blood."

"Booth!" Wendy exclaimed. "That's an awful story!"

Booth stared hard at her brother. "So, John, if a shark can find a dog in the shallows, how long do you think it would take one to find you in the middle of the ocean with fresh blood upon your hands and face?" John fell silent. "Would you still like Wendy to leave you in the middle of the ocean?"

Wendy couldn't hear what John mumbled.

"What was that, John?"

"I said, FINE. I'll stop struggling, you pretentious bore."

"Good choice, John, old pal."

John faced the ocean, which was whipping by at an alarming speed.

"I'm not your pal. I'm not your friend. Why would a Darling stoop so low to be friends with a Whitfield? Part of the reason we're in this mess is because you couldn't keep your filthy, working-class hands off my sister!"

Booth just snickered, but Wendy winced.

"John," she said, "if I weren't flying across the ocean right now, I swear . . ."

"You would what? Hit me? Like Peter? Like the other generals? Like Booth?"

Her brother's hurt passed through her like a sharp lick of wind. *He's right. I shouldn't have hurt him.* She was about to reply when just underneath her there was a flash of scales. Her head screamed to pull up, but by then it was already too late.

"Shark!" screamed Booth.

Worse, Wendy thought. The nose that peeked out of the water was white and hard, as if it were made of marble. Black eyes fringed with lashes of blue and violet and a crown made of human bones soon followed.

"Pull up!" shrieked John at the same time that Booth bellowed, "What the hell is that?"

Celestial blue and pale violet hair swarmed up like a beast from the deep. The queen's huge eyes met Wendy's as her pearled lips finally appeared from underneath the water, lips that Wendy had prayed she would never see again.

"Girl, it's so good to smell your blood again."

Wendy let out a cry and jerked up, but it was too late; the

queen's large six-fingered hand shot out and latched around Wendy's ankle. The three of them were jerked to a hard stop, hovering above the water as the queen of the mermaids looked on them with amusement. With a wicked grin, she drew a thin line across Wendy's skin with a sharp fingernail. A drop of Wendy's blood fell into the water, and the queen's eyes went wide with desire.

"Still pure, I see. Now, I must ask: what are you doing this far from Pan Island, little one?"

Booth and John instinctively closed their eyes at the sound of her pure voice, which was like a thousand choirs singing and was almost too much to bear. Wendy flinched, but she kept her eyes open and pulled up against her captor's grip. They didn't budge as Queen Eryne blinked her eyes lazily.

"Are you heading back to the *Sudden Night*? Hook's in the Eastern Sea, you know. Preparing for war, meeting with Jaali Oba—reimbursing him for the *favor*."

Wendy shook her head. "No. We're heading toward the mainland."

Booth finally opened his eyes and let out what could best be described as a stunned groan as Queen Eryne looked over him.

"Young man, I haven't seen you before."

"Hello, ma'am," he whispered, his eyes wide and dazzled by her beauty.

A tendril of jealously curled around Wendy's heart, and she looked over at Booth with annoyance. "Do. Not. Gush."

With a feral smile, the queen reached up with her other hand and traced a line down his face.

"When this is all over, you should come visit us in Miath. I'm sure my girls would love to try a piece." Her forked tongue ran over her lips.

"I don't think so," snapped Wendy, her patience wearing thin. Her heart was pounding hard in her chest, where the exhaustion of the escape and of hauling two others over the sea was settling in. Her wrists were sore, her hands were going numb, and they didn't have time for this little . . . distraction. Wendy cleared her throat and looked back at the mermaid queen. "Your majesty, if you wouldn't mind," she spoke with sharp tones, "we happen to be fleeing from a sociopath with supernatural powers at the moment, so could you please let me know what you need?"

The queen's eyes narrowed. "You're going to find the Shadow."

Wendy shook her head, John tipping ever so slightly with the effort to listen in. "No. We're going to learn how to defeat the Shadow. And then I'm sure it will find us."

The queen blinked twice, and the blackness that covered the surface of her eyes was siphoned back into clear blue glass irises. She tightened her grip on Wendy's ankle, and her words were like a hum of the waves.

"Do you really believe you can defeat it? Or will you doom us all?"

Wendy swallowed, the salt from the waves licking at her lips. "I will try my best."

"Your best?" The queen cackled, a mean look marring her stunningly beautiful face. "Your best may lead to the end of Neverland."

Without warning, the queen let go of Wendy's ankle and surged upward, both of her hands grabbing the back of Wendy's head. Booth and John tried to hold on as she struggled fruitlessly to pull back from the queen, but instead they were splashed into the choppy water. To Wendy's surprise, Queen Eryne pressed her crown holding a skeletal seahorse against Wendy's forehead.

"If you succeed, my people will sing your name deep into Sybella's halls and be forever indebted to you. And if you fail . . ."

Wendy twisted her mouth. "I know. My blood will feed your coral gardens forever. Etcetera."

The queen's breath washed over her face, smelling of sea salt and oysters thick with brine. "Yes, my dear." She pulled back from Wendy. "What a curious creature you are, girl from another world. Please make note that you don't destroy our world."

The queen's brow furrowed, and her grip on the back of Wendy's head tightened, and Wendy felt as though her brain was being torn apart.

"Go pick up your boys before they drown, and get to the mainland quickly. Peter is about, but I'll make sure he doesn't see you."

The queen gave Wendy a long look and released her. Wendy darted forward toward where the boys were struggling to keep their heads above the growing waves. Booth was lying on his back, one arm wrapped around her brother to help keep him afloat as he thrashed back and forth, screaming.

"John! Calm down!" Booth sputtered as John pawed at him, pulling him under. When he saw her approaching, Booth shot out his hand, and Wendy grabbed it as she passed overhead.

Water poured off their soaked clothes as they rose up beside Wendy, their hands linked together. As the wind whipped around them, Wendy smiled wryly at the position she had found herself in once again: *Neverland isn't safe above or below.* A broad swirl of water and moist cloud was rising to surround them as they flew, a camouflage of mist to hide them from navy eyes. They flew silently, all of them lost in their own thoughts. A minute or two passed before Booth broke the silence, muttering quietly.

"Wendy, does everything in Neverland want to kill you? Was that an actual mermaid?"

"Yes," replied Wendy. "And yes. They're quite mean."

"A mermaid!" Booth sighed happily, despite the fact that he had just almost drowned. "What is this place across the stars?" His face was delirious with that same delight that Wendy had once known herself. Though his smile remained, his eyes changed when they rested gently on Wendy's determined face. "Though truthfully, I must confess that in my imagination, they were much less inclined to the murder of young girls. Did she say she wanted your blood?"

He sounded so appalled that Wendy would have smiled if she had not been so shaken. She silently squeezed Booth's hand and focused on flying, faster. *Faster.*

"John!" Wendy said quietly. "What direction are we coming in from?" There was a long pause as John looked at her with surprise.

"You're asking me?"

"Answer her!" intoned Booth, but Wendy quieted him with a look.

"Yes. I need to figure out the best place to set down. The answer benefits you as much as it does me if you don't want to be hiking for days through the Neverland wilderness."

John stared at her for a moment before rubbing his glasses with his free hand. "Considering that you kidnapped me, you should be grateful for any knowledge that I'll give you."

Booth growled under his breath, and John relented.

"But, I guess that I would say that we are approaching on the south side, maybe just to the east of Port Duette?"

Wendy closed her eyes, trying to remember the map in Peter's hut. "So, we need to fly over the island heading northwest, correct? To reach the Forsaken Garden?"

"The Forsaken Garden!" exclaimed Booth and John at the same time, with very different tones.

"I need to think for a moment," she whispered. "Just a minute."

John gestured with his head and sighed with annoyance, as if he was put out by Wendy's request.

"Fly that way. We should be there by now," he said, and though Wendy didn't trust him entirely, she understood that John needed her to listen, and so she did. She turned them sideward, only ocean and mist visible around them; the swirl of invisibility also lent itself to blindness, each moment more terrifying than the next.

"John, are you sure this is the—"

But she didn't have time to finish her sentence, for just like that, the main island was upon them, a world of green rearing violently up from the water. Wendy didn't even have time to pull up as their ankles dragged in the surf, the mist around them dissipating quickly into the air. The waves began their steep ascent to the shore as Wendy saw the sand, the glorious pearled sand of Neverland, and her body collapsed in exhaustion, rapidly losing height as she dropped out of the air. The breath she had been holding since she spoke with Tink was exhaled in relief. Somehow, she had made it, and these three precious items from Pan Island had made it with her.

CHAPTER TWELVE

With a clumsy downward tumble, Wendy dropped Booth and John onto the shore, water splashing over their ankles as they sank to their knees. While she hadn't had to carry their weight, the exhaustion of their sprint rushed through her body like a poison released. She hit the ground hard and pitched forward into the sand, her hands jamming up against wet shells, her arms numb as she crawled forward, away from the waves. Booth bent over her, brushing the sand off her face as Wendy dry-heaved onto the shore, her limbs trembling with the effort.

"You brave girl. You got us here."

Then she felt something pulling out the marrow from her bones; the power of flight left her, tracing its way down her wrists and out through the points of her fingertips. Tink knew that they had made it. She sagged forward. "It's gone. The flight." She looked over and saw John watching her silently. "I couldn't leave either of you behind."

Wendy thought she saw her brother quickly blink away tears, but he turned his head so fast that she couldn't be sure.

She took a deep breath and pushed herself up, wiping the bile from her mouth. "We need to hike up underneath the trees. Quickly. Peter could spot us from here." Booth helped her to her feet as John watched both of them with narrowed eyes.

"Oy, John, can you help?" Booth demanded.

John looked skeptically at Booth.

"Why should I help you do anything? Neither of you care about me, not while you're mooning over each other. It's disgusting." Even though his words were sharp, his tone had taken on a defeatist tone. John Darling looked down at the sand and took a deep breath, filling his lungs.

Booth stepped forward. "I swear to God, John, if you yell . . ."

"I won't," snapped John angrily. He shoved himself up underneath Wendy's arm and began helping Booth drag her off the beach. "But only because you're incapable of helping my sister alone."

They shuffled across the empty beach, which was bare save the skeletal remains of some enormous creature that loomed over their heads. Its open jaws were occupied with fluttering teal birds that had dark black streaks marking their wings. They squawked angrily at the soaked intruders that had crashed into their nest, their cries growing more alarmed as the three of them made their way to the tree line.

From there it was a steep uphill hike—the jungle steadily climbed up from the shore, and soon they were all out of breath. Booth was still helping Wendy walk, and Wendy was very aware at how close he was to her, his arm looped around her side, his fingertips searing into the skin underneath her breast, their hips moving together as they slogged their way through the sand.

I am so tired.

As Booth staggered forward, Wendy hung her head, embarrassed at how much the flight had cost her, but even then she knew that it wasn't just the flight; it was Tink's words, Oxley's death, the way Booth looked at her. It was John's battered mind and Captain Hook and the Shadow and Michael somewhere far away from her.

It was Neverland, and it was draining who she was, drop by precious drop.

John shuffled behind them, offering infuriating commentary as the ground rose to meet them.

"You're not good enough, you know."

Booth raised an eyebrow at John. "What's that, mate?"

"You're not good enough for her, for my sister. You're below her level. Our level."

Booth turned his head back to look John square in the face, his handsome jaw clenched angrily, brown curls wet with saltwater plastered against his forehead.

"You'll hear no argument from me on that note. Wendy is far too good for me, for anyone, really. John, you may think me transient, but I assure you, my feelings for your sister are no retiring light."

John rolled his eyes. "I hate that way you speak, like someone far above your station."

"And how should I speak to suit you, John? Like a beggar?"

"If everyone could just shut up," snapped Wendy, surprised at her own irritability, "that would be fantastic."

Overhead, the canopy of trees stretched out as the three of them passed underneath, the cool shadow of the jungle swallowing them whole. They made their way upward, the sand giving way to soft black soil and tangled roots underneath their feet. Birds called out to each other overhead, and they watched as they feasted on lavender caterpillars that inched alongside them.

Wendy took a moment to look back, letting out a small sigh of relief when after about an hour of hiking she saw that they had left the beach far below them. Her body was spent, and so, with a graceful surrender, she pointed to an open area where an onyx rock sat surrounded by tree roots.

"Let's rest here for the night," she said.

Without a word, Booth reached out with his hand and thoroughly brushed the dirt off the rock before letting Wendy sit down on it. She stared at him as he gently helped her down and, without thinking about it, she took his face in her hands and kissed him, long and hard, the way that she had wanted to in the attic that day long ago.

Booth straightened as she took his mouth in hers, but he rapidly dissolved under her kisses like rain hitting a steaming street. The taste of his mouth hadn't changed since London; this boy still tasted like cream and books, but there was a tang of bittersweet now, a loss of childhood. He gave an involuntary moan and wrapped his arms hard around her, pressing his body to hers in need as their tongues tangled together. He was cool where she was burning alive, and she felt them being molded together, as if heated by a kiln.

"This makes me particularly vomitous," uttered John, and Wendy and Booth pulled away from each other, their cheeks burning with embarrassment.

"Umm . . ." Booth was nervous, his face beet-red. Wendy looked at John and then back at Booth.

"Booth, could you give us a moment?"

Booth had never looked more relieved in his life, and he ran his hands happily through his brown hair. "Yes! Absolutely. I'm going to just take a quick jaunt around the perimeter, get a lay of the land and, um, whatnot."

While Wendy wished that it were John who would give her and Booth a moment, she nodded, settling her sore limbs back on the rock. John stared at her for a long moment, his face confused as if he were seeing her for the first time. Wendy held his gaze. Finally, he cleared his throat.

"You know you've killed us all, right? Peter's revenge for this . . ."

Wendy sat up. *So this is how this is going to go.*

"Probably. But honestly, John, perhaps you should ask yourself, how did your loyalty go to a boy who would kill us for doing what we please? Maybe you should ask how much fear and hate Peter has wrapped around your heart that you would turn on your own family."

He ignored her question as he rocked back on his heels, swinging back and forth in the same manner that her father often did. John opened his mouth, and Wendy prepared for a tart response, but instead, the voice that came out was soft and needy:

"What do you think our parents are doing right now?"

Wendy blinked in surprise.

"I haven't thought of it, though I do think of them often."

Her younger brother sighed dejectedly and sat on the ground near her feet. In silence, he began drawing images in the sand . . . a house . . . their house in Kensington Garden, with eight windows and the iron fence around the small yard. Then John added her mother's window boxes, the latch on the gate, every detail something Wendy knew deep inside of her, in that place where your childhood home is carved forever. As he drew, his voice was careful.

"Assuming that we are in the same approximate world of time, I would say . . ." He closed his eyes, and a fat tear dripped down his cheek, surprising Wendy. His voice was strangled as he choked out the words.

"I would say that Mother is sitting here, in her bedroom, wearing that silly lavender robe, the one with the lace around the neck that always itched me as a child. She is reading a book—perhaps something that she picked up from your shelf, something light and womanly—Lewis Rand, perhaps."

He sniffed as he began drawing the old oak trees that lined the sides of the house, trees that all three children had climbed.

"She misses her children, and she never lets go of the cross around her neck, which she clutches tightly. She clutches it as if it will save us all."

Wendy bit her lip to keep from crying, but it was no use. Tears flooded her eyes, the stubborn love for her brother and a yearning for home so potent it swelled in her chest. John continued.

"Liza isn't there anymore to bring up tea—she's surely been

fired for letting us go missing—and so now Father brings up tea for them, and he takes our mother's hand and kisses it."

Wendy was openly crying now, moving off the rock toward her brother.

"Father tries to reach her, but they are both so lost in their grief that they can't even look at each other." John looked up at her, his eyes fixed on Wendy's face.

"I miss Father," he said.

His face crumpled. All the Darlings had been broken by this place.

"I know," said Wendy.

She tried to remember comforting words that her father would use with John when he was upset, but she couldn't find any; she had never cared. The chasm between them seemed almost impassable.

"And our mother," John continued. "Though she was silly and overbearing and fussy, I loved her too, even though I never told her. And our father . . ." John started openly sobbing, the man that he was becoming curling back into the little boy who had never been accepted, who never felt like he was enough.

"Our father is standing at the window, and he's looking out at the stars, because somehow I think he knows that's where we are. I know because I feel his eyes on me everywhere."

Wendy clenched her jaw to keep from losing herself completely and instead focused on being strong for John. *He is the only one that matters in this moment.* He looked up at his sister, tears streaming down his face.

"I had no choice, Wendy. About bringing Booth. It was either bring him here or let Peter kill me."

Wendy cautiously reached out, letting her hand linger on his brown hair.

"There is always a choice," she said softly.

At that moment, Booth came tromping back through the forest, louder than Wendy would have liked. In his arms was a pile of luscious dripping fruit.

"I found us some dinner! Though in my delight, I neglected to see that these might indeed prove poisonous and therefore be inconsumable."

Wendy stood up and walked over to Booth, kissing him lightly on the cheek. She took two of the fruits out of his arms.

"Only these ones," she said. Then with a smile, she reached down and picked up a bright fuchsia fruit, a misshapen sphere that dripped with syrup when she bit into it, her eyes closing at the honeyed taste. Booth looked like he was about to faint.

John stood up and looked down at his drawing in the soil— the Darling house, in all its glory, their childhood captured so perfectly. Booth stepped forward to see what it was, and John scuffed it with his foot, dashing it all back into the fertile Neverland soil.

Wendy stared at him for a long moment, wondering just how much to trust John. As she watched him sniffle and wipe his nose in the same way he always had—with two fingers and a pouty face—she realized that the choice had been made long ago, when John had emerged out of her mother, screaming and colicky; he was her brother whether she liked it or not. He was her family, and if Wendy was going to win the battle for John's soul, then he had to know the entire truth.

She settled herself back down on the rock, tucking her legs underneath her dress.

"Grab a fruit and sit." Wendy smiled kindly as Booth knelt beside her and John plopped down with a sigh several feet away. She waited until they were both settled and lowered her voice, remembering Peter's stories in the teepee, how she had watched him with worshipful and naive eyes.

"I'm going to tell you a little story about a boy named Peter Pan and his Shadow."

Wendy took a thankful breath when she finished her story hours later. It had come tumbling out, detail after hideous detail. She had spared nothing; not the truth of who Peter Pan really was—a rich landowner's son—not Hook's obsession to both kill Peter and save Neverland, not the Shadow and its unholy relationship to Peter, not the brutality of the mermaids or Captain Maison's allegiance with Peter. The only thing she had not mentioned to John was that Peter's pipes were currently pressed against her chest.

The looks on the boy's faces were vastly different; while Booth's reflected horror, John stared at her with an uncomfortable disbelief.

"It's not true!" he mumbled. "It can't be."

"It is." Wendy's eyes stared hard at John. "Every word."

"Peter would never . . ."

"Kill an entire race?"

John shook his head back and forth. "No! He wouldn't; he couldn't; it's impossible."

Booth's face erupted in rage.

"Not possible, John? I have known of Peter Pan's existence for about five minutes, and I already could tell you that he is absolutely capable and willing of horrors like that."

Wendy almost pitied John as he struggled with this new information; her brother was a boy watching the boy he worshipped fall to earth in a fiery pyre. His eyes shifted back and forth.

"Maybe the mermaids were lying. Maybe they control the Shadow."

Wendy shook her head. "No, they fear the Shadow. I saw it in the queen's eyes. She fears they are next."

John blinked rapidly, his eyes turning red and watery. "It's not true!" He stomped his foot. "It's not! It can't be!"

Wendy slid off the rock and took a gentle step toward John. "I didn't want to believe it either. I know the way that Peter Pan can make you feel, John." She lowered her voice to ease the blow.

"I loved him, too." Out of the corner of her eye, she saw Booth flinch, but now wasn't the time to hide. Her lips parted. "Peter Pan is a lie, John. He doesn't tell lies; he is a lie. He can't separate reality from his own delusions of grandeur, and the Shadow has corrupted everything he once was."

"No!" John stepped back from her. "No, I don't believe you! I won't! He wants me to be a general. He believes in me!"

Wendy's hazel eyes met her brother's.

"He doesn't, but I do."

John plunged away from them, disappearing into the thick folds of green around them, his footsteps echoing heavy through the forest. Wendy started after him, but Booth's hand gently pulled her back.

"Let him go" he said softly. "John needs time. He'll come back." Booth pressed his lips against her hair. "You've given him all that a sister could: faith and knowledge. The rest is up to him. Besides, as Nietzsche once said, 'All truly great thoughts are conceived by walking.'"

Wendy leaned against him, smiling at the fact that only Booth would quote a German philosopher in the wilds of Neverland. "Nietzsche never had to deal with Peter Pan."

"Or pesky little brothers," Booth replied, and Wendy's heart twisted. *Michael, where are you right now?* She closed her eyes. *What are you doing? Is someone holding you? Making you smile?*

"Wendy?"

The world returned, and she found herself staring up into Booth's handsome face, and she noticed that he had aged a bit since the last time she had seen him in London. The stubble on his cheeks was thicker, his brow stronger. The more she looked at him, the more she saw it; while Peter Pan was still a boy—an evil, charming boy—Booth was becoming a man. She took his face in her hands and kissed it again, relishing the goodness of him.

"Shall we lie down?" Booth whispered, and Wendy looked at him with surprise. He laughed. "To sleep, I meant. We have an eventful day tomorrow."

Wendy nodded, and they sank to the ground, Booth curling his body around hers to keep her warm. "You know . . . " she whispered, "I wouldn't have minded the first suggestion."

Booth froze behind her, and Wendy quietly laughed.

"Have I embarrassed you by my forthcoming nature, Booth Whitfield? Have I forgotten myself?"

Booth let his fingers trail down her cheek and onto her shoulder, resting just above her chest. "On the contrary," he whispered into her ear. "I feel like you have never been more yourself than you are here."

Wendy fell asleep quicker than she would have imagined possible. One minute, she was enjoying the closeness of Booth, and the next she was drifting in blackness. Wendy found herself walking slowly into a square white room, and in the middle of the room sat Peter Pan. He was floating in the air on crossed legs, and he was scrubbing manically at something on his shoe with a bar of soap.

"Peter?" His eyes met hers. They weren't navy anymore; they were pure blackness, and they bore into her with a freezing chill. She wrapped her arms around herself as he watched her silently. Then he went back to scrubbing.

"You took it from me, so I took it from you."

Wendy shook her head.

"Peter, I don't understand." He scrubbed harder now, violently, the soles of his shoes coming clean off, his hands becoming bloodied.

"You took it from me, so I took it from you."

Panic filled his eyes as he reached for her. She stepped back. He clutched the soap in a bloody palm. "I can't get it off! Wendy, I can't get it off!" He opened his mouth and turned toward her, and she again heard the thousands of screams, this time coming from his mouth, the sounds of a massacre pouring out between his lovely lips.

Wendy woke up with a jerk, her heart pounding. She opened

her eyes and pushed backward into Booth, who was still deeply asleep. Through the darkness, she saw the glint of narrowed eyes. Someone was staring at her.

"Peter?"

"No." John's voice was quiet. "It's just me."

Wendy took a deep breath.

"Sorry," she whispered. "Bad dream."

John sighed and let his body sink to the ground from his crouch. "I have them, too. Every night. Nightmares." She knew that it might be rejected, but Wendy reached her hand across the distance between them. John looked at it for a long time before cautiously taking it like a live grenade.

"I guess if you need me to hold your hand to sleep, I can do it. But it's annoying, Wendy, it really is."

Wendy bit her lip to keep from laughing, from crying. Her brother was back, in some tattered form of his wry self.

She wrapped his hand in hers and closed her eyes, this time falling into the restful sleep they both deserved.

CHAPTER THIRTEEN

Dawn came much too early. Wendy opened her eyes to the pitter-patter of light raindrops tapping her face. She rolled over, feeling soggy and damp, wriggling away from Booth before he had a chance to smell her. As she pushed herself up in the mud, she saw John staring at the sunrise, his face a mask of conflicting emotions. Booth rolled over with an adorable snort and woke up, his eyes displaying unbelief as he looked up into the lush green canopy above them.

"Oh. I dreamed I was home. With my father, in our bookstore."

"What a lovely dream," said Wendy as she pushed her hair back from her face and swept it into a curly bun. "I can remember the smell of the stacks at the back." What she wouldn't give for a lovely dream, free from the nightmares that Peter had wrought.

Booth smiled up at her. "Even here, you are without measure, so lovely."

"All right, that's enough!" John wheeled on them, his face twisted in annoyance. "Look, I've thought about it for rather a long time, and I've decided that I'll give you two prats a chance, but that means that you can't be making eyes at each other every minute. It's utterly revolting."

Booth glanced at Wendy and then back at John.

"I guess that's fair. She is your sister, after all."

"Yes," said John, giving Wendy a rare smile. "She is. So what now?"

Wendy pointed to the jungle. "I saw the Forsaken Garden from above only once. But I think if we keep hiking upward, we'll run into to it. If I remember correctly, it sits just above the edge of the waterfall that leads down into Port Duette."

John sniffed the air.

"We aren't far from Port Duette—I'd bet my nose on it. That disgusting town carries a distinct odor." He sighed. "Though honestly, a bath and a bed would be nice."

Wendy shook her head. "John, if you go into Port Duette, you will be skinned alive by one pirate or another."

He frowned. "Well, you didn't have to go and ruin my fantasy, did you?"

As they readied to go, Wendy turned away from them and reached into her blouse, checking for Peter's golden pipes. She could feel the heavy cold metal against her skin, feel the weight of what she was carrying. In her waistband, her jeweled dagger sat firm against the small of her back. Whereas the pipes were cool, the dagger emitted a pleasant warmth against her spine. With a grimace she hiked up her skirt and began walking toward the jungle.

"All right. Let's go, men."

John grinned at her choice of words, hiding his smile behind a shy hand.

Up and up they climbed, hashing their way through broken tree branches and twisty roots, a world of green palms and the lined shadows that covered the ground.

At first John and Booth bickered back and forth about everything imaginable: popular philosophers, the alignment of the stars in Neverland, how to best eat shepherd's pie, the best names for horses. Eventually their light conversation fell away as each of them focused on the climb. Before long they were soaked in a sweet Neverland sweat. The soil turned its deepest black as the trees closed in overhead. Wendy raised her hand up.

"Shhh . . . listen."

John stopped and rested on his walking stick, the very existence of it making Wendy smile. Somehow when they had been walking, her brother had found a stick, had broken it, and had begun whittling as they moved. He would always surprise if given the chance. Wendy tilted her ear to the west, where the rushing of water sounded like a whisper through the trees.

"The waterfall. We're close."

"Well, let's keep moving then!" Booth said, cheery even though he was covered with sweat. "I fancy a dip in the pool will do us all well. We're wretched." He saw the look on Wendy's face and laughed.

"Except you, Wendy Darling. You're positively glowing."

John looked from Wendy to Booth with confused eyes. "She's not glowing, you twit! She looks disgusting!"

The three of them burst into laughter.

Wendy rolled her eyes. "Come on. We're almost there. Keep moving."

They pushed forward, minutes dragging like hours. Behind her, Wendy heard the boys walking, their feet snapping twigs beneath their weight, the birds chattering overhead, a swish from the jungle to the right, the hiss of a snake . . .

And then she heard John's scream.

She whirled around in time to see a shape leap out from the jungle, its skin flickering like light on mirrors, its coat patterned to match the palm trees around it. As it leapt through the air on powerful hind legs, its coat changed to the color of the misty air around it, and then it transitioned again to the white of John's shirt as it sunk its claws into his chest. Wendy watched in frozen horror as a crimson stain blotted its claws, and then the color of the Keel cat's coat turned deep crimson.

MOVE! she screamed at herself, breaking through the shock.

"JOHN!"

The word burst from her mouth as she spun toward the cat.

John gave a gargled scream as the cat swiped at his face with its large claws, his hands struggling to protect his eyes and cheeks. Wendy sprinted toward him, reaching for the dagger and feeling relief as her hands closed around the handle. She went to pull the blade as she bore down on her brother . . . but the dagger wouldn't move.

No!

Wendy yanked again, letting out a scream of frustration as she watched the huge cat rear up above John's body, its mouth opening to sink its teeth into her brother's neck. John raised his hand to protect his head, his eyes wide with shock, leaving his neck vulnerable, so thin and white.

Wendy yanked again, but the dagger didn't move, and since she had no other choice, Wendy used what she could: her arms. She slammed into the big cat, attempting to tackle it, but she only moved it a few inches. As the cat writhed, Wendy struggled to hold on, but her small body was no match for this coil of muscles and teeth, desperate to finish its kill. With a feral scream, Wendy planted her feet and arched backward, somehow managing to temporarily lift the cat off her brother. With a mangy yowl, the cat whirled on her, and the heat of its mouth rushed across her face as it clawed at her.

She tried to keep her arms around it, but it was moving too fast. She couldn't tell what was happening, but she heard John screaming her name as claws tore at her in a blurry mess of blood and matted fur.

I'll die here, she thought. *I'll die before I let you kill my brother.* She saw its mouth open wide—wide enough to fit her entire head inside—and smelled the scent of her brother's salty blood pouring from the cat's teeth. With a howl, the cat reared back, and Wendy saw death swallowing her, but instead it slumped to the side with a whimper. Wendy pushed it off her body, confused about what was happening. She wiped the cat saliva out of her eyes and saw Booth standing beside her, the sword that she had given him on

Pan Island dripping with blood. The cat was stretched out beside him, a long cut slicing up its middle and out through its back.

Wendy leapt to her feet.

John.

"John! My God, are you all right?" Wendy ran over to her brother, where he lay curled on the ground. "Are you all right? John!" She leaned over him, her hands searching for wounds to heal.

John struggled to find his words.

"Yes, I think so, Wendy! I think so! I'm cut, but . . ."

With a trembling hand, Wendy picked up John's glasses from where they lay beside him and held them up to the light, and they both looked with amazement at the long cut across one of the lenses.

"These old things," John said. "Mother made me wear them, and I hated her for it, and here they saved my eye." With a groan, Wendy helped him up. John's face had a mean cut that ran across his cheek, and his hands were bloody and torn, but as he stood up, Wendy was glad to see that his injuries weren't severe. As she reached for John, he jerked his head away. "Stop fussing! I'm all right!"

From behind her, Wendy heard a pathetic growl, her heart breaking at the sound. She turned and bent over the Keel cat. Up close it was beautiful, roughly the size of a large dog, and its fur was rippling with the color of its own blood. It let out a soft meow, its eyes rolling back in its head as its tongue lolled out of its bloody mouth. Wendy looked up at Booth in desperation. They communicated wordlessly, and he leaned forward. Wendy watched as the boy she loved laid his hand on the cat's face and whispered the soft words of W. B. Yeats as he gently pushed the sword into the cat's heart.

> *On a morning misty and mild and fair.*
> *The mist-drops hung on the fragrant trees,*
> *And in the blossoms hung the bees.*

The cat's suffering ended. John looked over at Wendy as he wrapped his hands with strips of his shirt.

"What do we do now?"

Wendy turned back to the jungle, shaken but feeling more determined than ever.

"I guess we keep moving. The scent of blood will no doubt draw other predators, maybe more cats."

John sighed. "How did I know that's what you would say?"

They limped forward, much slower now, each of them lost in their own thoughts. As they walked, Wendy pulled out the dagger from her waistband, and this time it slid out easily. She turned it over in her hand, watching the way the blue gemstone sparkled in the light, feeling the heat of it warm her torn-up hands. *Did I feel resistance? What is it waiting for?* She looked at the dagger for another long moment, and this time she noticed a thin thread of her ripped dress wrapped around the handle. She burst out laughing, shaking her head at herself as she put it back in her waistband. It was a fact: Neverland was making her think some crazy things.

"Wendy."

She was struck at the awe in her brother's voice, and she turned. John's face was slack, and Booth looked speechless as well, and their wide-eyed stares drew her face up above the trees. Wendy found herself unable to even speak.

"By gods, I think we're here," muttered Booth.

The Forsaken Garden.

High above them, a stone archway soared into the air, marked with ancient runes and carved with two outreaching fairies on each end. It had once been beautiful, but now it was stained black with dripping, greenish condensation. Pale moss draped over most of it, and one of the fairy' eyes now held a bird nest, the white egg inside of it seeming to stare out at the three of them.

The image haunted Wendy. They slowly walked forward, an

eerie silence overtaking the jungle; apparently nothing moved here. Down a hill to their left, the towering waterfall that Wendy had heard earlier got its start, roaring down from a jagged peak above, and to the right was only jungle. As they made their way closer, a rising gray mist swirled around their feet. The once-grand entrance to the city lay before them. Beyond the gate, there was only mist, rising up above their heads vertically, the entrance to the garden like a wall of fog. Wendy went closer but turned when the uncomfortable sound of violent retching reached her. Both Booth and John were on their knees, trying desperately to keep in the contents of their stomach. When she reached them, they had both gone completely pale, their skin cold and clammy like milk.

Booth leaned over. "My body . . ." He pointed. "I don't know what's happening, but I feel like if I pass through the fog, I'll die." He retched again.

"Same!" mustered John as he emptied his stomach onto the ground.

Wendy stepped backward, wanting to help but also nauseated at the sight. John was rolling on the ground, clutching his stomach. "Wendy, I'll die if I go through there, I know it! Argh, my stomach!"

Booth leaned his head against the ground. "Maybe if you give me a few minutes," he said, "I will be able to stand and then I can go with you. We can wait for it to pass." At the end of his sentence, his body began seizing, and Wendy ran forward, wrapping her arms around his waist. Without hesitation, she dragged him backward, away from the gate. She had only made it maybe ten feet before his seizing stopped. Booth's color returned quickly, and his breathing slowed.

"It's gone," he said in amazement. He beckoned to John.

"Oy! Come back here, mate!" John followed behind him, crawling on his knees. When he passed by them, he sat back in surprise.

"I'm all right."

Booth was taking deep breaths as he rested his face against his knees. "Wendy . . ."

"I'm going in alone. We've come all this way." She brushed off her dress matter-of-factly. "I know exactly what's happening."

John could hardly contain his indignation at being left behind. "What *is* happening? And also, why should you get to go in but not us? Just because you're a *girl*?"

"No." Wendy straightened her shoulders as she faced the gate of gray fog. "I can go in because this is where the Shadow lives. And Peter controls the Shadow."

"And Peter loves you." Booth said it quietly, his blue eyes meeting her own. He didn't say it with emotion, or as a fact to be questioned. "He loves you, and so the Shadow would never hurt you."

"It's a working theory," said Wendy bluntly. "Either way, I have to find Qaralius. And if he's in there, I have no choice." She looked at her brother and Booth, both staring nervously at her.

"But . . . you'll be alone," sputtered John. Wendy pushed her hair back behind her ears.

"Yes. Alone, like I was with Peter Pan when he dropped me out of the sky. Alone, when I watched our brother almost drown. Alone, on a pirate ship full of men who viewed me either as something to be consumed or as something to throw overboard." She turned her back to them, facing the gate.

"Pray for me all you'd like, but don't ever think that being alone means I won't do what's needed."

"Bravo," muttered Booth. "Brave girl."

There was nothing more to say, so Wendy simply walked away from the boys, leaving them behind as the stone arch rose before her. Underneath it, the wall of mist churned, hiding everything that lay beyond it. When she reached the barrier, Wendy cautiously stuck her hand into it, feeling nothing but a slight dampness, not unlike a thick fog in London. There was a strange creeping feeling as her hand and then her arm disappeared into the mist, like the feeling of being watched manifested into a physical touch.

She looked back wistfully at the boys, who watched her with grave concern before she took a breath and stepped into the Forsaken Garden.

CHAPTER FOURTEEN

Wendy continued wandering forward, her hands out in front of her, blindly pushing her way through a mist that was denser and heavier than fog. The only things she could see were the wildly swirling patterns of gray, one like a breath, another a curl that danced in front of her eyes. She could taste it in her mouth, like heavy bitter greens that lingered on her tongue. After just a few steps, the fog enveloped her completely, leaving the boys in another world.

As Wendy walked, the fog pressed in, and she jumped at the feeling of a phantom hand on her waist. She spun. There was no one there. A ghostly finger of gray trailed a lingering touch across her collarbone, and Wendy felt the uncomfortable presence of a body pressing in behind her. She turned. Still there was no one there. She began walking quicker now, her steps swallowed by the strange silence of this place. The mist trailed down her neckline and rose up from her legs to wrap around her waist. Wendy started to run, and her breath caught as she watched the mist curl into a black skeletal hand marked with long jagged claws and reach out for her ankle.

Want, whispered this dark thing. *Want.*

She suddenly burst into a sprint, throwing her arms violently out in front of her, sending the mist billowing back in her wake.

It swirled back into form, this time whirling into a vortex that looked as though it could swallow her whole. *There.*

In front of her, a piece of sunlight pierced through the gray, illuminating where the mist began thinning. She ran desperately toward it as skeletal hands tangled in her hair and wrapped around her neck. Gold glinted on the ground in front of her, and Wendy threw herself forward with a determined cry, bursting through the wall of mist and emerging out into the light. Without a sound, the mist curled back from her, fading like smoke in the morning light.

A small city lay in front of her, and Wendy took a minute to breathe as she took in her surroundings, the glinting light assaulting her eyes from every surface. Wendy shaded her eyes with her hand and looked again, and she was at a loss for words.

Every place under her feet and above her head was *gold.* Under her feet were gold cobblestones, stretching out before her, the foundation of what once must have been a shining city on a hill. Wendy looked up, her eyes tracing the grand tree trunks that lined the remnants of the main road, a gentle curve pulling away from the stone archway, now so far away that she could barely make it out; she had traveled farther in the mist than she originally thought.

Ahead of her, the once-glorious Forsaken Garden rose up out of the ground, at once a cathedral and a tomb, its empty halls and windows a ghostly remainder of what had happened here. She began walking up the golden road, making her way to what looked to be the center of town. She hummed a quiet song as she walked, wanting to hear something, *anything.*

Wendy had once heard Hook say that if he could raid the Forsaken Garden, then he would never have to raid ever again, and now she saw why. Everything was made of gold: the road, the buildings, the signs carved in ancient runes, the curled candelabras that lined the street. Giant trees held up elegant, peaked gathering places far above Wendy's head; the city went up instead of out. Everywhere she looked, nature and treasure danced together in an intimate pairing—a home carved out of a tree here, a tunnel of twisting vines dotted with gold flowers there. Above her, bursting from the trunks of trees decorated with beautiful gold paintings, towers of glass and metal rose up into the sky; it was a city built for a people that had wings.

She would have been easily taken with the beauty of it all had it not been for the thick layer of ash that covered every surface.

The ash fluttered down from the buildings like snow, perpetually laying a fine dusting over the gold. Wendy passed by a hall of gilded mirrors, her heart pounding loudly as she watched her own distorted reflection through the smeared glass. Everything was covered with the gray substance: open doors held drifts of the ash; homes sat barren and still with ash covering the windows.

As she walked quickly, clutching her arms around her, it occurred to Wendy that she was standing in a graveyard, only instead of underground, everything here was buried above her. "A city of death," she whispered, hating it immediately.

Wendy thought she heard a whisper to her right, and she spun around, expecting to see something horrifying, but instead she found her eyes resting on an innocent play area built for fairy children. Above a soft floor of packed leaves, small golden trees intertwined and leapt up from the ground. Wendy stepped closer, seeing the lifeless building behind it—a school, perhaps? She stepped around the trees carefully, noticing for the first time the small huddled shapes that lay underneath. *No. No. No.*

With a shaking hand, Wendy reached forward and gently brushed away several layers of ash, expecting a skeleton underneath. What she found was far worse: a perfectly preserved fairy child, perhaps four years old. His lips were a deep pink, his face angular and otherworldly, his cheeks still maintaining a glowing flush. She stared at the face for a long moment, unbelieving; apparently the fairies didn't decompose—they just stayed here, forever. Wendy sadly ran her hand over the child's cold cheekbone and looked at his open eyes, a place she knew from Tink normally danced with the light of stars. Instead, this boy's eyes were black and wide with horror. She could tell from the position of his body and his head that he had been twisted, been broken.

Struggling to keep her emotions under control, Wendy bit her lip and gently tried to close the fairy boy's eyes, but his skin was the texture of marble and just as unyielding. With a cry of frustration, Wendy sat back and began piling the ash upon his face as tears streamed down from her eyes.

"I hope you are somewhere new," she whispered to him. "Somewhere magical, where you can grow and laugh." The dead fairy boy stayed silent as his face disappeared back under the ash. Wendy stood, and the anger that churned through her body made her fingers tingle. She was so tired of seeing dead boys in Neverland. So tired.

"Peter . . . how could you?" she whispered through gritted teeth. "You monster."

Beside the bench where the boy sat, a small puppet sat slumped over on one of the golden tables, forgotten forever. She picked it up in her hand. It was just a simple marionette, the basic, faceless figures of a human held together by a string, made of sturdy black wood. It reminded her of London's toy stores, their windows bouncing with dozens of them, all trussed up for Christmas holiday. With a sad smile, Wendy tucked the puppet beside the dead fairy boy and walked toward the pinnacle of the city: a shining tower made of seven pieces of glass, each peppered with ash.

Wendy felt the lurking presence watching her, and she turned, but there was nothing once again. "Go faster," she whispered to herself, but she kept her walk at an easy pace, restrained by the certain feeling that if she ran, something would chase her.

More and more huddled figures appeared the closer she got to the center of the city, the bodies of ash-covered fairies littering the ground. Her feet passed by an outstretched hand, its skin barely visible through the ash. In a tree nearby, a large piece of wing hung forever from the golden branches, translucent light blue and strung with tiny veins, the sun sparkling through it like stained glass. Wendy swallowed her fear and kept walking.

The tower rose before her, a massive tree with a dozen golden doorways carved into its sides, a building that in its glory must have been a vision of light and beauty.

Its loveliness passed through Wendy without a thought; she needed to find this fairy king, and fast, before this nightmarish place sucked her soul away. The door was slightly ajar, and Wendy slipped inside, her feet kicking over a mountain of ash on her way in. In front of her, winding stairs made their way upward—an afterthought, probably, for human guests visiting the city.

Guests like Peter, who had stolen their song, their Shadow, and their lives.

Upward she climbed, passing once-grand windows smeared with gray. The spiral stairs kept winding, and Wendy found herself out of breath by the time she reached the throne room at the top.

She bent over to catch her breath, stepping out onto a wide hexagonal platform graced with an empty throne of thin spun glass.

"Hello?" A ghostly silence answered her, and she walked farther into the room.

"Hello? My name is Wendy Darling." Nothing.

"Idiot," she mumbled to herself. *Why did I think I could just stroll in and find him? Why did I believe Tink?* Maybe this was all some elaborate trap to get her here, where she could be easily picked off by Peter or, God forbid, something else.

Wendy quickly walked around the room once more, the bottom of her dress swishing over elaborately painted scenes of feasting beneath her feet. There was a creaking sound, and Wendy spun around, her eyes on the door, her hand on the dagger at her back. Nothing appeared in the darkness of the doorway, and she had just stepped back when the wooden floor began shifting underneath her. She stepped to the side, unnerved, and when it barreled forward underneath her again, Wendy fell to her knees to keep upright. "What is this?" she whispered as the wood underneath her feet began spinning in a circle, the boards disconnecting and forming themselves into a whirlpool shape, curling down into themselves as the platform moved back toward the wall. Underneath the boards, something huge was rising up out of the darkness below. *The Shadow?* Wendy lowered herself to the floor, her heart pounding out the same sentence over and over again: *This was a mistake. This was a mistake.* What rose up, however, was very different than the horror that her mind expected, so different that a mad laughter burst out of Wendy.

It was a giant silver acorn. The size of a small home, it curled up out of the base of the tower and up into the room where Wendy was seated, her back against the wall. The boards underneath her feet shifted again as the acorn came to rest in front of her. She climbed to her feet, dazzled by its size and texture, and her mouth hung open in surprise.

Moving slowly, wondering what she was doing, Wendy gently laid her palm on the acorn. It was cool to the touch. Her fingers had begun to trace the metal toward the stem when the acorn gave a shudder and began a much slower rotation. The seeded top of it began to swivel outward. As the top opened up, the acorn sank downward until the lid of it was level with Wendy's feet. With a groan, it stopped moving and settled into its new position just below where she stood. Wendy stepped closer, peeking her head over its side.

The reality was not what she expected, and she gasped aloud, recovering as quickly as possible, bowing at the waist.

"King Qaralius, your majesty. My name is Wendy Darling, and I'm here because we need your help."

CHAPTER FIFTEEN

When King Qaralius finally spoke, his deep voice was dry as a parched riverbed.

"You sound surprised. Am I not what you imagined, human child?"

Wendy hoped to hide her shock in some quiet corner of her mouth.

"I have presumed nothing, great King."

"Do me a favor child, and do not flatter me. I am not the mermaids, who find praise a treasure worth hoarding. Your kind words will only fit to wound me further. You're shocked, are you not?"

Wendy smiled. "Perhaps a bit surprised."

The fairy king's eyes closed in shame.

"I have been surprised only once in my lifetime, and once proved to be enough."

Wendy tried not to stare, but it was impossible. The once-great fairy king lay now on a soft bed of gold velvet, a fur blanket pulled up to his withered chest. He was painfully old, his body so thin that bones strained against skin spotted with age. Wendy could see each rib in his concaved chest. When he rolled over slowly, his bones cracking with each movement, his face was a mask of pain. Wendy swallowed her disappointment, remembering the carving of Qaralius on Hook's chamber door: beautiful, strong, and otherworldly. Here he was, the fairy king, and he was a crumbling husk.

Wendy gestured to the platform above the acorn.

"Is it all right if I sit? I'm quite tired."

Qaralius blinked slowly, like a child woken from its nap.

"Yes, you may sit, human child."

Wendy saw no point in beating around the bush. "I've come for answers, King Qaralius."

"Of course you have. There are only two things that could make you venture into the Forsaken Garden; you are a person seeking either treasure or answers. And since you don't strike me as a treasure hunter, who never make it out of here alive . . ."

His voice trailed off as a sad smile crossed his face. "I'm sad to tell you that you will leave unhappy, either way."

Wendy looked down at him, her heart aching for such a pathetic creature. *How glorious he must have been once, how handsome with his star-streaked eyes and yellow-gold hair.* She felt safe in his presence, oddly reassured, even though he was the oldest being she had ever seen in Neverland.

"Why are you here, your majesty, in this strange contraption?"

At her words, he gave a shudder, and he turned to face her, though his frail body seemed not up to the task.

As he moved toward her, he clenched the edge of the platform, his wings unfolding behind him. They were enormous but broken; large holes bore their way through the translucent gold, and the top of one wing was ripped clean off. Long jagged scars stretched out from the middle of the wing and onto his body. Pity flooded through Wendy; the Shadow had ripped the fairy King from head to toe. Qaralius looked up at her before she could erase the pity from her face. His lip curled.

"They're a sight to see, I'm sure. Most days I forget I even have them. Sometimes at night, when I leave the roof open, I can remember what it feels like to fly among the stars."

Wendy's mouth curled in confusion. "Then why don't you? Fly? Leave?"

Qaralius shook his head, his eyes drawing back into his face in terror. "Because it's out there. And if it knows that I'm free, it will come to finish the job it started. I'm only safe here, inside this shell and my city."

"That is hardly a life, slumbering here in this acorn for almost a hundred years."

He cleared his throat. "Every time I wake, I wish for death, for the sweet release that it once promised. But now my death only lies in the hands of a monster, and I cannot . . . I will not . . ."

He was stumbling over his words now, lost in memory, and Wendy reached down for his hand, taking it in her delicate one, marveling at how his skin felt like paper. Wendy gave his hand a squeeze.

"You're afraid." Her voice was quiet, hoping to draw him out of his quite literal shell.

His brow furrowed. "If you had seen what I have seen, you would be afraid too. It was the darkest of all days."

Wendy folded her legs underneath her. "This is a dark land."

The fairy King nodded as he settled his tired body against the wall of the acorn. "It didn't used to be, child. Neverland was once a palace of celestial delights, a land carved by the fairies to live a life of pleasure and worship. My distant ancestors made this place to be as beautiful as possible, with magic sewn into every blade of grass, every grain of salt in the sea. They were happy, but greedy. With their endless strength they carved more and more for themselves, pulling the gold from the soil to build this silly city." He stopped to take a breath; even talking exhausted him. "Then more races found this place: first the mermaids, then the Pilvinuvo Indians, and finally . . . man. For a while we existed peacefully. But when men arrived, so did their many sins, and it blackened our world. The evolution was inevitable. One clever boy made sure of it."

"Peter Pan." It was the name of all Neverland was tuned to, set to vibrate at one destructive, lovely note.

Qaralius's face turned from sorrow to anger.

"Yes. That little snippet of a boy. I met him only the once, and while others around me were enchanted by him, I remained skeptical. Something ancient inside of me whispered not to trust him, that he was dangerous. I dismissed him out of hand, reminding him that I was a Fairy King and he was merely a mortal. Humans, I felt, were not worth a fairy's time." He paused, watery red eyes lingering sadly on Wendy's face. "Every day, I wonder, perhaps if I had taken him under my wing, then I might have changed his fate. If I had been kinder, would my subjects be here with me today, watching our children play?"

Wendy thought back to the dead fairy child, buried forever in the ash. Her heart ached for this pathetic creature. "And so this is your penance? To stay here in this . . . tomb for all eternity? Your own circle of hell?"

His voice nervously rose several octaves. "This tomb, as you call it, is the only safe place from the Shadow."

Wendy stared at him for a long moment. "There is a world out there that needs you. I'm here because we are trying to defeat Peter and the Shadow. His evil must and can be stopped, and you can help us."

Qaralius pulled back from Wendy and began wringing his hands together. "No, my dear. What you are doing is ensuring your death and the deaths of everyone you've ever loved."

His voice croaked as he spoke, his eyes opening wide. "You've no idea the horror of it. To emerge from your home to see your people being ripped from limb to limb, to see the bodies of children twisted and wrenched apart by a creature that you couldn't have conjured in your nightmares. We had no warning, no threats or requests. The fairies ruled one moment and were annihilated the next." His face paled at the memory. "There is no way to beat it. I've seen it. Faced it.

Fought it. I couldn't save my people, and you won't be able to save yours."

Wendy's temper rose. "Not if we rip it from Peter Pan and then destroy it." She paused and leaned forward, her eyes on Qaralius's eyes, which sparked with the light of dying stars. "Not if we know the song that will pull it out of Peter."

"The song." The King laughed dryly, his whole body shaking with the effort, his atrophied muscles contracting with each chuckle.

"Yes. The song that calls the Shadow. I was told that you know it."

"Know it?" The King's wry smile disappeared. "What could you, a mortal, know about the song? How could your small brains even fathom the depth of such a call? How could you even begin to understand what it means for the stars to call you out of your soul and into their arms?"

Wendy slammed her hand down on the outer lip of the acorn with a clang, harder than she meant to.

"You know, the mermaids may have betrayed you, but you have more in common with them than you may think. It may have been Peter who called the Shadow, but the pride of both your races went before the fall."

The King blinked at her.

"Who are you to speak to me in such a way?"

Wendy was getting angry. "I'm no one. Just a girl from London, but I'm one of a few people who is trying to save your world and thousands of innocent lives while you sleep away your regrets."

He shuddered away from her.

Wendy almost growled at him. "You know the song; I know you do."

"I will never call it again, The Shadow. I can't." His voice was shaking. "The last time it was called, it performed an act of violence so brutal that it ripped a hole in our sky." Wendy closed her eyes as hopelessness carved out a place in her heart. *He will not tell me the song, but can I blame him? If something had ripped apart my family, would I call it back again?*

No.

There was nothing she would not do for her family. Which is why she would do what she needed to do. She pulled Peter's golden pipes out of her blouse. The King curled back against the wall.

"What are you doing?"

Wendy shrugged. "I'm probably wrong about the song, but there is no danger in just trying it out, right? I can cobble together a melody. Besides, I bet the Shadow enjoys music—and these are Peter's pipes, so it probably heeds them no matter what." She pursed her lips in the same way that she had seen Peter do so many times. "I'll start with a C, I think."

Qaralius was on her in a flash, betraying his body and leaping across the wide mouth of the acorn. The white heat of fairy magic blasted across her face as their eyes met, and for a moment, she saw his true age glimmer; he was young, attractive, and powerful beyond belief. In a breath, he was an old man again, and his eyes were pleading, desperate.

"Don't! It lives here, in the city, lurking in the dark places where it took so many lives. It's not free to do as it pleases, but we can still attract it. Put those away!" Wendy raised them to her lips, uncomfortable at bringing this pathetic being any more pain, but she was unable to think of any other way.

"Tell me the song and I'll stop!"

He looked at her desperately. "A fairy's word is law. I will never let it pass my lips again." He paused. "But there is another way." Wendy waited with the pipes at her lips, looking over the golden metal at Qaralius, the sunlight glinting through his tattered wings. She continued to stare at him, unwilling to break the silence, unwilling to beg. He fell to his knees.

"It killed my wife. It ripped her wings from her before it broke her body in its cruel hands. Our eyes met as the life was extinguished from her, and I could feel her heart slowing, so connected were our bodies. As I fought—unsuccessfully—to save the lives of our children, she opened her mouth and sang as the last of our race was extinguished, as our warriors fell like leaves from the trees. My mate gave what I could not: hope."

Wendy clutched the pipes.

"How?" she gasped. "Tell me now."

"She wrote the song into something that would never completely disappear, onto something that would pass through the hands of hundreds of people every day, so that many would have a chance to defeat this evil."

Wendy paused for a moment. "A book?"

The fairy shook his head. "Something more durable. Something people desire above all other things."

Wendy sat up as the memory struck her: *She is in Peter's battle room, full of overflowing chests of treasures, still a girl in love with a flying boy. She picks up a heavy golden coin. It burns in her hand. On one side, there is a single tiny skull with wings stretched behind it, covered with a large X. On the other, spiraling lines are interspersed with small dots. Peter comes up behind her, and she can feel his presence like a fire on her skin. He pops her hand from underneath, and the coin goes spinning into the air, where he quickly catches it.*

Wendy gasped: *The dream. He said, "You took it from me, so I took it from you."*

Everything was spinning as she stood. Qaralius reached out for her arm to steady her.

Her eyes matched his own, and she understood. The fairy queen had sung a hope for the future of Neverland, a whispered prayer carved into something not even Peter Pan could make disappear, no matter how hard he tried, into tiny skulls stretched out on a line . . . like notes.

The song to call the Shadow was carved into the fairy money.

And Wendy knew a pirate captain who probably had some.

A wide smile stretched across her face, and she laughed out loud at the hope flooding through her. They could win. It wasn't just a vague dream anymore; this was a concrete hope. She leapt up from where she was sitting, landing hard in the acorn. Qaralius stepped back in alarm, but it was too late; Wendy was hugging him hard against her chest. He froze for a moment, but then his body sagged with relief against her; how long had it been since he had been held?

"Thank you," she breathed, his white heat around them both. "Thank you." She stepped back from him. "I'll come back for you when we've defeated the Shadow. You won't have to be afraid."

His eyes were sad. "There is no place for me out there. I'm the last of my kind. Neverland will never again be my home." Wendy looked up at him, gently pulling his face down until their eyes met, ready to share the ace in her pocket.

"You aren't the last."

"What . . . could you possibly mean by that?" Golden fairy dust was pouring from his wings now, circling around them both in a violent vortex. He gave her a hard shake. "Speak, child!"

Wendy smiled, happy that for once she had good news to tell someone.

"There is one fairy left; she was only a child when the Shadow came. Peter spared her life, and she remains with him on Pan Island. She . . . loves him." Wendy paused as tears began welling in King Qaralius's eyes.

"No. It can't be. I'm the last! I would know if I wasn't alone . . ." He trailed off, lost in thought as she pulled away from his grasp and walked to the side of the acorn.

"Perhaps you have been in hiding too long." Wendy climbed up and out of the acorn, awkwardly heaving herself onto the platform, which was beginning to spin now, swallowing the acorn bit by bit as Qaralius stood silently stunned by this news.

"It can't be."

Wendy looked back.

"Come with me and see for yourself. Please. We can do this together."

The fairy king's eyes narrowed suspiciously. "This is a trick, to get me outside. To use me as bait for the Shadow."

Wendy shook her head. "No." She paused. "Your majesty, if I may be honest: I've been afraid almost every day that I've been in Neverland. I have seen and experienced horrible things. I've a thousand reasons to curl up in a ball and just wait for things to pass, but I've found one very good reason to stand." He raised his eyes, and Wendy could see in the waning light the outline of where a heavy crown had once sat.

"And what's that?"

"Because fear doesn't care if you are lying down or standing; it comes either way." She didn't look at his face as the acorn closed over it, sealing the fairy king back inside his fortress.

"And I would rather be standing when it comes for me," she whispered.

The Forsaken Garden was still when she stepped out of the gilded tower; too still. It was as though all the sound in the world had been sucked away; Wendy's breaths rang out like hammering drums in the silence. Something wasn't right. As Wendy stepped forward, her foot knocked into something hard and small. A horrified scream rose in her throat, and Wendy covered her mouth to muffle it.

The marionette she had placed by the dead fairy was now seated on the ground in front of her, its head tilted sideways. Watching. Someone had moved it.

The Shadow. It was playing with her.

Her thoughts became jumbled together as she sprinted away from the tower, her legs flying underneath her before she even understood what was happening. Dread coiled around her heart as Booth and John screamed her name, their voices muffled, as if underwater. In the distance, the gray mist that had once been contained by the stone archway was slowly seeping toward her, pulled forward by claw-like hands made of black smoke. The hands were moving quickly, each one clutching at the dirt before dissolving and letting others take their place. Wendy looked around for another possible exit into the jungle, but the fairy city was ringed with walls of gold, and she cursed the fairies for their greed as she ran. When she turned to glance behind her, the small marionette was rising up in the air, it head beginning to turn as Wendy sprinted away.

The wall of fog rose up in front of her, but the only way out was through, and so with a deep breath, she plunged into it. The invasive mist was everywhere then, the tendrils creating shapes in front of her: There were figures of slaughtered fairies, figures of Lost Boys adorned with weapons, and, finally, there was the figure of Peter, his silhouette appearing before her, his hands resting haughtily on his hips. Wendy burst through him with her hands outstretched, turning Peter Pan into a whirling fog that tasted like him   salty skin and adventure. Hands made of smoke clawed at her as a thick rope of mist circled about her form like a python, wrapping itself around her torso. Wendy turned, unsure of which direction she was headed. *Is the gate this way?* She took a few steps forward and then back. *Which way am I facing?* The mist seized her pause and rushed at her, swallowing every part of her so that she couldn't see and couldn't breathe. Wendy let out a strangled scream and sank to the ground. The mist was darkening, turning from gray to black, curls of night rising from the damp soil. Wendy rolled over on her back as the darkness began piling on her chest, heavy like stones, pressing the light out of her. She could see the black claws creeping up her side, reaching for her beating heart. *Is this what happened to Peter when he called it?*

There was a shout, and something solid was pushing against

her. No, not pushing. Pulling. A hand—a real hand—was pulling her forward. She heard the awful sounds of retching as her head lolled to the side. As she struggled to breathe, she remembered everything about these hands: how they traced their way across a bookshelf, hesitating once and then manically plucking a book from the stack, quickly paging through to see what the prose sounded like.

She knew these hands well.

"Booth . . . ," she muttered, and then everything went black as night, black as shadow.

Chapter Sixteen

Something hard was hitting Wendy in the face, and Wendy jerked awake. Above her, John's pale face appeared.

"Ow!" Wendy gasped. "John, stop hitting me!"

John looked over his shoulder, his voice deadpan. "She's back."

Booth knelt in front of her. "Wendy, are you all right?"

The gentleness in his voice made Wendy want to cry.

"Yes. No. I don't know."

She was grasping at memories, at what had happened in the garden. The garden. The acorn. Qaralius. She sat up quickly, the world spinning around her. Booth grabbed her arm, his voice strict. "Wendy. Sit down. You're still not well. I insist." Wendy swayed a moment before surrendering, sinking back down to the ground.

"The fairy money," she whispered.

Both boys stared at her like she was insane, and maybe she was, just a little bit.

She took a deep breath and told them everything that she had learned from the fairy king.

John frowned.

"What now?" he asked.

"We need to get to Hook. As soon as possible. Now."

Booth laughed at her just a little bit, but he stopped upon her look of reprimand.

"I'm sorry, it's just . . . Wendy, look around." Wendy did, finally noticing the hazy dusk that was rapidly approaching; it was almost night.

"How long did I sleep?" she sputtered. John snorted.

"Enough time that I told Booth every bad thing you've ever done, and now he's through with you."

Wendy grinned. "Is that true, Mr. Whitfield?"

Booth shrugged. "Unfortunately. But I heard there are some brothels down in Port Duette, so I wager I'll be just fine. I bet they love a man who can quote poetry."

Wendy laughed, and it rang through her chest like a clear bell, pushing out the darkness. "Watch out, whores, Booth Whitfield is coming to town! Everyone gird your loins." Wendy rolled her eyes while John groaned at their delightful banter.

"Honestly, Wendy, there's no way we can go anywhere tonight. In the morning, we'll start out fresh. How do you wager we find this pirate captain of yours?"

Wendy bit her lip; it tasted of blood. "I think if we go into Port Duette, he'll find us. Or at the very least we can find out where he is docking next." Wendy missed Oxley something fierce; if he were still here, they could have used him to get an immediate message to Hook. She let her mind linger on his kind smile and his optimistic grin, and her chest ached in return. She laid her hand across her chest as if to staunch the bleeding.

"Let's hunker down here for the night, and in the morning, we'll try to find Hook." She sighed. "What I wouldn't give to sleep in a bed tonight."

Booth tucked one of her curls up behind her ear. "And have a good meal."

"A warm drink."

"A book, and a pillow to sit on."

As they spoke, Wendy noticed that John had become fidgety, something that she knew he did when he was in trouble.

"What is it, John?"

John blinked. "It's nothing."

"Don't lie to me, John Darling."

He shifted back on his heels.

"Wendy, Captain James Hook has good reason to kill me."

Booth turned to look at John with surprise. "What reason would that be, mate?"

John stared at Wendy for a long time, his face drawn.

"Because I killed someone," he whispered quietly. "The blind pirate in the crow's nest. When I rescued Wendy. I shot him, and then I threw him onto the deck, just like Peter told me to do." His confession hung in the air.

"Oh, John." Wendy's face crumpled as she looked at her brother, too young to have this weight around his neck. "I had hoped it wasn't you." *In my deepest of hearts, John, I had hoped.*

"Well, it was," John snapped. "I killed him, but it was Peter . . ."

Booth raised an eyebrow. "How long are you going to use that excuse, John? You were complicit."

"I KNOW I DID IT!" John screamed, his shrewd face twisting. He threw his bag to the ground. "I know, all right? I think about it every minute, so I don't need your guilt. I'll never be like you, Wendy. I'll never be *just good*."

Wendy watched him, her mouth frozen in shock.

"I know you look down on me, you and Booth and Michael, even! John, the bad one." His eyes turned cold and his voice flat. "And I guess I am, a pathetic self-fulfilling prophecy. Only now I'll never sleep again because killing that pirate didn't wash off me the way Peter said it would."

Wendy waited a long time before she let quiet words fall from her tongue. She wanted to reassure him, to convince him he was wrong, but she couldn't muster the strength to lie. Instead, she kept her words short and clipped.

"I'll speak to Hook for you, John. The captain knows that you are my brother and are not to be harmed." John looked like he wanted to argue back, but instead he gave a nondescript shrug, his emotions exhausted.

The hours ticked quickly into nighttime, and the three of them settled into the unyielding ground for rest, falling into their own thoughts.

"I could be in my hammock right now," muttered John angrily as he punched at the leaves underneath him. "Belly full, rocking to sleep."

"Under the control of a psychopath," added Booth in the same tone of voice. "On the wrong side of history, prisoner of a maniacal dictator who has romanced you with a mix of unrealistic idealism and a healthy dose of fear."

"Or that." John turned over with a huff. "But the bed was rather nice."

As Wendy pushed some leaves together to make a suitable sleeping place, a bead of sweat rolled down her forehead. She raised her hand to wipe it away and was disgusted when a smear of dirt came with it. She sat back, stunned by how revolting she felt while still mentally arguing away the silliness of it all. It was just dirt. Or was it? She rolled it between her fingers, and the brown fell away, leaving a trail of gray. Ash. Wendy choked back the nausea rising inside of her. She desperately wanted it off her skin, this reminder of that place.

"You all right?" Booth came and settled beside her, their knees touching. "We have some time to talk, you know. It's not like falling asleep out here will be easy, not with what you've seen today, what happened to John—"

He was interrupted by a loud snort from John's nose. Wendy and Booth looked over their shoulders. John was deeply asleep, his chest rising and falling with each long breath.

"No rest for the wicked, I guess," muttered Booth, but Wendy smiled as she watched her brother. There was a peaceful look upon his face, as if he had finally untangled the burdens weighing down his heart. *John deserves rest.* Most of the time, he deserved a punch in the mouth, but right now he deserved rest. She stepped over to him and carefully pulled his glasses off his face and set them beside his arm before brushing a lock of curly brown hair off his forehead. Booth watched her silently return to his side.

"You're too good for him, you know."

Wendy nodded her head. "Perhaps. But he's still a Darling."

Booth reached out his hand, and Wendy took it in her own . . . and then she sat a few feet away from him.

"Have I done something?"

"No. Not at all. It's just that I feel so disgusting right now. We're both . . ."

"Utterly revolting? Putrid? Like the filth of London's deepest alleys?"

"I was going to say *unclean*, but those work too." Wendy laughed. She had forgotten how Booth could make her laugh, how he was like a mirror that reflected her own light back upon her.

"You know there is a small stream just past those trees, right?"

She was already standing. "What? Where?" Booth gestured with his head.

"See where those trees sort of make a *Y*? Under those huge leaves? There's a small stream over there. I saw it when I was searching for fruit earlier." Wendy was following his point.

"And you didn't say something until now? What kind of person does that?" Booth looked discombobulated.

"A person who doesn't think of bathing in a shallow stream, maybe?" He shrugged, amused. "Wendy, you know me. I was looking for food."

Booth disappeared behind her as Wendy pushed back the heavy blue leaves that draped overhead, which were dotted with tiny white flowers illuminated by the moon. Beyond the canopy of leaves, there was exactly what Booth had described: a small stream, maybe waist-deep and four feet across. She dipped her foot into the stream, sighing with delight at the water; it was cool but not cold, just right.

In a flurry of movement, Wendy dropped her dress to the ground, followed by her undergarments, slipping the sticky pieces of lace and silk off her feet. Then with a delicious sigh, she slipped into the water. It came up to her waist, and she bent her knees, dipping her entire head underneath the cool surface, feeling her hair swirl around her; it had grown so long since she had left London. She gasped as she came up for air, feeling whole again, feeling clean.

Using her hands, she sloughed off the levels of dirt, scrubbing every inch of her skin, occasionally scratching herself in a rush to get clean. She dunked herself under the water again, reveling in the stillness, in the sudden void of sound—that fathomless place where she was only Wendy. She sat underneath the water until her lungs pulled her upward, back to the surface. Then she lay on her back and floated, letting the air kiss her bare chest, taking in the stars overhead, those Neverland stars that simmered a thousand times brighter than they did at home. She wasn't the same girl that had come down from those stars with Peter Pan so long ago, that girl who had bowed to her parents' desires, to their rigid social constrictions.

She was wild and free, and at the same time, she was still the good girl she was once was. It seemed as though the stars were whispering to her, and Wendy titled her head to listen, smiling when she heard them say she could be all these things at once. Her feet found the bottom of the stream, and she stood, droplets streaming down her chest as she pushed back her soaked hair.

"Booth."

She called his name loudly. She knew what she wanted. She wanted him. He came, his quick steps betraying what he wanted as well. He stepped onto the bank, and his sharp intake of breath was the only sound as he saw her topless in the water.

"Wendy . . ." His voice trailed off. She wouldn't wait a moment longer for him, not after she had hesitated in London, not after she had betrayed him to Peter and he had forgiven her so easily because that was his way. His kindness, his intelligence, his desire for her, they were lighting Wendy from the inside, and she desperately needed him to meet her there.

"Can you see John from where you are?" she asked.

Booth looked back. "Yes. He's sleeping soundly."

She moved her hands quietly under the water. "Then get in."

Booth silently dropped his clothes to the ground—his tweed pants, his blood-splattered white button-down shirt, all of it fell into the dirt without a word, and Wendy gasped at the way the moonlight reflected off his lean, hard chest.

God, he is so beautiful. Her body was on fire.

Booth slipped into the water without a sound and stepped toward her, Wendy conscious of every waning inch between them.

"Darling . . . " he whispered as his hands found her bare waist under the water. Wendy arched against him, pressing her breasts forward. Booth roughly pulled her against him, and when their mouths met, the Booth she knew fell away as he kissed her with pent-up desire, his hands tangled roughly in her hair. He pushed against her, and for a moment they could have lit up the sky with the heat between them. To Wendy's annoyance, Booth pulled back, his face struggling to contain his raging desire.

"You must know, if we were back in London, I would wait for you to be my bride."

A smile carved across her lips. Even here, as they were cresting a wave of passion, Booth was still a gentleman, through and through. It made her want him even more. She rested both of her small hands upon his cheeks and softly kissed his lips, which were glistening with river water and the taste of her own mouth. Her heart pounded as desire flooded through her, and all she could see was him, and all she could feel was their temperature rising under the bright stars. She leaned her head in the crook of his shoulder and kissed underneath his chin.

"I know you would have, Booth Whitfield. But we're not in London anymore." Then she jerked him hungrily down toward her, her mouth combing across his ear as she spun around. "So call me your Neverland bride, and then take me."

Booth's spine straightened, and his arm pulled her tightly against his chest, their eyes meeting as they dissolved into each other.

"I do," he whispered, pulling her mouth to his, letting his tongue trace her bottom lip.

"I do," she whispered in return. The water around them seemed to give a sigh as they both surrendered, falling deeply into the passion that would make them one.

Booth wrapped his arms around her, his hands moving every-where as he pressed her against the bank of the stream, his mouth never leaving her skin. Wendy gave a whimper as his body began lavishing hers with attention, the smell of him everywhere as she wrapped her legs up around him, her eyes clenching shut as she quietly gasped with delight and surprise. As Booth's mouth found hidden places, she cried out and clutched to him, hoping to ground herself as her body threatened to float into the night sky. The strength of what Booth was building inside of her was staggering, and Wendy felt as though she was on verge of being blown to dust by the power of his touch. Wendy heard the words coming out of her mouth, hungry words, selfishly begging for more as every muscle she had drew taut.

"I love you," he whispered into her mouth. "I love you. I love you. Wendy . . ."

She let out a cry. It was almost too much. *Why is Booth so damn good at this?* Her body was quivering with desire, her limbs pulsing in the water, their frantic movements making tiny splashes. She grabbed his hair, yanked and pulled him closer, not wanting even an inch between them.

He let his hands run over her bare sides, his fingers trickling up her ribs and back down, his touch hitting her in quiet spots that turned her gasps into moans. Wendy shuddered against him, her legs quaking in the water, and when he finally slowed to look up at her, she saw that she had pulled his hair into a wild tumble and that his face was glowing in the darkness with childlike delight. Then he stopped moving, and she almost dissolved with disappointment.

"Booth . . ."

"Wendy," he whispered, his voice aroused. "Look up."

When she lifted her head, a small laugh pulled from her lips. Above them, the white flowers that dotted the leaves of the canopy were slowly falling from their stems, the warm Neverland breeze blowing them toward the water. They fell around them like snow. Booth smiled and lowered his head, his hands finding her hips under the water. Without a sound, he lifted her onto the bank, her legs opening for him.

Wendy let her body fall backward, raising one hand over her head to let the white flowers brush her open palm. Then her eyes met the stars as she fell apart into his open mouth, her other hand grasping desperately at shoulders as he caressed her. He pulled back again, toying with her until Wendy felt his mouth at her ear, his tongue tracing around it as he breathed magical words to her, words that poured over her skin like rain. Booth, a lover of words, a lover of Wendy. She opened like a flower, her heart bursting toward him with violent delight.

"Wendy. The Eve of my country, your lips are drawn with infinite might. I am the mountain your water runs over, giving life to my mossy forests, my dry deserts."

She gasped as his hand found her again, his touch one of tenderness and gratitude.

"Your name is my heart's cry. It knows you the way an infant knows its mother. Each syllable of my lips is spoken in your native breath."

He hungrily drove his tongue inside her mouth, the blossoms reigning down around them. "Your planets map my sky. I was once shadow . . ."

His body met hers, and then they were one as Wendy cried out in the darkness.

"But now I am light, made only of you."

Wendy clutched the earth underneath her as the Neverland sky stretched overhead, Booth's words playing her like an instrument, her heart and body surrendering to the one she had saved herself for. She gasped for the air that wasn't there as Booth's body moved above her, and Wendy silently thanked the stars that she had not given this away to Peter, that she had kept herself for the one whose heart worshipped her own.

CHAPTER SEVENTEEN

Wendy awoke the next day, her body sore, and the memory of what they had done sent a blush rising up her cheeks. Self-consciously she turned over, her eyes searching for Booth, but he was gone. With a groan, she rolled over and brushed off some muddy leaves that clung to her cheeks from sleep, her eyes lingering on her hands as memories flooded her mind. *These hands traced Booth's muscular back. These hands ran down his chest and into the water. These hands clutched the sides of his face as the water splashed around us.* She brought them up to her face to cover her burning cheeks, her eyes closing.

Who was I last night?

Her lust for Booth had brought out something primal in her, and she had unleashed it, consuming him completely. She laughed quietly behind her hands, cringing at the memory of a few awkward moments, but glowing in the rest of them. She was a woman now. Wendy ran her hands down her dress, wondering if she looked any different. *Am I different?* Her fingers brushed her lips. Surely, yes, and yet . . . she was the same Wendy as before. The world had shaken off its axis and somehow remained exactly the same. A bark of laughter escaped her mouth at the delicious absurdity of it all.

"What are you grinning about like some blimey idiot over there?"

John's harsh voice cut through her memories like an ax.

Wendy looked up. "Nothing."

John narrowed his eyes suspiciously. "Are you laughing at me?"

"No, John. It has absolutely nothing to do with you." Wendy stretched her arms over her head before walking a few feet into the jungle from their small clearing. With the dazed smile still tracing over her face, she found a palm branch on the ground and gave it a hard shake. The brown spindly spider crouched on top scuttled to the ground, and Wendy turned back, brushing up the area where she had slept pressed hard against Booth, her body never wanting to be separated from him again.

"Are you cleaning?" John looked so flabbergasted that Wendy almost laughed. "Wendy, we're in a goddamn *jungle*!"

"Watch your mouth, John! Would Mother appreciate those words?"

"I don't know. Would Mother appreciate you throwing away your honor to a bookseller's son?"

Wendy stepped backward, her cheeks flaming.

"You're honestly terrible at hiding things, Wendy. It's written all over your face."

She braced herself for the onslaught of judgment and snide comments, but instead John shrugged with an easy smile.

"At least it wasn't Peter, eh?"

Wendy blinked, the corner or her mouth pulling upward. This was new territory with her brother, and she entered it cautiously.

"There is that."

John shifted awkwardly. "Should I congratulate you, or, rather—can we please be done talking about this now?" He looked like he was about to faint.

"Nothing would make me happier," Wendy breathed, flinging the palm branch into the jungle. "There. Now Peter won't see our tracks."

"Good thinking!"

Booth exploded from the jungle, looking the opposite of how

Wendy felt. Where she felt a bit like hiding, Booth was glowing with confidence from head to toe, the smile on his face so large that it threatened to crack at any moment. "Ho, Darlings!" He flung down some fruit wrapped in a banana leaf. "I have procured us a bounty beyond our wildest dreams!"

"Ugh." John looked at Wendy with exasperation. "Is he going to be like this all day?"

Booth's eyes flitted from John back to Wendy. "You told him?"

Wendy rolled her eyes. "I haven't told anyone anything, but with your grand strutting about this morning you might as well have screamed a message into the sky."

"Oh." Booth ran his hand along the stubble dotting his chin. "Should I not have done that?" Then he winked at her, and Wendy's knees actually trembled, remembering how he had lifted her up out of the water, his hands clutching her bottom. *Oh no, I'm doing it again.* She turned away from him to hide the smile rising on her face and peered at the daunting jungle in front of her.

"How long of a walk do you think it is from here to Port Duette?" asked Booth, his voice reaching through the trees.

"A few hours," John answered quickly. "Best get a move on before it gets too light. But could you tone down your glee a bit? It's positively unbearable."

Booth gave a small shake of his head. "No can do, John."

The two boys began making their way back down the rocky trail. Far ahead of them, Wendy could see the steam rising out of the jungle where the waterfall snaked off into the smaller rivers that flowed through Port Duette. Just before their bodies were swallowed up by the thick jungle, Wendy looked longingly back at the small creek at the base of their makeshift camp, searching in vain for the girl she left behind, but there was only a unremarkable stream dotted with white blossoms.

Thankfully the hike to Port Duette was mostly downhill, and to Wendy's happy surprise, Booth and John chatted amiably this time around. The trio stayed alert for any sign of Keel cats, but none made their appearance, though a sea-glass-colored snake had dropped down from a tree overhead, its tongue flicking in Booth's face. Booth had screamed, and Wendy's stomach had hurt from laughing so hard with John, a much-needed feeling of joy emitting from the siblings.

Maybe we won't die. Maybe this will work.

After a couple of hours of walking, the scent of the port hit her nostrils: the briny air of the sea mixed with simmering meats and heavy spices. Wendy's mouth watered.

"The first thing I'm doing when we get to Port Duette," John declared, "is *eating.*"

"We have to find a way to Hook," Wendy muttered, but as the words passed her lips, she found herself dreaming of a dripping hunk of turkey leg. "Never mind," she corrected. "Let's eat first. We can't save the world if we're starving."

Booth began happily humming an old Victrola tune behind them. As John walked ahead, he looked back at Wendy. "Remember those lemon rosemary tarts that Liza used to make, with the white frosting roses?"

"You're cruel, John." Thoughts of delicious food were actually painful at this point, but John seemed invigorated by them as he wove under tree branches.

"She would put them on a tray with all different sorts of cheeses, and maybe a little porridge . . ." John kept walking as he disappeared into a fold of green ferns that whipped backward as he passed.

"Hey." Booth gently grabbed Wendy's arm from behind. Wendy stopped walking as his fingers traced over her bare skin, her follicles rising at his touch. "Why won't you look at me?"

How can I explain that I can't bear to look at him, not after the things I said to him, the noises I made?

"Wendy?" His fingers found her chin, tilting it upward. "Are you quite all right?"

Their eyes met, and when Booth saw the look in them, he

tilted his head sideward, a seriousness appearing. "Do you find yourself full of regret this morning? That is what I had feared most." He pulled her against his chest, and Wendy breathed him in. "Can you accept an apology for my obnoxious, inappropriate happiness in light of your feelings? Have I offended you with my forwardness?" He blinked, probably remembering a scene from the night before. "I must confess, I got lost in the moment, and when I saw the moonlight on your hair . . ."

"No." Wendy smiled shyly. "No. I have no regrets whatsoever, Booth Whitfield, but . . ." She paused, and Booth leaned forward, his hand on her face. "But I can't help wondering if your opinion of me has changed."

His lips pressed against hers before she even finished the sentence, a bemused smile on his face tracing across her own. He pulled back from the long kiss.

"Do you think any less of me, Wendy? After last night?"

Her body was pulling toward him again, like a fish on a hook. "No, of course not."

His bright blue eyes smiled. "Then why should it be any different for you?" With a grin he nipped her bottom lip and snaked a hand around her waist. "If anything, last night made me wonder even more at the natural phenomenon that is Wendy Darling of Kensington."

As she rose on her tiptoes to fully kiss him, Wendy felt an uncomfortable change in pressure, as if the earth was pulling her downward. She felt him, as she always did, a second before she saw him, a lick of flame in the furthest corner of her brain, a bond yanking her like a leash. "Run," she whispered quietly.

There was a thud behind them, and a snide voice cut through the clearing.

"Am I interrupting something?"

Peter Pan's tone was dark with resentment.

Wendy turned around. There were thick trees all around them, the cover of green leaves concealing where the voice was coming from. Booth pulled out his sword and stepped in front of her, his body tensing.

"In the light of the sun . . . " Peter sang. A black shadow passed overhead. The mocking tone was coming from the trees above them.

"Two lovebirds stopped to make a sight."

No, it was beside them.

"They thought they could hide."

It moved again, and Wendy spun, struggling to keep track of where he was. Peter was everywhere, his voice bouncing off the trees as he sung the lullaby in a deadened tone.

In the jungle directly behind Booth, the trees quivered as if breath had passed through them. Peter's voice was bone cold as he stopped singing and said flatly, "Instead, they'll die."

She knew what they had to do. Wendy reached out and pulled Booth against her. He stopped breathing as she looked over his perfect face, clutching it desperately between her hands.

"I love you," she said, the thought that she might never touch him again tearing her heart from her body.

"Go," he whispered. "I'll fight."

He'll lose.

"Distract," she whispered. "And don't die."

Booth took her hand and put it against his chest, Wendy feeling his heart give a single beat. Peter's voice was closer now, and the jungle foliage parted for him as if he were a god.

"Go!" Booth yelled, and Wendy spun away from him, sprinting forward, screaming her brother's name. She plunged into the jungle beyond the clearing, slashing with her arms as she ran, using the roar of the falls ahead to guide her. Her brother was here somewhere; she had to find him.

"John!"

"Wendy?" His nervous voice rose up somewhere in front of her.

Behind her, the harsh clash of sword meeting sword rang out as Booth bravely faced a demigod. *Please don't let him die;*

please don't let him die. Wendy exploded through the jungle into an open clearing. The ground turned from the black soil of Neverland into moss-covered rocks, the water beyond them so loud that she could barely hear her own panicked breathing.

She stood on the side of the waterfall that cracked Neverland in two. Far above her, the waterfall started its drop; she had come out in the middle—a short grassy incline stood between her and the water. Beyond that, a vertical drop ended in a cloud of roiling mist. John was standing at the edge of the drop, his eyes wide with fear.

"Wendy? What's happening?"

She sprinted toward him, pulling him back from the edge, her breath coming now in ragged chokes as she struggled not to think about what was happening to Booth.

"Peter's here."

"Where's Booth?"

Wendy shook her head. "He's giving us a chance."

"Wendy?" He looked to her now, and in his eyes she saw Michael, looking up at her, asking her to keep them safe. And she would. If she had to die here today, she would.

The ground gave a slight tremor beneath her feet, and Wendy turned, her heart pounding in terror. Peter Pan stepped forward, dust settling around his boots from where he had just landed.

"Oh, look, it's my Neverland bride and her traitorous brother. Who shall I take first?"

He put his fingers against his chin and tapped lightly.

"Such a hard choice. The girl who has betrayed me for the second time, or a boy so weak he's hardly worth my time."

As he stepped closer to them, Wendy tried to dart back toward the trees, but Peter launched into the air, spun, and landed in front of her, blocking her path. The Darlings were cornered now, trapped between Peter and the waterfall. Wendy's eyes flitted to Peter's and back to her brother, who was standing taller, his eyes locked on Peter. She spun around. All the world stopped as she pulled her little brother close, their shoulders pressed against each other, their backs to Peter. Silently, she passed the pipes from where they were concealed inside her bodice to under her brother's shirt. His eyes widened as the gold pressed against him.

"John."

"Don't say it. You don't get to tell me what to do. You're not my mother . . ." His voice choked off.

Wendy whispered her quiet words directly into his ear. "Get these to Hook. Tell him what Qaralius said, about the fairy money, about the song, about everything. He's the only one that can save us now."

Wendy followed John's gaze as he looked fearfully over her shoulder at Peter, who was gleefully tossing a dagger to himself in the air as he eyed them both.

Wendy touched her brother's chin. "I will never, ever let him take you prisoner again."

John's brown eyes looked up at her through his cracked glasses. "But you can't leave me."

Wendy pressed her head against her brother's. "Never." A tear dripped down her cheek.

"Oh, WENDY!" Peter was almost on top of them now, and he wasn't alone; Wendy could hear the sounds of other Lost Boys running through the trees. "What could you two kids possibly be whispering about?"

Peter stepped closer as the Darlings turned to face him, John tucked protectively behind Wendy's body.

"It's good to see you, Darlings!" Peter leapt up in the air and landed just a few feet in front of them, forcing Wendy and John backward. Dirt was crumbling off the edge of the ledge now, disappearing into the spray below. Peter's eyes were sparking navy, and a small waft of black mist curled off his skin.

"What's your excuse this time, John?"

John looked at Peter for a long moment before he stepped out from behind Wendy, his hands trembling, but his voice confident.

"You lied to us. You used us. Me, and all the other Lost Boys!"
Peter rolled his eyes.

"We mean nothing to you. You promise adventure, but what
you are selling is death."

Peter looked at his fingernails, his red hair moving ever so
slightly, despite the lack of wind. "And your point is? I did nothing; I simply took an insecure bratty whelp who was jealous of his
sister and turned him into an admired general, a boy who actually had friends." Peter shrugged, his eyes lingering on John's
face. "Though truthfully, no one really wanted to be friends with
you, John; they just did it because I made them. Because there's
the honest truth: you are a weak, unlikeable worm."

John raised his chin, his eyes meeting Peter's. "Someday someone's going to kill you for the things you've done."

Pride blazed through Wendy.

"Doubtful," laughed Peter. "But I know one thing. It won't be
you, because how could you? You couldn't fight me in your wildest dreams."

Wendy curled her lip at Peter, pure hatred rushing through her.
"He might not be a fighter, but you know what he is? A DAMN
GOOD SWIMMER."

And with that, Wendy turned and shoved John off the ledge.

Peter stepped forward, his eyes wide with surprise as John's
body disappeared beneath the cliff. Wendy watched him fall into
the roaring stream of water. As he fell, his arms were crossed over
his chest, protecting the pipes, protecting his heart.

Her brave, smart brother.

Peter crouched to spring into the air, but Wendy launched
herself at him, all ladylike pretense gone. Their bodies collided
as Wendy curled herself around him, her nails reaching his face.
Jagged lines of red appeared across his cheek.

"WENDY!" Peter's voice was surprised. She pushed him onto
the ground and climbed on top of him. Peter put his hands
behind his head.

"Where are the pipes, Wendy? Is this how we are going to do this now? Like two children at play?" His hands began roaming her waist, searching for the pipes.

Wendy thought of the dead fairy child and the hundreds of ash-covered bodies in the Forsaken Garden. With a cry, she brought her hand hard across his face, the slap echoing across the valley.

His eyes turned navy, and his arm snaked quickly up, grabbing her wrist.

"You little bitch," he hissed. "That hurt."

Wendy tried to move, but Peter pulled her downward.

"Is this how you are now, Wendy? Throwing everything away for a nobody?"

Wendy pulled her face back from him. "Booth is worth a thousand of you. A million."

"And soon he'll be dead," smiled Peter. "In fact, soon, everyone you love on this island will be dead. And when that's done, I'm going to fly to London and make sure that the entire Darling family line is wiped clean." He snarled and flipped her over, his body pressing hers into the ground. "Why can't you just be mine? Why can't your heart just do what I need it to do?" He pressed his lips violently against hers as the pressure of his body pushed her into the ground. Harder, harder.

"Stop! Peter, you're hurting me!"

"Good," he hissed. "You should know pain . . . and loss. You've betrayed me twice now. I can't trust my heart around you, can't trust my better judgment. I need you away from me, until I have finished this war and taken every single distraction from your life. I know that you have feelings for me—I can tell in the way your blush rises to my hands, even now." He grabbed her hair roughly, lowering his mouth to hers. "You could have been a queen."

Wendy raised her chin in the haughty way her mother had taught her and looked directly into Peter's eyes. "I would rather be his beggar than your queen."

A thin tendril of black smoke curled across Peter's skin. He flinched, but her insult had landed true. "This is why I have to send you away, Wendy, because your words, they do something to me. They weaken me, and right now, just on the dawn of war, I can't have you pulling my strings. I could kill you, but what good with that do in the end?" He gave a snort. "No, you and your beau will both be getting exactly what you deserve—and I'll get something in return."

I hate you, I hate you, she thought, and her hand reached for the dagger behind her back. It slid easily out of her waistband this time, its weight just right in her hand. As she brought it out from behind her, the blue gemstone winked in the light. She shoved hard against Peter with her shoulder, and he tumbled underneath her. Wendy snarled and brought the blade against his neck. Peter froze as the sharp tip of the knife kissed his jugular.

"Do you mean to kill me, Wendy Darling?" Her hand was shaking as she pushed the blade against his neck. He grinned at her. "Not such a good girl now, are you?" Wendy stared down at him, her eyes lingering on his neck, which was dotted with small brown freckles, and the knife pressed against it. "Do it," he hissed. "Do it and see what happens."

But she couldn't. Wendy wouldn't draw blood, not now, not ever. It wasn't who she was, and if she lost herself here . . .

"That's what I thought," he snarled, batting the knife away. Wendy barely had time to slip it into her pocket before he was yanking her violently to her feet. "No more games." His hand bent her wrist backward as he yanked her after him. "Boys!"

On command, an army of Lost Boys emerged from the jungle. Wendy's heart ached as she saw the boys' eyes burning with anger as they marched toward her. The last Lost Boy to emerge was Abbott, and he was dragging something behind him: a body.

Booth's body.

Wendy screamed and lunged out of Peter's arms, screaming Booth's name. Abbott's apologetic eyes met her own. The boy she loved didn't move. The left half of his head was covered in bright blood.

"Stop your hysterics!" Peter sighed. "He's not dead, but he's going to wish that he were."

Wendy looked at him. "You're a monster."

A flicker of sadness passed over his face, but it was quickly replaced by a hard stare. "So they say." Peter looked back at Wendy and ground his teeth together. "In a minute I'm going to go retrieve your brother's watery corpse out of the river, so I need to know . . . where are my pipes?"

"I don't have them."

Peter nodded slowly for a moment before exploding, his hands shoving hard across Wendy's shoulders. Wendy's feet left the ground, and her body flew backward in the air, landing about ten feet from where she had started. Something hard punched her side as she landed, and she felt a ripping just below her ribcage.

Wendy moaned and rolled over, her fingers frantically finding a thin branch jutting out just below her breast. Her fingers came back bloody. Wendy stumbled to her feet, the Lost Boys watching with blank faces as she yanked out the branch with a painful gasp. Thankfully the wound wasn't a deep one, and with a grimace she flung the stick to the ground.

Peter shook his head back and forth. "I didn't want to do that, Wendy—I didn't! But when you lie to me, you force me to do things like that." He was above her now, hovering over her head. "I'm going to ask one more time. Where are the pipes?"

She turned her head up, her mouth full of salty blood from where she had bit her tongue. "I don't have your silly pipes. I never did."

Peter took one last look at her, his mouth carefully forming terrible words. "You're about to learn that there are fates worse than death. I know it very well." Then he floated back from her. "Boys!"

Wendy tried to run, but the aching pain punched through

her side, and she fell to her knees. When she looked up, Abbott was walking toward her, a club in his hands, an apology written across his face.

"Abbott . . ." That single word was the only thing she could get out before he swung the club at her head and everything around her faded into a pleasant buzz.

Chapter Eighteen

Wendy Darling was dreaming. Even now, as she walked through the hallways of her home, there was something about the hazy, crystalline light that whispered that this was not quite real. Down the hall, she could hear the loud voices of her brothers as they chased each other round the furniture; the signature booms of their feet on the hard floor came bouncing up the hallway. They sounded so happy, their shrieks of laughter putting a smile upon her face. She heard a quiet shuffling behind her and turned in time to see her mother brush past her. Wendy reached out her fingers just to touch her mother's shoulder. Mary Darling turned and looked back at the empty hallway, not seeing anything.

"I miss you," Wendy whispered. "I'm sorry."

Her mother blinked once before turning away, walking back to the family that was now clustered in the doorway, eagerly awaiting their tea. John and Michael rushed toward her mother, John grabbing the cup with a thankful smile, Michael burying himself in her skirts. Her father kissed her mother's forehead and rested his hand protectively on her mother's swollen belly.

It was as if Wendy didn't exist.

She reached out to them from her place in the hallway, but suddenly she couldn't raise her hand. She looked at her feet, and they were frozen as well, unmovable.

"Mother! Help me!"

But the Darling family had disappeared, and by that time it was already too late. The door at the end of the hall burst open, and black water swallowed Wendy. She opened her mouth to scream, but the water filled in, flowing down her throat and into her lungs. She felt herself drowning and turned her head back to the light under the door, to the place where her family waited for her.

Wake up.

Wendy swam up toward consciousness and finally jerked awake. *It was a nightmare, only a nightmare, but why am I still choking on water?* Wendy screamed, causing a stream of black bubbles to rise up from her mouth—someone was holding her face underwater. Her head jerked backward, and her feet kicked against something hard, but the sounds around her were muffled by the water.

I'm going to die. There were no flashes of life before her eyes; there was just one thought: *Air, air, air.*

Just when her chest went slack, Wendy's head was yanked back out of the water. She gave a violent gasp and fell forward, her lungs expelling water all over the floor. After a moment she sank to her knees, treasuring each precious breath, the air bringing her back to life. Once her ribs stopped heaving, she became vaguely aware of the form standing over her. A calloused hand grabbed her arm and yanked her to her feet.

"Ah, I see you're awake now, lass! Just thought I'd give you a bit of a bath to help wake you up." The body pressed her up against a thick wooden barrel, the same one that she had almost drowned in.

"Let me go!" she shrieked.

"I don't think so," hissed the voice in her ear, sour breath washing over her face. A filthy hand caressed her cheek. "Do you think the captain will care if I take a little something for the journey? A trollop like yourself won't mind . . ."

Beneath their feet, the ground bucked and rolled to the right, a familiar sensation. Her sea legs weren't what they used to be, and Wendy would have fallen if the body behind her hadn't braced itself uncomfortably against her.

"'Tis a rough sea today," the pirate spat, just as the ship pitched forward, the starboard groaning. Water sloshed over her hands as the man behind her uttered a guttural curse.

Wendy bit her lip, hard, hoping to wake herself up. *Get your wits about you, girl.* She was on a ship; that much she knew. Her hands quickly slipped out of the coarse rope binding her wrists while at the same time she aimed a kick backward into the man's groin.

He let out a girlish scream at the exact moment the sickly stench of rot hit Wendy's nostrils. Wendy choked back a mouthful of bile as she realized exactly where she was.

The Undertow.

It was the ship of one Captain Maison, a man who had aligned himself with Peter Pan and betrayed Hook; a man who had wanted Wendy for his own reasons; a man who had shown himself to be without mercy, or decency.

He possessed an evil of the purest kind. And Wendy was on his ship.

"Larcenous whore bait!" the pirate cursed as he doubled over. "I'll take a finger for that, you little cur."

Wendy frantically looked around, trying to get her bearings. She could tell by the water level that splashed against the port windows and by the fine grains of salt crusting halfway up the walls that she was somewhere near the bottom of the ship. Possibly the level above the food stores. Her eyes quickly found the stairs on the side of the room and she bolted forward, away from the pirate curled on the ground, protecting his goods.

She flung herself up the stairs and pushed open the trapdoor. Another level opened up above her; there was a narrow warped oak hallway, red paint splashed upon the walls in gruesome arcs, knives dangling from hooks. She turned and found the next stairway and then the next, the ship passing by in a blur of ugliness. When she turned one corner, a rat dashed past her feet and disappeared into a hole in the floor, where licks of seawater drips calcified walls. She couldn't breathe; she just had to get up—and out. Two pirates stepped out of the kitchen as she darted past them, their confused faces turning hungry.

"Oy, look at this! A wee bird come to the cat cage for a little petting!"

Wendy spun around and headed the other way, her breaths coming fast, panic rising inside of her. She tore past a glittering room overflowing with coins and jewels. A young guard standing outside the door stared at her wide-eyed as she passed.

"Hey, get back here!"

Her eyes found the next set of stairs, jutting out from a wall like broken teeth. She leapt up them, slamming her hand against the shut trapdoor above her.

"Girly, don't be afraid." One of the disgusting kitchen pirates leered at her, his teeth stained with wine. "You've got plenty of time to get to know us."

Through the slats above her she could see light, and Wendy pushed, using every ounce of her strength. She let out a primal scream as she jammed her shoulder hard against the trapdoor, her neck feeling like it would snap with the pressure. Pirate hands grabbed at her legs, their filthy words washing over her as she was pulled back down, down into an unimaginable hell.

She gave one last shove that sent the door bursting upward, and Wendy shielded her face from the scorching sun before scrambling up into the light. A hand grabbed her by the collar and yanked her out of the belly of the ship, flinging her onto a deck covered with slimy silver fish. Wendy slid over their bodies, and her hands were shoved deep into their slit bellies as she struggled to stand. She gagged once and heard the laughter of men all around her as she got to her feet, though she kept her back crouched defensively. Wendy snarled, feeling stripped raw; she was a cornered animal.

Captain Maison stepped forward. He was just as she remembered from that day in the privateer when he had murdered Captain Xian Li in cold blood; he was more viper than man. Slick black hair was pushed back from his pockmarked face, his left ear was missing, and a red raised scar covered his cheek where Hook had ripped his face open. Wendy—the prize Maison had once desired—now stared at him with blank hatred.

"What do you want with me, Maison?" she spat wearily. "Why am I here?"

Maison stepped forward. "It's Captain Maison to you."

Wendy didn't flinch. "There is only one man that I call captain, and he's the one who gave you that scar."

Maison's confident face twisted into a look of pain but then moved quickly back into an unhinged grin. The captain of the *Undertow* was certifiably crazy, and that was more dangerous than anything else. He ran a finger down Wendy's cheek, and she winced.

"Actually, Miss Darling, the only captain that matters is the one that *owns* you. Peter Pan needed some ammunition of mine, so he sold you to me, his prized filly to hold for the time being. Not only will you now have a front-row seat for the grand reordering of Neverland, but you'll also get the pleasure of my company. Of its most intimate nature."

Revulsion rose up in Wendy's throat as she stared at the scar that nearly split Maison's face in half.

"Where is Booth?"

"Booth?" Maison stroked his gnarled black beard, and Wendy saw a tiny speck of white lice crawl for cover. *I'm going to vomit.* Without warning, Maison grabbed both her hands and began swaying back and forth with her, dancing a waltz. Wendy tried to pull away, but he yanked her back toward him. "Dance with me, and I'll tell ya. Refuse, and I'll take one a your purty eyes."

Wendy stared hard at his face before she leaned softly right and left.

"Ah, there it is. It's been a long time since I have waltzed with a proper lady."

A tear ran down Wendy's cheek, and Maison leaned forward and flicked it off.

"Where we were? Oh yes." He turned her slowly in his arms. "You were wondering about the boy with the blue eyes. I'll tell you something, my dear: I haven't seen one like him in *decades*. He's so clean, so polite, even when he's begging me to take his life for yours." He spun her around, and their feet slid over dead fish. "One more gentleman brought low by the power of my ship."

Wendy's head jerked up. "What have you done to him?"

Maison reached forward, his fingers delicately tracing the lace of her collar. "Don't worry, dear, he's been put to work."

Booth is alive.

Wendy's shoulders sagged in relief. He was alive, and that was all that mattered in this one tiny moment, even as Maison twirled her under his arm. Wendy was vaguely aware of the crew watching them, growing closer with each step. "You have yet to mention my impressive ship, girl. You best notice it before it notices you."

Wendy glanced around at the pathetic hunk of twisted wood, mangled skeletons adorning every possible surface, a mast slick with mud. Above her, tattered black sails snapped in the wind, and a faint song was carried on the breeze, perhaps sung by some pirates below deck. Wendy didn't want to see anymore, didn't want to feel these men's eyes resting hungrily upon her form. Her mouth twisted as she turned back to Maison, anger surging through her.

"I don't give a shit about your disgusting ship, or the men that sail it."

It was the first time she had ever said that word, and she meant every letter of it. Maison laughed.

"Aye, I like your spunk! Peter said you were a handful, and I didn't believe him. I thought, how could a girl so lovely cause so much trouble? I thought maybe he didn't understand that a girl like you has one purpose."

Wendy longed to rip open the other side of his face. She stared hard into his eyes, which were a surprising pale green, far too light for such a dark heart.

"And men like you always take what they want because they know that girls like me would refuse every time."

Maison stopped dancing and absentmindedly scratched his beard. He turned his head and spoke quietly to himself, his voice rising as if he were in an argument. Then he snapped his fingers.

"I'm supposed to show you something, little lamb." Maison lunged forward, quick like a snake, and caught her by the hair. Before Wendy could pull away, he was dragging her over to the side of the boat. Wendy struggled against him as he shoved her hard up against the gunwale. "Look out there. What do you see?"

Wendy raised her eyes and took in the endless Neverland Sea before her, an ocean of turquoise lapping quietly against the sides of the boat.

"I see your grave," she snapped.

Captain Maison gave a hollow laugh and shook a crooked finger at her. "I like you so much that I might keep you just for myself and never give you back to Peter Pan." He cupped his rough hand underneath her neck, holding her head in place as he jerked her chin upward and squeezed. "Now, tell me what you really see."

Wendy strained against his tightening hand as fear ran through her veins. "Nothing. I see nothing."

Captain Maison bent over her, his mouth on her hair, his breath as putrid as the fish that suffocated at her feet. "Exactly. Nothing. Nothing to save you, not in any damned direction. It's just me and you and the wide blue, and I plan to make the most of it before Peter's damned battle begins." He chuckled once before spinning her around and thrust her away from the side of the ship. "Now tell me: did you like the little pink present that I sent to Pan Island?"

Wendy exploded, lunging for Maison with a deranged scream. Two pirates grabbed her arms and restrained her as she kicked and screamed.

"You sent the bomb! You killed Oxley! He was my friend!"

Maison shrugged.

"Peter was dragging his feet—distracted by you, I imagine—and I was getting anxious. I needed something to light his fire. And so I risked lighting him on fire, though I'm delighted to hear that the bomb did its work. I put that lovely bow on it, just for you, a little treat."

Wendy looked at him with cold hatred. "You have no soul."

Maison ran his tongue over his teeth and looked nonchalantly at his blackened hands. "No doubt. For now, you can spend the night in the abyss, come face-to-face with your future." He turned to the pirates holding her. "Know that if you touch her, I'll cut off your balls with me own hand. I promised Peter Pan that she would remain unblemished." He winked at her. "The boy who can fly even made *me* promise to leave you be, but you know what they say about pirate captains. *Can't be trusted.* Now, does an upper-crust girl like you fancy a swim?"

Wendy bolted forward, twisting out of the pirates' arms, but it was too late. Maison grabbed the back of her dress before hauling her across the poop deck. In front of her, a filthy pirate struggled to open a heavy wooden trapdoor in the floor.

Maison shoved her forward, grinning madly. "We're going to have such fun, we are! Starting right now. Sorry for the inconvenience, but the stairs are for crew members." He laughed wickedly as the door opened up underneath her. "I'll see you soon, Wendy."

Like hell you will, she wanted to spit, but instead she cried out as the pirates picked her up and threw her inside. She plunged down into murky brown water that sloshed over the top of her head. The trapdoor lid slammed shut above her, sending every-thing around her into deepest black. Wendy held her breath as her head went under the water, her heart pumping wildly. Something slimy brushed against her legs, and a scream threatened to escape from her lips. But instead her hands reached downward, feeling for the sides of the wood. Her panic threatened to rise again, but she held it in, her inner voice speaking calmly. *I know where I am.* Her legs found the bottom, and she pushed swiftly upward, her head breaking the surface of the water just seconds after it had been covered.

"Breathe," she said to herself. "Breathe."

She stood, the water hitting her at the chest. She wouldn't drown, not in here. Wendy was inside a large wooden contrap-tion filled with brine and live fish—the storing place for the food to feed the men on long ship journeys. The *Sudden Night* had one as well, though she had only used it a few times, when she gathered fish for Keme to cook. And she knew the one on the *Sudden Night* held a lever. Her hands felt around the sides of this one, searching for a groove, a plank, anything.

There.

Wendy's hand found a small groove in the side of the contrap-tion, just above her right shoulder. She followed the groove with her fingers and found a wooden lever. She took a deep breath of air, plugged her nose, closed her eyes, and pulled the lever. The contraption opened up at the bottom, and she was sucked down-ward with the fish. There was a feeling of weightlessness as she fell, as her body cut through the ship's levels, and then she landed hard on her bottom, the fish underneath her padding her landing. Silence surrounded her, and Wendy wondered what fresh hells the *Undertow* had in store for her this time.

She was not prepared.

CHAPTER NINETEEN

She was first struck by the sight of an enormous gun, its base a circle of iron, pointed into the depths of the keel. To her left and right, there were cages, *actual cages* of thatched bamboo that lined the edges of the wretched ship. They stretched out on either side of her, disappearing into the darkness.

Wendy slid forward off the pile of stinking fish and squinted her eyes. In the middle of the room, a small fire crackled and leapt, its flames contained in a cast-iron pot. After a moment, Wendy found a long piece of wood—perhaps once a weapon of some sort—and shoved it into the fire. The wood began to glow, and Wendy stepped back, brandishing the makeshift torch in front of her eyes.

She wasn't alone; she could feel it. Wendy made her way forward, the light spitting tiny embers. She began to be able to make out thick rows of shapes stretching from the port to the starboard side. As she got closer, she realized the shapes were human forms. Wendy stepped backward, a cry escaping her throat as a familiar voice resonated sadly through the chamber.

"Move slowly so you don't scare them. And hold the torch behind you."

It was Booth's voice, the sweetest sound she had ever heard.

Wendy did as he said and put the torch behind her back. She

stepped into the middle of the first row. Everywhere around her were children—little boys and girls, their faces so streaked with dirt that it made it hard to tell the difference between them. Torchlight bounced off them as they stared at Wendy with starving eyes and cracked lips, pitiful creatures of want.

"Are you our mother?" a young one whispered as she passed, and Wendy's heart clenched tighter with each slow step. A long, rounded plank of wood sat across their legs.

Eight children sat in each row, their eyes blank. The smell was inhuman, and Wendy was forced to cover her mouth with her sleeve as she made her way deeper into the keel. She passed one row after another, making her way toward the head of the aisle, where a taller figure sat hunched in the dark.

"Booth?"

"I'm here, Wendy, I'm here."

One of the children reached out as she stepped past, his fingers brushing her skirt. Wendy gave him a kind smile, and the child inhaled sharply, as if no one had ever smiled at him before. There was a branding on each child's hand as if they were some sort of livestock.

Tears flooded Wendy's eyes, hot and unstoppable, and she let them roll down her face as she made her way toward Booth.

He was strapped to a tall leather drum, ropes binding him at his chest and waist. The side of his head was covered with dried blood, and one of his eyes was black and swollen.

"Wendy . . ." He croaked her name, and Wendy leapt toward him, her hands longing to heal the wounds that maimed the skin she loved.

"You may not touch him!" snapped a deep voice. She had been so focused on Booth and the children that she hadn't even noticed the ferocious pirate standing silently in the corner. He eyed her warily, his gnarled hands holding a sword and scabbard.

"Me names is Fresh Graves, and I'm in charge down here in the 'byss. Now back up from yer pretty boy before I take yer arm offa you. Back up!"

Wendy took a small step back from Booth; moving away from him was a sheer act of will.

"That's right, deary. Pretty boy gots work to do."

Wendy turned back just in time to see Booth's face collapse into desperation.

His voice was shaky as he raised his head to stare at Fresh Graves. "Can't you just beat me instead? Man to man, there must be some remnant of honor, some quality within you that bespeaks to your better nature."

The pirate stomped over, shoving Wendy sideward as he made his way to stand in front of Booth. He withdrew his dingy sword, the blade stained a dark red.

"No!" Wendy shouted, fearing for Booth's life, but the pirate turned away from Booth and headed for a small boy at the end of a row.

Booth screamed, "Stop!"

The pirate brought his blade up against the neck of a blond-headed boy, probably no more than seven years old.

"Tell them your name," the pirate demanded.

The boy's lip quivered as the blade pressed higher against his neck.

"P-p-pier," he stuttered.

The pirate patted his head. The blade didn't move as he looked at Booth. "Now, I don't talk the way you do, all fancy-like, but I know we made a deal when you came down here yesterday, didna we?"

Booth nodded. "Yes. I remember. Please, don't hurt him."

The pirate roughly shoved the boy's head aside. "Then you know what you need to do. If you don't bang that there drum, little Pier gets a taste of this." He licked his sword, and Wendy's stomach lurched.

"Wendy." Booth eyes were on her now. "Forgive me for what I'm about to do."

"Always," she whispered. Her heart ached as the boy she loved raised his arms and brought two wooden sticks down upon the leather top of the drum. The children wordlessly picked up their oars. He brought them down again, and the children began a rhythmic pulling of the oars, first in and then up before wearily pushing them out. The boat gained speed as they continued to row.

"Faster," hissed the pirate. "They have to earn their supper."

Booth stared at the pirate with raw hatred—a look that Wendy had never seen grace his kind features—but the speed of his drumming increased.

BOOM.

BOOM.

The ship shook with the rhythm of the drum. The children, their tiny arms trembling, struggled to pull the gigantic oars. Sweat poured down their faces, and their eyes were blank as they stared ahead. Some were more seasoned than others, but none of the children were more than ten years old. *No more than ten . . .* Wendy gasped. "The missing children of Port Duette."

Fermina had spoken of this: young children kidnapped from the arms of their mothers. Hook had even told her once that Port Duette was not safe for children.

The pirate spun around. "What did you say, deary?"

Wendy took a menacing step forward, rage thrumming in her veins. The pirate, to her surprise, stepped back. "You took these children from Port Duette, from Harlot's Grove!"

He shrugged. "Aye, and from houses and street corners. What of it? What are those whores in Harlot's Grove going to do with them?"

"Love them!" cried Wendy, throwing her hands up in the air. "These children have mothers who want them!"

There was an audible intake of air when the children heard her words, their melancholy faces lighting up like the sun. Sniffles sounded underneath the pounding of the drum.

"These children belong to Captain Maison. They eat and sleep in this ship, and when they die, their bodies will be thrown from this ship, and they will join the trail of souls that follows in its undertow." The pirate spun in a circle, his sword pointing slowly at each child. "We need rowers to maintain its speed, and besides, they make for good workers. Nimble hands. Easy to feed. That's the end of their pathetic story. Now, sit!"

Wendy glanced around and then quietly took a seat next to a small girl. "What's your name?" she whispered.

"Bekah," the girl answered shyly.

"Hi, I'm Wendy."

When she took Bekah's hand with a kind smile, the girl's gloomy visage notably brightened. Booth's drumming continued, and so Wendy picked up the oar, happy to do something to help these children, and if it broke her back, she would lighten their load. The speed of the *Undertow* increased as the ship fought its way through choppy waters. This was why the *Sudden Night* couldn't catch Maison; it was extremely hard to find a ship on the open seas, and the *Undertow* would always be faster.

Wendy's anger slowly curdled into despair, pulling her deep into her mind. *Has hope ever been so far away?* Escape in the middle of the sea was impossible, and the evil that lingered here in the abyss was less terrifying than the evil that strutted up on deck.

"Faster!"

A thin strap of leather slapped across Wendy's back, and she gritted her teeth, pushing her body harder.

"Drum, you silver-spooned twit!" the pirate screamed at Booth. "Watch your girlfriend row, or watch a child die."

Booth wouldn't meet her eyes as he brought the sticks down harder and faster, the look upon his face a despair Wendy hoped never to see again. And so she rowed. She rowed for Booth, for all the children of Neverland, and for herself—anything to distract her from her own morbid thoughts.

The day clawed by; the agonizing hours stretched like years. The sun had set in the sky when Fresh Graves finally relieved the children from rowing. Bekah gave Wendy's hand a squeeze before placing the oar onto the riggers between rows. Wendy slumped forward, her body exhausted beyond measure. Silently, the children stood up from the oars and scampered to their cages, shutting the doors behind them. Once they were in the cages, Wendy heard the first sounds of life: quiet chattering between the children, clapping games, and songs as they rested.

It lifted her spirit and broke it all at once.

The skin on her hands had blistered at first, and then, after several more hours of rowing, it finally broke, and the cracks on her palms stretched out into a river of sores that bled openly. She couldn't even feel them anymore. Her spine felt as though someone had put a torch to it, and in the spot where her back met her hips, a sharp pain made it almost impossible to stand. As she attempted to walk, strong hands circled her waist.

"I've got you." Booth's arms looped around her, trembling even as Wendy sank against them.

"Where can she rest?" he snapped at Fresh Graves, who was picking something from his nose.

"Don't care much, long as you stay down here. Besides . . . " his mouth curled up into a repulsive grin, "where are you going to go?"

Booth tucked Wendy against his shoulder and led her to a quiet corner where extra oars lay in a bed of shallow hay. Together they both kneeled, Wendy almost collapsing under the weight of her exhaustion. Booth leaned back against the wall and pulled Wendy up against his chest. Then the trapdoor to the abyss flung open, and Booth's arms tightened around Wendy.

"I won't let Maison take you. I'll die first."

Wendy prayed that it wouldn't come to that as a pair of boots descended the stairs. But relief washed over her as a handful of pirates appeared carrying bowls of porridge for the children, who reached out through the bars with open hands. Two bowls were slapped down in front of Wendy and Booth amid a litany of curses. Booth picked up his bowl with a disgusted look.

"Do you suppose it's poisoned?"

Wendy was already eating hers, and she raised an eyebrow at him. "Would it matter at this point?"

Booth sighed and ran his hand through his sweat-soaked hair. "It most bloody well will. I don't plan on staying in this hell for much longer."

She smiled in spite of the direness of their situation. "And why is that?"

"There are so many reasons. For one, I have to . . . no, I *need* to see the look on Peter's face when he is beaten. And because I want to watch you hug your little brother again—Michael, not John, *obviously*. And . . ." Wendy raised her eyebrow. "And I want to do what we did the other night again. Mostly, it's that. It's almost the only reason, really."

Wendy kissed him under his chin, thankful that even here he could lighten her mood. "I want all those things too. More than anything."

The pirates in charge of feeding the children stomped over to Wendy and Booth and growled, "Hands!" They both reached out their hands, cringing as rusted iron shackles were locked onto their wrists.

"The captain wants this one bright and early tomorrow morning," one pirate said.

"Try and take her from me." Booth's eyes filled with blazing heat.

"Won't be a problem once you walk the plank. That'll also be happening bright and early tomorrow morn. Sharks like to eat best at dawn."

Wendy gasped, and Booth tightened beside her. The pirates took their leave, chuckling as they headed up the stairs. Nausea washed over her.

"I won't let it happen. I'll bargain with Maison. Whatever I have to do. I'll keep you safe. I'll keep us all safe."

That uncomfortable thought, the one Wendy had been wrestling with since she had left Pan Island the first time, brought itself to her lips as she turned to Booth, her eyes serious.

"I need to talk to you about something."

An hour later, Booth leaned back, his eyes red.

"So it's decided." Wendy nodded.

Booth said quietly, "Then let's sleep now. Save our strength. God knows what the morning will bring."

Wendy acquiesced, her eyes closing as sleep pulled at her, but she thought she heard Booth's voice at the edges of her slumber: "I pray this isn't the end of our journey, my love."

Later, though, she wondered if she'd dreamed it when she awoke to the feeling of the bodies of the children pressed around her, piled like puppies, their warm breath on her face. When she cracked her eyes open, she saw Bekah snuggled up against her chest, a look of peace crossing her face.

"Are you out of your cage?" whispered Wendy.

Bekah smiled. "Always."

Wendy turned over in time to see two boys snuggled up against Booth's back. He harrumphed once before falling back into loud snores, his arms tightening around Wendy. With a half-awake smile, Wendy gently laid her hand on Bekah's hand. As she fell back into unconsciousness, Wendy found herself remembering that there was still innocence in this world worth fighting for, no matter how hopeless it seemed.

CHAPTER TWENTY

Wendy woke up and her hands reached for Booth, but she found only cold hay. The children that had kept them warm were seated back in rowing position, oars clutched in calloused hands, blank looks upon their faces. Booth was once again strapped to the drum, a look of abhorrent misery upon his face.

"C'mon." Fresh Graves eyed her nastily. "Captain wants you upstairs." She barely had time to shake the sleep out of her eyes before she was dragged up through the levels of the wretched ship, the pirate practically flinging her through the trapdoor. Light exploded into her eyes along with misty gray air; the dawn was breaking over the sea with a melancholy creep. Maison stood a ways in front of her, his eyes red-rimmed and bloodshot. He'd been drinking.

"Come here, girl!" he shouted. Another pirate tried to yank her by the arm, but Wendy pulled back with a snarl.

"I can walk there by myself, thank you very much." She walked toward the starboard side, toward Maison, and she listened to his voice rising and falling as he argued loudly with himself. They met beside the railing. To the right of her, a long wooden plank pushed out from the side of the ship. Was that for Booth? Maison turned and handed her a glass of red wine.

"Your boy walks the plank this morning." He raised his own

glass. "Am I not a man of mercy, giving you this? Drink will help with the sting. Also, once he's gone, you and I are going to celebrate, and I love the taste of wine on a woman's breath."

"Maison . . ." She was prepared to bargain for Booth's life, whatever the cost, but he suddenly leaned out over the water, his focus on something else.

"Debris off the starboard side! Come about!"

The *Undertow* gave a nauseating lurch, and the bottom of the ship bumped up against something hard with a resounding crash.

"What is it, captain?" called Maison's first mate.

Maison ran his lips over his sharpened teeth.

"Looks like a rowboat. Make sure it's secure before we bring it aboard."

A rowboat. A possibility of escape. Wendy's eyes lit up at the idea, but she stayed perfectly still. Maison came quickly up behind her, his hand wrapped around her waist as he pushed her against the gunwale.

"I want you to look there!"

Wendy followed his point down into the water, where the large rowboat rocked gently beside the *Undertow*. She leaned farther over the side.

"What do you see?"

Her stomach heaved.

"Bodies," she whispered.

There were two of them—two men, both bloated and long-dead. One of them had a knife wound across the front of his shirt, the linen cracked with dried blood; the other had a dark stain at the back of his head and a hole between his brows. Their eyes were open, staring lifelessly up at the *Undertow* as flies crawled across their lips. Underneath their bodies was a rich damask blanket and what looked like burlap sacks peeking out from underneath it.

"Do you recognize these men?"

Wendy squinted. "No. I mean . . . it's hard to tell, but no." There was no need to lie; she had never seen these men before. Maison spun her around before lowering his face to hers, his eyes searching for signs of a lie. Wendy swallowed as his wretched breath washed over her face.

"Good." He turned and yelled for his crew. "Wade! Inch! Check the bodies, you scallywags! Anything of value comes aboard. Throw the bodies into the sea. Every gold piece goes to me, and if I find one disappearing into your pocket, we'll be feasting on your innards tonight."

Two pirates tightened ropes around their waists and leapt over the edge of the ship, scurrying like spiders fearful of the light. They dropped down onto the rowboat, which gave a creak under their weight.

"Oy, they're dead, all right!" the one called Inch cried.

The other pirate, Wade, reached over and began flopping the dead man's arm back and forth. "Looks and smells like they've been dead for days, aye, Captain!"

Maison pushed his tongue in and out of his mouth. "Then bring the boat up! We don't want a single piece of gold missed."

The *Undertow* swayed slightly as the rowboat was brought up. From the edge of the deck, Wendy watched as it crept ever higher, threatening to buckle under its own strain. The smell of rotting corpses hit her once the boat was level with the deck.

Maison stepped past her. "Strip the bodies and the boat clean."

"What do we have here, men?" Wade shouted. "These poor souls probably killed each other over this load. Lucky us, gents, that it's ours for the taking." He bent over again. "Gold and . . . what's this?"

A sharp shot rang out from the rowboat, and everyone froze. Inch stared straight ahead, his eyes wide open in shock. A large hole had opened up in the center of his forehead, and a ribbon of smoke curled lazily out of his brain. Wendy gripped the railing as the pirate fell facedown into the rowboat. Three more shots rang out, and three more pirates' heads opened in the same manner.

What is happening? What is happening?

Wendy stepped back as Maison stepped forward, confusion playing across his face.

"What the devil?"

"Takes one to know one."

The familiar deep voice sent shivers up Wendy's spine.

The blankets that covered the bottom of the rowboat were flung upward, the dead bodies that covered them pushed off the sides of the boat. The barrels of two pistols emerged, followed by thick forearms covered with coarse black hair and inked demons. Smith's crazed eyes came next, wide with bloodlust. Voodoo and Black Caesar emerged from behind him, their guns poised at the ready. It was too much to process; Wendy's heart leapt in her chest.

"Smith" she shouted. Their eyes met for just a second.

"Good to see you, Wendy." He aimed the gun at Maison, who watched with sheer unbelief.

"But how . . . " Maison sputtered, caught off guard. "You can't catch us."

"We can, and we did, and we came for our girl, you son of a bitch." Smith fired. Maison grabbed Wendy's wrist and dove to the side, the shot narrowly missing them both before exploding against the mast. Wood splinters stung Wendy's face.

"I'll kill her first!" Maison grabbed Wendy's neck with blackened fingers.

No, he will not.

Wendy cocked her free fist back and smashed it into Maison's mouth, feeling his teeth splinter on impact. Then she brought her leg up and slammed it against his midsection. Blood poured from his mouth. Gunshots were echoing all around her as she twisted free of his grasp and darted away from him. Maison was reaching for his sword. Smith and Voodoo were now firing on anything that moved, and Black Caesar aimed his gun at the deck. Voodoo grabbed the lines and yanked the rowboat closer to the deck.

"Ah, the *Undertow*. Smells how you look, Maison!" Voodoo shouted.

Smith leapt off the rowboat and landed hard on the deck, followed closely behind by Voodoo and Black Caesar.

"Get off my ship!" Maison screamed, his eyes crazed.

"Don't think so," snapped Smith. With a mean grin, he flashed his knife and severed the lines holding the rowboat.

Smith was moving forward now, his gun firing rapidly. Wendy shot to her feet and tried to run back for the stairs, but she was blocked by a chorus of gunfire as Maison's men ran to defend their captain.

Smith stood calmly in place, his pistols taking them out one by one.

"Kill them!" Maison screamed. He grabbed his sword and lunged at Black Caesar, who spun aside. Maison struck again, and his and Black Caesar's swords clanged off one another as Smith gunned down every pirate emerging from the bottom of the ship. An alarm bell sounded, and Wendy knew that any minute the deck would be swarming with the crew of the *Undertow*.

She heard a terrible scream and turned just in time to see Maison slowly pull his bloody sword out of Black Caesar's heart. Black Caesar blinked twice before slumping to the ground. Maison raised his sword and watched the blood drip down the blade. He looked toward Smith with a crooked smile upon his face.

"Does your captain always send his pirates to do his dirty work? I knew he was a coward."

"I'm not here to kill you, Maison." Smith raised a hairy eyebrow. "I'm here to destroy you." Maison lunged at Smith, who sent a shot just past his head.

In the chaos, Wendy moved. Two gunshots whizzed past her as she headed toward the back of the ship. Pirates were streaming out from below deck now, most of them falling a second later in a collapse of blood as Voodoo took them out one by one.

Something changed in the air, and a cool wind rippled across the deck when Wendy reached the poop deck.

A high-pitched whining sound hit her ears, and Wendy paused and looked down in surprise at the wineglass still in her hand. All that had happened, and she hadn't let it go. The glass was vibrating in her hand. *Oh God.* Wendy almost laughed. She had chalked it up to another silly pirate superstition, and yet . . .

One of Maison's pirates was crawling past her, a trail of blood in his wake as he tried to make his way toward a captain who couldn't care less.

"Captain, is that a storm?" he asked. A black thing took shape on the horizon. Wendy turned to Maison with a wicked smile and raised her glass to him. "That's not a storm, Captain!" she said loudly. "That's a night. And it comes suddenly."

Maison was scrambling to his quarters with Smith following behind him.

"Get the coin and get off the ship, Wendy!" he yelled over his shoulder. "NOW!"

"There are children below deck!" she screamed.

"Well, you'd better figure that out then!" He swiveled his gun from the hip and fired at a pirate coming up from behind her.

Wendy had just stepped near the stairs when the front of the *Undertow* exploded into a mess of fiery splinters and burning shards of wood. The wineglass went soaring into the water. She fell against the railing, holding on as the *Undertow* swung hard to the right. Through a pillar of smoke, she could finally see the black ship on the horizon.

BOOM.

A second explosion came, this time near the mast. *Hook is not waiting.* Wendy climbed to her feet, ears ringing. Smith was on his back, blinking hard.

"Get up!" Wendy raced over to him, yanking him upward and pushing the gun back into his hands. "Are you all right?" Blood ran down the side of his head.

"Don't wait for me; I got plenty more men to kill today. AARGGH!"

Smith leapt to his feet and disappeared into the haze of black smoke screaming like a mad man. Wendy ran across the burning deck. The front of the ship was pulling down into the sea as pieces of it burned.

BOOM.

Another hit landed from the *Sudden Night*, which she could clearly see approaching now, its cannons leveled at the *Undertow*. The *Undertow* shuddered underneath her feet as the mast began to fall toward her. Moving as quickly as she dared, Wendy flung open the fish hatch and leapt inside just as the mast crashed above her. She plunged deep into the dirty water, her hand hitting the lever on the way down. Then she was falling, landing on dead fish. She was on her feet before she even knew what was happening.

The rows in the abyss were empty, the oars lying abandoned on the floor of the keel. In the flickering light of the fire, Wendy saw Booth standing protectively in front of the children. Fresh Graves lay behind Booth in a pile of blood-soaked hay with his sword and scabbard in his hand. Booth was trembling as he met Wendy's eyes.

"He was going to kill them. I couldn't . . . I couldn't . . ." There was no time for his explanation. Wendy took a step forward, and the floor rocked beneath her as the front of the ship began to tear from the middle. The children screamed as they slid out from behind Booth's arms. Wendy ran forward, snatching two of them before they were impaled on a wall of weaponry.

"Bekah!" she yelled, "Is there any way to get out of here without taking the stairs?"

The girl's face was pale, shocked. She had seen a man killed. Wendy understood. She grabbed the girl's chin and looked gently into her eyes.

"Look at me, Bekah! I'm right here." Bekah's eyes came into focus. "We need a way out."

"Yes," she said slowly, waking. "Yes! There is a hatch, underneath there, behind the gun. It opens to the outside, but most of the time it's underwater." When Wendy turned, Booth was already making his way toward the swivel gun. He pressed his body hard against it, but the gun didn't move an inch; it was iron, large, and secured to the floor.

"Everyone!" Wendy ordered. "Push!"

Several of the children rushed to help him, and Wendy lent her strength as well. They strained, and after several attempts, the gun pitched over, taking a large chunk of the floor with it. Above them, guns roared. Smith, she feared, would not make it out alive.

"There!" shouted Bekah, her hand clutched tightly in Wendy's, though Wendy didn't remember taking it in the first place. "That latch there—it opens to the outside."

Booth slammed his shoulder against the hatch. It stayed shut.

"I hate this ship, I hate this ship, I hate this ship," he muttered. He backed up and positioned his body above the hatch, but just then, the ship lurched violently forward. The *Undertow* gave a shudder as the scent of gunpowder carried past Wendy's nostrils. Above them, some sort of tar dripped down from the ceiling, and then there were horrible sounds: the sounds of shrieking wood and the sounds of shrieking children.

Wendy dove to the ground as a part of the ship was ripped away.

Where there was once a bow there was now open air and seawater rushing up toward them. A black net coated in burning tar sizzled where it had seared through the wood. The ship pitched forward, and seawater flooded into the chamber.

"Get them out!" screamed Wendy just before water rushed over her. She swam upward, dragging Bekah with her, pushing her above the surface, both of them gasping for breath. Bekah's voice rose above the screams of the other children, who clung to the walls, desperate to keep their heads above the water.

"You have to jam it!" Bekah shouted. "Wait!"

Without warning, Bekah ducked under the foaming water, and Wendy screamed her name as her hand disappeared from her own. Smoke was curling down now from above as the wreckage of the *Undertow* was swallowed by sea and flame. *Good*, Wendy thought for a moment. *Let this abomination be pulled into the deep.* She looked over at Booth, their heads bumping up against the ceiling as the water rose. There was a moment of eerie silence as the ship groaned around them.

"Aren't you glad you came to Neverland?" she sputtered. Under the water, his hand wrapped around her own.

"Yes," he said without hesitation. "Dying with you is better than living without you."

She closed her eyes, waiting for the ship to pull them under, but then Bekah's head reappeared.

She held out an iron wrench to Booth.

"Here! This was Graves's, but he always used it wrong."

Booth's eyes lit up as he grabbed the wrench. "Yes!" he shouted. "Bekah, with me!" They both ducked under the water. Wendy blew out a stream of air as the water covered her lips.

Then there was a heaving sound beneath her feet, and a great current pulled at her legs.

BOOM.

She heard another blast, and then another. Two new holes opened up in the wall across from them, and seawater poured inside. Wendy braced for the flame and death that would follow, but there was no fire. She opened her eyes; remnants of barrels were popping up from under water. Barrels, not cannonballs. *Hook is giving us a way out.* Booth began shoving the children through the holes and out into the open water.

"Swim up!" he screamed at them as he pushed one through the hole. A girl's tattered dress swirled around Wendy as she kicked her way to Booth. Her eyes widened.

Girls. In the water.

"Bekah!" The girl turned toward Wendy at the sound of her name. "When you get out to the surface, make sure the girls get onto a piece of wood or a boat right away! They can't be in the water! Booth! The mermaids!" Booth was struggling to shove a pudgy boy out through the hole, and once he got him through, he reached back for Bekah.

"I heard you!" Booth shouted. "You're the last one, right? Go!" Bekah took a deep breath and ducked under the choppy water, disappearing out into the open ocean. Booth looked frantically around the sinking vessel. "Wendy, you're next!"

Wendy heard Booth's words, but it was as if he were underwater. Something was pulling her toward the stairs, up into the burning husk of the ship, as if her heart were tied to a string. There was something distinctly magical about it, and Wendy knew what she needed to find.

"Go!" she shouted at Booth. "I have to find something first. Go without me, and get the kids to safety. And I swear, Booth, get those girls out of the water!"

Booth looked at her incredulously. "What do you mean, go? What could you possibly need right now?"

Wendy was already swimming to the stairs, the tops of them licking with flame. "It will take too long to explain. Booth—the kids! I'll meet you on the other side of this; I swear it! Trust me."

Booth could have argued. He could have forced her into the opening and pushed her out, but he didn't. "The mermaids!" he yelled. "You can't be in the water either!"

Wendy turned to him with a cheeky smile as a burning shard of wood floated by her face. "Booth, they don't want my blood anymore, remember?"

Booth took a second before bursting into crazy laugher, and for a moment, in this hell of fire and death, Wendy loved him more than she ever had.

"That was quite improper, what we did."

Wendy smiled. "I have no regrets. Now, go! Hurry!"

Booth nodded at her once before ducking under the rising water, pushing his way out into the open sea.

CHAPTER TWENTY-ONE

Everything was falling as Wendy clawed her way up the stairs, her feet pounding past the flickering flames. On the other levels of the ship, the world had exploded into chaos—men screaming and fires burning. She made her way quickly toward the room where she had seen the piles of treasure, stepping over corpses so damaged they made her stomach turn.

The fire and smoke made it almost impossible to tell where she was, so she found her way by following the macabre decor marking the hallway. Wendy ran up two levels, the ship giving dangerous creaks underneath her feet. The door that she was looking for appeared ahead of her, and she lunged at it just as a bloody hand snaked around her ankle. Wendy fell forward, twisting defensively, expecting Maison's horrendous face to appear before her. Instead, it was a young pirate, his body burned from the waist down. A pool of blood was leaking out from an unseen wound on his back. He was handsome, with dark skin and brown eyes fringed with thick lashes.

Wendy recognized him; he had been standing guard in front of the treasure room when she flew past it yesterday morning.

How much had changed since then.

"Please . . . " he pleaded. "Could you help me?"

Wendy looked back at the room wistfully, but she knew that

who she was in this moment mattered. She knelt by the dying man, resting her palms across his pale face and watching as his lips turned blue. Her voice dropped to a gentle whisper.

"You'll be fine. A doctor is coming to attend to you."

"Liar." A small smile crossed the pirate's face. "I'm dying, aren't I?"

Wendy swallowed the lump rising in her throat and nodded. "What's your name?"

The boy blinked. "They call me Seaweed, but my real name is Joseph." His eyes had trouble focusing on her. "It's been a while since I've said my own name. Almost couldn't remember it." His ribs contracted hard as his breathing slowed. Wendy clutched his hand between her own. "What do you think it's like?" he asked. "The place that comes . . . after?"

Wendy wiped the blood away from his eyes with the sleeve of her dress. "I think after this comes a place of rest, where you will wake whole to a new dawn. Where there are birds and songs and trees—"

"And girls?" he mumbled, his eyes now staring past Wendy, who nodded. The ship gave an ear-shattering groan. Water trickled up through the stairs.

"Girls sweet as a meadow's wind."

He nodded. "I never did get to know a girl like you."

A tear dropped from her face as Joseph's heart stopped, and a single word pressed between his lips on his last breath: "Mother?"

Wendy reached forward and closed his eyes. He wore a strange medallion around his neck, and without thinking, Wendy quickly slipped it over her head, not wanting all of him to disappear into the sea.

"I'll remember you, Joseph," she promised, before flinging open the door of the treasure room, the dull thudding of her heart echoing in her ears. Piles of treasure rose up on the floor around her; there were overflowing chests of coins and jewels, goblets and golden plates—all of it worthless except what she was looking for, a rare collector's piece: the fairy money. Her eyes darted desperately from chest to chest.

The water rose, and the ship began leaning to the port side as water flooded the chamber. *This is it*, Wendy thought. Then there was a bright flash in her mind: *Don't use your eyes; use your hands.* Wendy plunged her hands into the coins, closing her eyes as water rose over her shins. She remembered the burning heat of the coin, that white-hot heat that marked the fairies. Her hands shifted the coins underneath her, and with fingers spread, she tried to call the coin to herself.

Hundreds of pieces of gold passed under her palms. The water rose to her waist. To her breasts. There was nothing more than gold and jewels, just endless treasure, and her fingers trailed over sapphires and crowns, a strand of pearls . . . *WAIT.*

There, just below her pointer finger, was the smallest whisper of heat. Wendy stopped moving and centered both of her hands over the rising warmth. Slowly, she began pushing back the coins one by one, and then handful by handful, the heat growing. The water rose up to her chin, and Wendy took deep gulps of air as her fist reached down into a pile of coins . . . *there.* Something burned her knuckle, and she focused her hands on the spot.

She pulled the coin—no larger than an acorn—free just as the water passed over her lips. There it was: the skulls, the lines. *The music.* It burned in her palm as she lifted it to her mouth. Time was running out, and Wendy took a long breath before ducking underneath the door of the treasure room and swimming out into the half-submerged hallway.

An enormous creak ripped through the remains of the *Undertow.* The trapdoor that led up to the deck was missing, but luckily, the front of the ship was also missing, and so Wendy ran toward the light. She came out through an opening made of spitting flame and charred wood, just before the break in the ship. Below her, seawater churned with flailing bodies and curls of black smoke. Muted screams echoed over the waves, and Wendy watched in horror as a black-tipped shark fin slashed through the debris. *I can't go this way.* She turned, pushing her way past two dead pirates blocking an exit, their wounds from Smith's gunshots still fresh upon their brows.

She emerged onto the remains of the deck. And there, on a narrow section that had stayed level, Maison and Smith were still fighting, their swords clanging together in a flurry of metal screeches. Both men were bloodied from head to toe, their clothes burnt and their expressions wild. Maison swiped across Smith's midsection, his sword scraping the edge of Smith's belly as Hook's first mate leapt back to avoid the blow. Smith spun and brought his sword down near the side of his opponent's head, but Maison—a nimble swordsman—ducked. The ship buckled again, and both men stumbled, their swords pointed at each other as they struggled to stay upright.

"YOU!" Maison screamed when he saw Wendy. "You're the cause of this! When I brought your aboard, you brought a plague of death upon my crew! Witch! Sea witch!"

Smith shook his head and laughed. "A witch she's not, but a load of trouble she is, indeed!" He slashed out toward Maison, missing by inches. "But she belongs to the *Sudden Night.*"

Quick as a viper, Maison flung a small dagger out from his coat pocket. Wendy screamed as it buried itself in Smith's shoulder. He looked down at it with shock and then turned back to Maison with a crazed smile. "Wasn't expecting that!"

Smith reached up and slowly pulled out the dagger, blood rushing down his shoulder. Wendy's stomach heaved as Smith held the bloody knife up in front of his face.

"I think I'll be using this to kill you."

Maison lunged toward Smith, his sword leading. Smith deflected the blow and sent Maison sprawling by his sheer strength.

BOOM.

The gunpowder stores below deck were exploding now, and

the ground beneath Wendy's feet rocked violently as wood shards showered around her. She looked back toward the pirates and saw Maison crawling toward Smith, who lay motionless on the deck, his sword nowhere to be seen.

"Smith!" Wendy shoved aside planks of burning wood, trying to make her way to him, but it was too late. Maison gave her a terrible smile as he stood over the first mate.

"After you watch me kill him, I am going to cut you into tiny, adorable pieces."

"SMEE!" she screamed at the top of her lungs, the sound tearing from her throat. Maison raised his sword, but before he could bring it down, Smith had shoved his own sword—hidden underneath his body—into Maison's abdomen. The captain gasped, wriggling on the sword like a fish. Smith gave his sword a shake, and the captain of the *Undertow* slid toward him on the blade.

"You can't kill me," Maison sputtered. "Hook is supposed to kill me."

Smith reached out and lovingly patted Maison's cheek, his finger tracing the scar that Hook had left once upon a time.

"Ah. That's where you are mistaken. You fancied yourself Hook's greatest enemy, but that title belongs only to Peter Pan." Smith leaned forward. "You were never anything more than a gnat to my captain, a fly that he swatted away." Smith tossed the dagger he had pulled from his shoulder into the air, and Wendy watched it twist in the light before he caught it and plunged it into Maison's heart.

"Getting to kill you was my Christmas bonus this year."

Maison's body thudded onto the deck. Smith turned to Wendy.

"That was fun, but we need to—" His words were cut off by the deck tearing up the middle. Wendy was sent backward, her feet sliding against the buckling wood. When she looked up, Smith was gone; there was nothing but smoke and air now filling the space where he had once stood. Wendy clung to a torn piece of netting as the sea began rapidly swallowing the remaining half of the *Undertow*. As the churning water came closer, Wendy knew that she was in danger of being pulled downward . . . by the ship's undertow. She laughed at the grim irony of it all before clamping her teeth shut and diving under the water. The sea was cold and angry, swirling as it yanked her downward.

She kicked as hard as she could, resisting the pull of the ship as it was swallowed into the Neverland Sea. It was no use; the ship was too heavy, and the current pulled at her even though she was only a few feet below the surface. Wendy's arms flailed above her as Joseph's medallion floated up in front of her face, winking in the sunlight that was so close and yet so far. *I need to breathe.*

Above her, a large shadow rippled across the surface, and muddled voices followed a loud splash. There was a kick of legs, and then a hand reached down for her.

Only it wasn't a hand. It was a hook.

She grabbed it readily and was yanked upward, toward the sunlight, toward the air.

"Ahhhhhh!" She emerged from under the water with a hungry gasp. Hook was beside her in the sea, his signature navy coat floating around them both.

"Miss Darling, this is hardly a time to make such a fuss."

Wendy leaned her head back and smiled, taking in all the air she could. Hook helped her to the side of a large rowboat bouncing on the waves, both of them struggling against the pull of the ship.

"Get in the boat. Hurry, girl, there are sharks."

Another set of hands reached down for her, and these ones she knew better than any in the world. Booth lifted her up and out of the water, his arms crushing around her.

"Thank God," he murmured into her hair, and Wendy felt overwhelmed with relief at seeing his face again. Over his shoulder she saw the children huddled in the corners of the large rowboat, their eyes staring at a hulking figure who was lying on the bottom boards.

"STOP STARING AT ME YEH BLOODY URCHINS!"

Blood splatters covered most of his face, but Smith was alive. Booth's eyes froze on the figure behind her, and Wendy turned with a smile to see Captain James Hook, soaked to the bone and beaming.

"This is the second time that I have yanked you out of the ocean wearing a dress. One would think that you might revise some of your survival tactics." He shook dripping gray hair out of his eyes. "And while I rejoice that it was not your corpse I found, I am completely unsure why you have brought me an orphanage worth of children, and this rosy-cheeked boy who ordered me around like I was some bookstore patron."

Wendy smiled at Hook for a long moment before throwing her arms around him and wrapping the pirate captain in a gigantic hug. At first Hook went rigid in her arms, but he eventually succumbed to the embrace and wrapped his arms around her in kind.

"It's good to see you, too, Miss Darling. You've been missed."

Wendy said nothing, needing this happy moment to last, intoxicated with the relief pouring out of her. Finally, Hook pushed her away.

"All right, let's not lose our wits here. Smith, has our problem been taken care of?"

"Maison's dead. Stabbed him myself." Smith smiled. "I'm getting a little teary-eyed thinking about it."

"Right." Hook exhaled. "And you, Miss Darling, why are you not speaking? If I remember correctly, your voice never stops. Are you all right?" Anger quickly flooded his face. "Has Maison done something to you?"

Wendy smiled and opened her mouth, her fingers gracefully pulling the single piece of fairy money from just inside her cheek.

"No, but we have stolen something from him."

Hook's eyes lit up at the sight of the gold. "By Jove, you found one." He tilted his head. "How seemingly insignificant, this tiny token that contains all the power in Neverland."

Wendy didn't like the way Hook was staring at the coin, so she curled it back into her palm. "A power that has destroyed the fabric of this place." She looked down at the children, who were sitting silently at the back of the rowboat, huddled together, their eyes wide with fear. "How did you find us?" she asked the captain.

James Hook smiled. "Ah, yes, well, you have your brother to thank for that."

Wendy let out a cry of relief. *John is alive. John did what I asked.*

Booth was grinning and shaking his head. "The prat. I didn't know he had it in him!"

Smith jerked unsteadily to his feet, adjusting his pants, which were ripped from heel to groin. "Yeh want to know how we found yeh? The cap makes it sound like it was no big thing, when in reality, this man moved heaven and earth to get to yeh, Miss Darling! Look at the ship!"

Wendy leaned over to see the *Sudden Night* past Smith's wide girth. While most of it looked the same, there was one noticeable difference: the bottom level of the ship now resembled a spider, with eight long black oars—double the length of the oars she had seen in the *Undertow*—sitting still on the water. She whirled on Hook, her face furious.

"Rowers? You added rowers?" She would claw his eyes out for this.

The captain put a hand on her shoulder. "I can practically see steam coming through your nostrils. We made quick adjustments to the ship in order to catch the *Undertow*. The crew rows—not children."

Smith snorted. "Meaning, we compromised the structural integrity of the *Night*—and put our best men to rowing—just to find yeh! When we caught the *Undertow*, we had to find a way to keep Maison from killing yeh—and that meant sending me aboard. It took an entire night to get us in position! And while I love making dead bodies, I don't relish sleeping under them."

Wendy tilted her head to look back at Hook.

"For me. You did this for me."

He growled. "Don't let pride get the best of you, lass. When I told Maison that I'd meet him on the open seas, I meant it. He should have feared me then, but when he took the daughter of the *Sudden Night* . . ." Hook shook his head. "Maison's death certificate was signed with my blood long ago."

A hundred yards away, the cries of men rose from the swirling mass of fire and wood as survivors began swimming toward the rowboat. Captain Hook planted one leg up on the side and peered out.

"We best move, Smith, lest those crew members overturn our boat."

"Aye-aye, Captain."

"But there may be survivors. Shouldn't we at least try to help them?" Wendy's fingers brushed Joseph's trinket around her neck. Hook shook his head.

"I've been a savior already today, Miss Darling. Don't ask me to be a saint."

CHAPTER TWENTY-TWO

Climbing aboard the *Sudden Night* felt like coming home, and most of the faces that greeted Wendy Darling filled her with abject joy; the crew smiled at her with good cheer, Redd and Hawk waved over-excitedly, and finally beautiful Fermina emerged, her black curls thick with salty air. When she pulled Wendy against the folds of her robe, Wendy's body breathed in a relief so palpable her shoulders shuddered.

"You've done well, my girl."

Wendy nodded, wanting to stay here forever, comforted by this woman who reminded her of her mother.

"My word, what have you brought us?" Fermina pulled away from Wendy, seeing the children from the *Undertow* just over Wendy's shoulder, who were huddled together in a large bunch, their eyes terrified as they clung to Bekah. Fermina stepped forward, her voice soothing as she reached out her hand to brush the cheek of a silent little boy. "My God—I know these eyes. You're Magnus, Thea's son."

The little boy's mouth twisted. "On the *Undertow*, they called me Barnacle."

Fermina knelt before him, taking his hands in her own.

"Your name is Magnus, and I know your mother prays for you every night." She stood. "In fact, I would wager to guess most of you have mothers waiting for you in Port Duette."

"And if our mother's dead?" asked Bekah, stepping forward boldly. "The pirate who took me killed my mother in front of me."

Fermina's eyes went cold. "That bastard." She spit onto the deck. "May the sea tear his body to pieces," she said. Then she reached out and laid a hand on Bekah's shoulder. "How would you feel about staying with me, then? I won't take the place of your mother, but I'll make sure you have a home." Fermina saw Wendy looking at her carefully. "And not at Harlot's Grove."

Smith pushed past Wendy. "Don't you go adopting all these brats, Fermina!"

"Hush, love," Fermina said plainly.

Smith's face twisted angrily, but he offered no retort. Instead, he turned and walked away grumbling to himself, his face flushed. Wendy raised a surprised eyebrow to Hook, who simply gave a nod. It was a happy reunion aboard as Booth met the crew and Fermina took the children to their temporary bunks.

Someone handed Wendy and Booth a hunk of bread, and they tore into it with abandon, feeling ravenous now that they were safe. Wendy wolfed it down in a minute, swallowing the last piece as a familiar face appeared, though the sight of him caused her heart to feel as though someone had punched through it.

He stood before her, silently, the hope on his face more painful than any wound she had ever felt. It was Voodoo, a pirate . . . and Oxley's father. Wendy sucked in her breath.

Booth gave her hand a squeeze from behind. "Do you need me to do this?" he asked.

Wendy shook her head and let herself be momentarily calmed by Booth's warmth against her own. "No. It needs to be some-one who loved Oxley." Wendy brushed off her dress and walked toward Voodoo, the deck of the *Sudden Night* feeling like a vast ocean.

When she reached him, Oxley's father's face fell.

"I can see by your expression that it's true. He's gone."

Wendy reached her arms around his shoulders. "Will you come sit with me?"

Hours passed—hours of tears and anger, hours of laughter that returned to sadness again—and Wendy was vaguely aware of frantic activity taking place on the ship behind them as the sun set in the sky. Voodoo stared out to sea, his face thoughtful.

"I wish Maison hadn't died. Then at least I would have the fire of revenge burning inside me. Instead, I feel nothing. Empty."

Wendy shook her head. "It wasn't fair. If anyone deserved to make it through all this, it was Oxley. He made all of us feel like we were the only people that mattered in the world. He made me feel that way. And yet, underneath all those jokes, there was a fierce bravery. He had more to lose than anyone else, and yet he continued in spite of it."

Voodoo smiled through his tears. "A father couldn't be more proud of his son." He took a sip of the rum that Hook had poured for him. "Do you know, I told him that the last time I saw him? I told him I was proud of who he was, what he had done for those boys."

Wendy wiped a tear away from her cheek. Even though it hurt, it felt good to mourn Oxley with someone who loved him.

"He loved those boys," Voodoo said. He turned to her. "Promise me that his death won't be in vain. That we'll make sure those boys are cared for."

Wendy laid her hand over his, her heart aching. "I promise." Then she heard steady steps coming up the deck behind her.

"Wendy?" It was Booth. "I think I'm going to turn in; we don't know how much sleep we'll get in the next few days."

Voodoo staggered to his feet. "The boy is right. God only knows what lies in store for us now. Hook thinks Peter will make his move tomorrow now that the *Undertow* is destroyed." He reached down and gave Wendy a swaying hug. "Thanks for talking to me about my boy. Makes the heart a bit less heavy."

"I feel the same," Wendy whispered, just as Booth slid next to her. Voodoo left as Booth pulled her close, his eyes clouded with concern. "Hey. I haven't seen John anywhere. I think Hook may be lying—"

"About what?" a voice said, and they both jumped. Captain Hook stood behind them, silhouetted in the setting sun. "Pray tell, what is the captain lying about?"

Wendy got to her feet, her limbs trembling with exhaustion. "Where is John? You said you have him and that he is safe."

"That wasn't a lie, Miss Darling." He looked over at Booth. "Will you excuse us?"

Booth looked at Wendy. She nodded her head. "It's fine. I'll meet you below deck."

Booth gave the captain a look of warning before disappearing into the black night.

"I like him," pronounced Hook. "He's a good lad, your bookseller."

Wendy spun on him. "Where is my brother?" But the captain was already making his way up to the poop deck, relieving the sailor there and taking the wheel.

"Come and sit with me, Miss Darling. One last time, let me talk with you with only the stars as a witness."

She lifted her tattered dress and followed behind him. "Don't change the subject. Where is my brother?" Her hand shot out and grabbed the wheel. "I'm losing patience."

The captain reached out with his hook and gently tapped her fingers. The ends of it were razor sharp. "I am not yours to command, Miss Darling. Do not forget your place aboard this vessel."

She dropped her voice. "Please."

Hook cleared his throat. "Before I speak, let me remind you that your brother killed Owl. Shot him through the heart before throwing him off the crow's nest, almost inadvertently causing your own death."

She dropped her eyes to the ground, remembering the thud of Owl's body hitting the deck. "I know," she whispered. "But he's sorry for that, I swear to you. He's changed. After all, he found you."

Hook coughed. "Yes, he did. And what a righteous, unlikeable little chap he is."

"He's still my brother."

Hook smiled. "I quite like the other one better, the little one. Anyway, John found us in Port Duette. He told me about the fairy king, and about the pipes." Hook reached up and patted his coat pocket. "Which I have, thanks to him."

Wendy straightened her spine. "Tell me where my brother is, or you'll be very close to losing our allegiance. And may I remind you that it wasn't John that spoke to the fairy. It was me, and I almost died in the process."

Night fell around them, the stars like bright beacons.

"Your brother is safe, but I couldn't risk his life aboard the *Sudden Night*. He killed Owl—and Hawk, Owl's brother, is still aboard this ship, as is an entire crew missing their mate. I don't need to explain to you why John could not stay aboard."

He is right; of course, he is right.

"Then where is he?"

"Do you remember the vault?"

"You put him in the vault?"

"You may remember one particular room in the vault, a room with a spinning cage, built to contain a flying boy."

Wendy stepped backward. "Why put John there? He can't fly. That seems cruel!"

"On the contrary, when I saw your brother, he could fly. After a few hours with him, I began to suspect it—though he was trying carefully to conceal it—and I put it to the test by picking him up and throwing him. It turns out that he can fly very well. He was hard to catch after that."

Wendy's mind was whirling. "Flight? But how? He certainly couldn't fly when I saw him last. I would know—I pushed him off a cliff."

"I heard. What a clever girl you are, Wendy." Hook checked his compass and adjusted the wheel to port. "We caught him in a net and took the pipes. John told us that you had been taken by Maison and that I needed to make some very quick decisions if we wanted to catch you. I sent your brother with a few men to the vault and got on my way. I have since heard that he is being well fed and well rested, though he is probably fairly dizzy at times."

At Wendy's shocked face, Hook relented.

"Oh, fine—he's only in the spinning cage for an hour a day. Don't get all worked up. He murdered one of my men. Normally the consequence would be a gruesome death."

Wendy crossed her arms over her chest and looked out at the inky water. "I'm grateful for his safety, though I don't like having my brothers away from me. I never knew how much I had taken for granted having my family in one place, under one roof, and safe."

"Hmmm . . ." Hook stroked his beard. "If I may be honest, having a family alone sounds quite wonderful." Hook's face darkened, and Wendy saw pain flit across his eyes. "Let's speak of something else; what's that trinket you have around your neck? Some moony-eyed gift from your bookseller?"

Wendy's fingers found the medallion, and she handed it to Hook. "Hardly. I took if off of a dying sailor on the *Undertow*."

Hook's face dissolved into such shock that Wendy almost burst out laughing.

"It's not what you think."

"Well, I should think not! You've surprised me at every turn, but a grave robber is not a path that I saw you taking." He smiled. "I'm not sure if I would be proud or horrified or both." He squinted at the trinket. "Probably both."

Wendy sank down onto the bench that sat behind the wheel, her dress gathering around her. "His name was Joseph, and he was dying. He was alone and afraid."

"And you thought you would take his necklace?"

"I didn't want him to disappear." Wendy said softly. She held it up in front of her face when Hook handed it back to her. "Perhaps it was wrong."

"I think it was a kindness. Also, that's neither a medallion nor a necklace."

Wendy raised her head, taking in Hook's strong figure outlined by a thousand stars. "No?"

"Here, take the wheel."

Wendy smiled, shivering in the cool night air. "Really?"

"Of course." Hook stepped away, lighting a pipe and giving a long exhale. Wendy grabbed on to the polished wooden handle, watching as Hook's smoke curled up into small tendrils that disappeared into the night air. Hook pointed to her neck. "It's an equinoctial ring dial. They're rare, but you will see them on sailors now and then."

"What does it do?"

"Well, in nautical terms, it measures latitudes and stellar altitudes, common in the Spanish colonies back in your world. It also allows the time to be read at noon. However, among sailors here in Neverland, the somewhat superstitious belief is that the ring dial always is pulling you toward home. No matter where you are, this dial hones your every decision, eventually leading you to the place where you should be."

Wendy held up the necklace, taking in the gold etchings along the edge and running her finger along the glass bulb at its center. "It must not work very well," she said sadly. "Joseph found his home at the bottom of the sea."

"Well, I hope it works better for you, Miss Darling." Hook raised his eyebrow at her, blowing a smoke ring into the night air.

"You seem different, and not in a good way," Wendy stated plainly.

Hook sighed. "I'm tired, and what I long for most in the world I cannot have without great risks."

"You speak of Lomasi."

"I speak of peace." He took a deep drag and threw his arm over the side of the ship. "And, yes, of Lomasi, though I would prefer not to speak of that. Her name can be a stumbling block or a ray of light, depending on my mood."

"And what is your mood like now?"

The night air blew around them as she waited for his answer.

"Pensive. Hopeful." He paused. "Frightened. Peter will strike tomorrow now that the *Undertow* is gone; losing his best ally will make him desperate . . . and careless. But don't worry; we will see him coming from the air long before his army gets near the ship. You cannot hide a hundred flying boys, not by sea or sky." He smiled nastily. "Though we have a secret weapon up our sleeves that I guarantee Peter won't be expecting."

Wendy's hair swirled around her as the breeze lifted. "And what comes next? After all of this has settled?"

"You mean, assuming we're alive?"

"Of course."

Hook shook his head. "I have never thought that far ahead."

Her sarcastic grin was invisible in the dark. "Liar."

Hook paused. "Indeed. But I think I'll keep that dream to myself. I am, after all, a selfish man at best."

"No." Wendy turned the wheel slightly. "At best you are Captain James Hook, my dear friend, and the man who will free my brother when the time is right."

"If you say so, Miss Darling. John's fate is not one I have thought about."

"Well, I think about it every minute, because he is mine to protect." She stepped back from the wheel, filled with the sudden longing for Booth's lips on her own, for his arms around her waist.

"Catch," Hook said, and the golden pipes flew toward her, and Wendy caught them easily.

"I'm going to bed now, Captain."

The captain tipped his head toward her. "Goodnight, Miss Darling. Sleep deep, for God knows what the daylight will bring."

Wendy found Booth on the steps leading below deck, his head leaning against the wall, half asleep as he waited for her. Without words, Wendy took his hand and led him to what once had been her secret room. She turned the iron knob and pushed in the wooden lever, and the door swung open, revealing the small chamber with the wooden bunks. She closed the door behind them and led Booth to the bottom bunk, losing her dress in the process.

His hands were warm on her hips as he lifted her up around his waist, his palms running up her bare back and into her tangled hair. They tumbled forward into the bed, Wendy's body burning so hot that she feared she might burst into flame.

The night closed in as they lost themselves to each other.

Later, while Booth slept, Wendy crept out of bed wearing only a blanket. She bent over and pulled the fairy money out of her dress pocket, the heat of it warming her palm. Reaching underneath the bed, Wendy found the box of letters from Hook's father that Michael had once found. She turned one over, smoothing out the white paper as she reached for the quill inside the box. Placing the fairy money facedown on the bed, Wendy reached forward and began drawing lines across the paper, being ever so careful not to hum the notes that were appearing before her.

The song of the Shadow.

CHAPTER TWENTY-THREE

The next morning Wendy and Booth were seated on deck, eating with the crew, and Wendy was feeling at home in a way that she hadn't in a long time. There was no sign of Peter or his army in the sky, and it was a relaxing morning, the tiniest of gifts. Booth got along swimmingly with everyone; he and Hook easily fell into long discussions about philosophy, while the crew delighted in having Booth repeat filthy phrases to them in his perfect British cadence.

One pirate suggested, "Say, her fanny's so tight that you could bounce a quarter off it!"

And Booth responded, with a smile, "I dare say that her posterior is quite shapely and capable of orbiting a pound."

The mainland of Neverland sat a mile or so away, a green behemoth rising out of turquoise waters. The Teeth jutted out of the side of the island, the jagged cliffs angry and severe. Sunlight glittered on the water as a flock of blue herons took flight from the shore. As Wendy spooned tasteless porridge into her mouth, she took in the island, thinking of how easily beauty hid a litany of sins. Behind her, the crew of the *Sudden Night* roared at something Booth said as her beloved leaned back, quite pleased with himself. Wendy laughed but found her smile fading as her eyes met Hook's at the end of the table. Without a word, he climbed to his feet.

"SILENCE."

His voice was deadly serious, and the crew quieted instantly. "The birds," he whispered. Wendy turned, following Hook's eyes to the shore. Above the canopy off the shore, hundreds of birds were taking flight, rising out from the center of the jungle. Sparrows and hawks shot out of the trees, their cries echoing across the water as they fled.

"It's probably nothing," muttered Redd. "Probably just a Keel cat that's got 'em spooked."

Hook sprinted up the deck to his spyglass, swiveling it toward the jungle. There was a moment of silence aboard the ship, and every person on it heard only the pounding of his or her own heart. Hook stepped back from the spyglass, his eyes blinking rapidly. Then his hand went to his sword, and Wendy knew it was happening.

"PETER PAN!" Hook screamed, and the table erupted with pirates sprinting to their stations. Guns went up as Hook's father's flag was raised up over the water.

Cannons wheeled past iron turrets that were being raised on the port side.

Wendy ran over to Hook, and he handed her his spyglass.

"Look, girl! Look to the trees, where the birds came from!"

Wendy looked through the spyglass, turning the lens until she stopped breathing. Shadowy figures were rising up through the tree branches, *hundreds* of them, pushing the birds out as they neared the peaks of the trees. It had been a trap; Peter wanted to catch the *Sudden Night* just off the shore.

Hook had assumed they would see them coming from the air, but how could they see what lay in wait overnight in the branches of the trees?

Peter's army surged past the treetops, plunging into the morning light, rising up like a flock of eagles. He was at the head of the formation, brandishing a golden sword that flashed in the sun. He slowed for a moment to look down at the *Sudden Night* below him, his Lost Boys fanning out in combat positions on either side of him like a pair of great wings. Wendy watched the boys she once loved from below, exhaling one long breath, knowing that this was it. The game was ending.

With the sun at his back, Peter Pan tipped his head back and crowed.

Peter's great war has begun.

"ALL HANDS ON DECK! MAKE SPEED, AND COME HARD-A-PORT!" Smith yelled, brandishing a sword as he leapt up onto the starboard side. "Keep a weather eye open on the water to make sure we aren't boarded from below!"

All around Wendy, the crew of the *Sudden Night* flew over the deck, each pair of hands well-trained and disciplined. Pirates scaled the nets around her, rising into the air like spiders. Hook was screaming orders as he ran up and down the deck, double-checking each weapon before taking his place at the wheel. The chaos swirled around Wendy as she stepped up onto the main mast for a better look. Peter Pan was leading his army out to sea; hundreds of boys followed behind him. There were so many of them they almost blotted out the sun.

"LOAD THE GUNS!" Wendy heard Smith scream, and his words shook her out of her stupor. Picking up her legs, Wendy slid down the rope, hitting the deck hard before sprinting to where Hook had taken the wheel. "Cannon men to the starboard side!" he yelled.

Wendy stood before him now, her eyes blazing. "You promised me you wouldn't hurt them."

"Miss Darling, may I remind you that we are about to be attacked?"

Wendy stepped in front of the wheel so that he couldn't see past her. "Keep your word, Captain Hook. They are children."

When their eyes met, Wendy knew she had won. Hook sighed.

"I'll not see my men die needlessly."

"I'm not asking you to."

Hook growled at her and cursed, "God damn you, woman." Then, with a long sigh, he stepped out from behind the wheel.

"Here now, men! I'll thank you to be warned by my words: this may be the *Sudden Night*'s last stand, and a grand one it will be. It has been a pleasure serving as your captain, and by the gods above, I hope to be your captain tomorrow."

The crew erupted in cheers.

"What I'm about to say isn't going to make you happy, but it's going to make you right to meet your maker." Silence folded over the deck. "We aren't trying to kill those boys. The boys who fly toward us now are children, and they have been brainwashed by Peter Pan. You know it to be true. Why, some of you have lads back at Port Duette no bigger than they."

Wendy saw one of the pirates nod in agreement.

"I'm not saying don't protect yourself, and I'm not asking you to sacrifice the *Night* for one of them urchins. But for me—and for Miss Darling here—try not to kill. *Try to catch.* Today is the day we defeat Peter Pan, not the day that we stain our hands with the blood of innocents." Hook raised his sword. "Today, the *Sudden Night* fights on the side of good! And if you aren't with me, then feel free to walk the plank!"

Smith thrust his sword into the air without hesitation, a show of support.

Voodoo followed, his voice shaking. "For Oxley, who was once one of those boys flying toward us."

Redd raised his short sword. "For Wendy, and for Hook, and for the bloody *Sudden Night*!"

Booth raised his own sword into the air, and Wendy watched him with pride; her bookish lover was now tanned and fierce, his shirt open at the collar, his face determined. He was a force to be reckoned with.

Hook cleared his throat. "Now, defend this ship! Take as many prisoners as you can—alive!" His voice lowered to a growl. "And bring me Peter Pan." He stepped away from the wheel of ship to face Wendy. "And you, Miss Darling . . . you know what you have to do? You may be the only one who can truly end this."

Wendy nodded. She started to walk away when Hook grabbed her arm.

"You know I'll kill him if I have the chance."

Wendy leaned forward and kissed Hook's cheek, surprising him. "Thank you for being my friend," she said, and then she darted below deck, taking the steps two at a time, running back to the bunk that she and Booth had lit up the night before.

Her hand reached under the mattress and yanked the golden pipes out from below the ratty blanket. Then, from inside her blouse—because she never let it be far from her—came the fairy coin, and then came the music, written out on Hook's father's letter. Wendy studied the notes, trying not to let her own fear overtake her. Fear, she believed, was the key.

Peter would call the Shadow when he got desperate, but not before; he'd call it when his cockiness turned into that cold fear. And when it appeared, Wendy would call it out of him. She had almost everything she needed—everything except the confidence that she could do this. Panicked voices rose up on deck above her, and she hastily tucked the pipes and the folded paper into a small bag that slipped over her shaking shoulders, and then, without a second thought, she tucked the coin inside her blouse.

Breathe, she told herself. *Breathe, breathe—*

BOOM.

A cannon blast shattered her calm, and she raced down the hallway and up the bone staircase onto the deck of the *Sudden Night*.

Peter's army flew low over the surface of the water and was shaped like a blade and moving just as fast. Just before they reached the *Night*, Peter jerked violently upward to stay out of cannon range, and the boys continued straight toward the ship. Then, when they were about to collide with the *Night*, the boys flew straight upward, curving around the body of the ship, plunging into the air above them.

It was as if the *Night* were being attacked by a flock of harbingers. The Lost Boys were all wearing maroon cloaks with wide hoods, making it impossible to tell them apart, and they swarmed over the deck of the *Sudden Night.* They attacked from up above the mast, from the port side and the starboard; the Lost Boys were everywhere, and they were armed. Screams echoed over the deck as the Lost Boys hoisted their guns onto their shoulders and opened fire on the pirates below. The crew of the *Sudden Night* took cover as quickly as they could, each of them raising a metal shield that came up and out of narrow slits in the deck. The gunfire peppered the *Sudden Night*, tearing the sail into ripped pieces that fluttered in the open wind.

The Lost Boys began to run out of bullets, and soon most were reloading their guns. Corpses littered the deck. Wendy darted for where Hook was turning the ship, and she zigzagging as she ran to avoid the burning pieces of coal that were being dropped from above. They flew down like meteors, leaving trails of black smoke in their wake. When she stopped to catch her breath, she watched in horror as a large rock caved in the head of Bloody Blair.

Above her, Peter gave a joyful hoot. Hawk was screaming from the crow's nest, and then she saw the still body of a Lost Boy thrown down into the ocean. At the other end of the ship, the Lost Boys hovered just above the starboard side, where Booth was running toward the main mast, the body of a bloody Lost Boy slumped over his shoulder.

Wendy pressed herself up against a wall as a cascade of gunfire peppered the wood above her head. The Lost Boys were terrible shots—thank God—and the water around the ship exploded as bullets sliced harmlessly into the waves.

"LINE UP THE BANSHEE!" screamed Hook.

Redd swiveled a harpoon gun toward a large group of Lost Boys clustered in the sky.

"FIRE!"

Two harpoons at opposite ends of the ship exploded in a scream of black smoke, and a long net stretched between them. As the double harpoons arched into the sky, the Lost Boys scattered to avoid their sharp ends, putting them right where Hook wanted them: in range of the net that dangled between them. The harpoons detached, plunging into the open sea, while the boys remained netted together, a sinking clump of limbs and frustrated shouts.

"Fire!" Hook cried again, and the same weapon fired on the opposite side, only this time one of the boys brandished a sword and sliced upward as the net hit, sending it falling harmlessly into the sea. The boy's hood fell back, and Wendy saw Abbott looking fiercely down upon the ship, a flock of Lost Boys circling around him like birds.

"Now!" he screamed, and the Lost Boys plunged forward toward the deck, grabbing pirates by their arms before launching back into the air, using their power of flight to drop screaming men into the churning sea. The *Sudden Night* gave a strong lurch as Hook spun the wheel, and the base of the ship slammed into the Lost Boys throwing dynamite into the ship's open portals.

"WATER CANNONS!" the captain yelled, and thick plumes of water erupted from the sides of the *Sudden Night*, shooting straight into the air, sending Lost Boys scattering and many of their weapons falling into the water.

Wendy watched in amazement as Smith turned a wide gear as fast as he could, his thick arms using the wheel to propel seawater up and away from the ship. The plumes of water arched overhead, soaking them all and creating a protective tunnel of water over the deck of the *Sudden Night*. Most of the Lost Boys trapped onboard looked around in a panic; where they were once winning, they were now rats in a cage, and the pirates descended on them quickly.

Wendy moved to be near Hook's side when she heard a jovial laugh.

"Oh, children—have I scared you?" Above her, the water parted as she saw Peter's face emerge through the foaming wall. His body followed, passing through the funnel as if it were nothing.

"Such grand tricks!" shouted Peter, with his arms raised. "I am flattered by your welcome, James Hook!"

Wendy's hand unconsciously closed around the dagger behind her back, its handle warm against her palm. Peter smiled once at her and spoke in a voice loud enough for all to hear: "A gift for the *Sudden Night*, to repay them for their generous present."

Peter disappeared behind the water, but his hands returned, and they held a white box, bound with a pink ribbon.

"HIT THE DECK!" Wendy screamed, just as Booth screamed, "BOMB!"

Booth's body collided with Wendy's as he threw himself over her. The pirates scattered as the box smashed against the port side. Then: the explosion, which Wendy felt in her bone marrow. Smoke and fire. Screaming. The mast was burning, and a black pirate flag landed at her feet, its edges singed. Next to Booth, a foot landed with no body beside it. The deck of the *Night* would not burn due to its shiny black coating . . . but everything above it would.

The delay from the bomb was the opening Peter needed. At his shout, Lost Boys plunged through the water tunnel on every edge of the ship, gunshots ringing out as the footsteps of pirates pounded the deck. Chaos erupted as the Lost Boys prepared to board.

"Bayonets to the helm!" yelled the captain, brandishing his own sword.

A grinding sound rang out from below deck, and all the harpoons on the deck of the *Sudden Night* swung inward on Hook's command.

"LIGHT UP THE NIGHT!" screamed Hook, and Wendy

found herself sprinting toward a black cannon that sat below the mizzenmast. She pulled a trigger, and a large plume of blue flame shot up out of the lip and onto a piece of flint that ran along the decking.

The edges of the ship flared to life, sparking with mad flames that shot up the railing of the deck, making it impossible for some of the Lost Boys to land. Peter dodged it easily, but the flames caught the edge of his coat. With a disgusted look, he threw it down at Wendy's feet.

In front of her, Smith was cutting his way through the fold, dragging a pile of bleeding Lost Boys behind him as he made his way toward midship. Gunshots rang against his metal breastplate as he punched one Lost Boy in the face and grabbed another by the foot, slamming them both against the deck.

Wendy watched with her heart in her throat as Smith—the man who she had once seen slit a Lost Boy's throat—did his very best to disarm and capture every boy he came in contact with. *Almost every boy.* As Smith turned back from an easily won sword fight that left an older Lost Boy bleeding but not dead, he failed to notice the tiny boy making his way across the threshold near the plank.

One of the boy's small hands was on the netting, and the other was on a pistol that he held with total uncertainty. It was Thomas, and he was trapped and alone, and as Smith turned in his direction, the little boy raised his weapon with a shaking hand. Wendy was already running by then, her arms out in front of her, her voice screaming his name.

"Thomas! Stop! THOMAS!" Thomas turned at the sound of his name, his terrorized face meeting Wendy's as his voice lifted with hope.

"Wendy?"

Smith lunged—a mistake—and Thomas pulled the trigger in fear. Wendy screamed as a bullet tore between Smith's eyes and his head snapped back in an explosion of black smoke. Wendy was on Smith now, her hands wrapped around his meaty face as she knelt over his body. This giant of a man, gone in a second.

Smee was dead before he hit the ground.

Behind her, Hook screamed in agony.

"Thomas!" she breathed, turning to the boy, who looked as shocked as she felt. He dropped the weapon, and it clattered to the deck as he covered his face with his hands.

"Get out of here! Go! Now!" She waved her hand, and Thomas fled upward, disappearing into the water streams. Hook was beside her now, his voice rising over the chaos.

"Smith?"

Wendy shook her head and reached for him, but he shoved her away, his face distorted with rage.

"Turn them off!" he quietly ordered Voodoo, his eyes still like death.

"Sir?" Voodoo looked perplexed.

"That's an order from your captain."

The water cannons ceased, and the seawater fell back into the sea as Hook stomped up the top deck.

"PETER PAN!" Hook screamed. "Come and fight me!"

The world went silent as both pirates and Lost Boys stopped moving to watch Peter Pan descend before Hook, looking every bit like the dark god he fancied himself to be.

Chapter Twenty-Four

Wendy watched Peter descend. He wore dark green pants sewn with leather stitching underneath a green tunic patterned with gold leaves at the shoulders and waist. Upon his head sat a crown made of hammered golden moons. His navy eyes glittered as he watched Hook. His body pulsed with the white tendrils of flight. He smiled that beautiful smile.

"Is it time, Hook, old boy, for us to finally dance? To finish what we started so long ago?"

Hook threw off his jacket and brandished his sword, his graven face betraying the calm that he normally exuded. Smith's death had thrown him—Wendy could see it; he was barely holding it together. Peter stepped in front of him.

Hook raised the sword and leaned it against his forehead. "For you, Father."

"Your father?" Peter gave a hollow laugh. "Why, I had almost forgotten about that pathetic old man." The flying boy raised his sword as though he were seeing it for the first time. "I do believe that this is the same sword I ran through him! How fitting that your blood will stain its blade as well, a family legacy of defeat."

Hook wiped the sweat from his brow and took a fighting stance. "You always had a way with words, Peter. Such clever words."

Peter gave an exaggerated bow. "Only a clever boy can become a god."

"Especially if he's one only to himself," Hook answered. "And it's quite a pathetic god who can't hold on to either of the women he loved."

Peter snarled and lunged forward, his temper stoked perfectly. Hook met his sword in midair as the two stared at each other over the ringing blades. Peter was quick to parry Hook's cutlass and spun outward, whipping around at a terrible speed to clash steel once again. He held the blade steady, a horizon of steel pointed at the captain's face. A wretched grin split Hook's lips as he swiveled his blade back and forth.

"My guess, Peter, is that you've come to rely on tricks over the years, but one must ask, how is your sword play?" He shoved forward, his speed not a match for Peter's, but the elegant arch of his sword was just enough. It caught the side of Peter's shoulder, ripping open the patch of golden leaves on his collar and piercing the flesh below.

Peter let out of a roar and flung out his arm, his body lifting off the ground in the wake of his backswing. The blade flashed as he brought it over his head, and Hook met it with an upswing, the swords humming when they were brought low. Wendy could barely breathe as she watched them fight, the bag tight across her back. *When he calls the Shadow, I will be ready. When he calls it, I will be ready.*

Peter pushed off the deck, flying up a few feet, his back arching as if he were in an elegant swan dive. The tip of his sword flicked up and caught the captain's chest, carving a thin bloody line from belly to chin. Blood splattered the deck as Hook screamed, clutching at the wound before swinging again, his sword arm shaking. Peter blocked the blow, pushing forward as the captain struggled to stop his advance.

Again and again the swords rang out over the deck of the *Sudden Night*. Peter pushed faster now, moving in from above the captain. Hook danced away each strike of his sword, but Peter's speed was something that no mortal man could match, no matter his skill.

Wendy felt hands on her shoulders and sensed Booth behind her, bracing her for the inevitable: that Hook would die, and she would watch her greatest friend perish in front of her. Peter leapt up and kicked Hook in the mouth, spinning in the air and bringing his sword down on Hook's arm. What should have been a scream of pain was instead the sound of scraping metal as Peter's sword met the captain's hook. Using Peter's surprised pause, Hook reached forward with his free hand and punched Peter hard in the face, shattering his nose. Blood poured out from his nostrils as Hook picked up his sword once again and gestured to Peter.

The boy who could fly leapt up with a roar of frustration and struck back, using precise strikes that pushed Hook toward the edge of the ship. Hook was defecting the blows, but he was losing ground as his strength waned. He gave Peter a tired smile.

"As long as I breathe, you will not have what you want. But you don't have it in you to kill me, because you know the truth: without your greatest enemy, you're nothing."

With a cry of rage, Peter shot off his feet and shoved Hook backward. The captain of the *Sudden Night* went flying hard into the wheel of the ship, his body crumpling over the handles as he slid to the ground. After a moment, the captain tried to climb to his feet, but he stumbled forward, unable to hold on to his consciousness.

Peter's eyes were bleeding with navy, the color pouring down his face as he looked down at his enemy. He sheathed his sword and turned away, his cold words echoing up the deck of the *Sudden Night*: "What I want is for you to suffer. And suffer you will."

With that he leapt into the air and shot across the deck toward Wendy, moving so fast barely anyone had time to react, save

Booth, who leapt in front of her with his sword out. Peter would have killed him had it not been for Abbott tackling Booth around the waist, pushing him down to the ground just before Peter swept over them like a hurricane.

Peter landed in front of Wendy, black curls of mist wafting off his skin as he pulled her hard against his chest. Within seconds they were soaring off the deck of the ship, and Wendy struggled in his arms.

"HOLD YOUR FIRE!" screamed Hook as Peter crossed over the bow.

He soared out over the sea with her curled around him. Her body went slack in his arms as they left the *Sudden Night* and flew quickly toward the shore.

It is going to be okay, Wendy told herself, grateful that Hook still lived, but when Peter reached around her back to tear at the small bag, Wendy exploded. She fought, her fingernails raking new lines down his already-blood-splattered face. His flight veered at her attack, sending them plummeting downward toward the shallow water below, the foaming white caps crashing underneath them.

"Is this what you want to protect?" Peter snapped, finally tearing the bag from her back with a sneer as its leather strands broke. "Your grand plan with Hook? All that pressure carried on the back of a shy girl from London." He laughed cruelly. "As if a Darling could ever order the Shadow."

Wendy blinked. *Of course he would think I mean to control it.* It would never occur to Peter that one would throw away such power, that one would want to destroy it. She lunged for the bag, kicking as his torso as he pulled them up away from the water. Peter dangled the bag in front of her.

"Let's see what we have here . . . oh, my pipes, hullo. And what's this?" He turned the letter over in his hand, seeing the musical staff written there. "Ah, well that's wrong. Oh, Wendy . . . how dramatic you are, writing your plan to defeat me on a note from

Hook's father. A man I delighted in killing." Peter snickered as he crumpled it up in his bloody hands, and Wendy's heart sank.

"Just as I will delight in killing his son." And then Peter dropped the bag, pipes and all. Wendy's hope died as the bag plunged away from her, splashing into the ocean far below. Hot tears sprang to her eyes as she turned to face Peter with a look he'd never seen from her before: pure hatred. He flinched as it hit the mark, his body falling out of the air just a hint, but he said nothing as the landed on the pearled sands just below the Teeth. He roughly shoved Wendy to the ground upon landing.

"Stay down!" he growled, all joviality gone. "Or I'll be forced to hurt you."

Peter leapt up into the air, landing beside her on one of the sharp rocks that lined the edge of the Teeth. He looked out to the *Sudden Night*, where Wendy could see that the fighting between pirates and Lost Boys had stalled since their departure.

A large bunch of Lost Boys were confusedly following Peter to shore, their maroon cloaks fluttering behind them as they soared over the sea, headed for their base in the trees. Cannons were blasting out from the side of the *Night* as it gave chase, followed by nets and harpoons that were managing to snag Lost Boys left and right. Pirates clamored up the masts as the ship turned toward the shore; Peter's army was dissolving before his eyes.

Peter stepped forward, a crazed look passing over his face. "They're losing," he hissed. "After all that training, they're losing."

"They're boys," snapped Wendy from the sand below him. "Children fighting grown men. Of course they're losing without you! But you're not a quite a man either, are you?" Peter whirled on her, the madness on his face terrifying, but she refused to be quiet. "No. Not you, Peter Pan—you're something else."

Peter ignored her comment and watched his Lost Boys make the shoreline and head to the trees.

"I do not lose," he said furiously, anger consuming him as he threw his hands forward, flight whirling around the tips of his fingers. "And they will pay for their lack of devotion."

My God.

"No! NO!" Wendy was hurtling toward him now, scaling her way up onto the jagged rock that he stood on, her bare feet slipping on the sharp stones that cut into the pads of her feet. She saw his face above her, his eyes wide with rage, his mouth twisted in anger. "Peter . . ."

Peter Pan uttered three words: "No. More. Flight." He smiled savagely, and the white light that danced over his fingers began pulling back inside his body, lighting up his veins as it went.

And the boys began falling.

They dropped out of the sky like rocks, their surprised screams echoing out over the water, screams that Wendy knew she would never forget. Some boys had been flying low over the water and harmlessly splashed into the ocean. Others fell from greater heights, and some were over the trees, the rocks.

Over the waves, Wendy thought she heard the echo of Hook screaming, and then something dark shot out from one of the cannon holds on the *Sudden Night*. But instead of a following a straight trajectory, whatever it was soared upward, moving impossibly fast.

Peter stepped forward, his eyes wide in confusion. "How?"

Wendy couldn't help the prideful smile that cracked across her face as she watched Hook's secret weapon explode into the sky.

John.

But how? Wendy closed her eyes, sorting out what she was seeing. John had never been in the vault. Hook had lied to her, but he had also lied to his crew to keep John safe and hidden. Because John hadn't gone straight to Hook. He had gone back to the Forsaken Garden. And Qaralius had given him something in return.

"I take his flight!" screamed Peter. "I take his flight!" But nothing happened . . . because John's flight wasn't from Peter, or even Tink. It was from the fairy king. And it was fast.

John soared after the falling boys, catching them one after another, his touch stopping them midfall. As he caught them, the boys linked hands, forming a chain that John wielded at impossible speed. John whipped his arm out, cracking the chain of boys like a whip, catching as many as he could. His movements were sharp and precise; his flying skills seemed unmatched as he caught dozens of Lost Boys who would have hit the sea below like concrete. Then he plunged quickly downward, dropping them harmlessly into the ocean as he soared toward the shore before veering east, to where a fellow general was falling. Wendy covered her mouth as she watched him fall.

Abbott was tumbling down, his body falling the entire length of the Teeth, his maroon cloak fluttering around him. Wendy's heart stopped beating as she watched him plunge downward and watched John rushing up to meet him. *He's not going to make it.*

"Impossible!" Peter mumbled through gritted teeth as he crouched down to fly. But he didn't get a chance, because Wendy launched herself onto him, wrapping her limbs around his body and covering his eyes with her hand.

"Argghh!" Peter struggled to get her off, but Wendy held on, her heart hammering in her chest as she clutched tightly around his neck. His hand snaked around her thigh, and with a yank, he pulled her forward to face him before reaching his hand around her neck. It squeezed as she clutched his wrist.

"Peter . . . stop."

"I should finish what I started in the ocean that day . . . the day you left me behind with a broken heart." Wendy was kicking her legs beneath her, where the sounds of fighting on the *Sudden Night* bounced across the water.

"Tell me how, or I will crush your windpipe. HOW IS JOHN FLYING?"

A voice came from beside them—no, behind them. John spoke

quietly as he said, "Because you aren't the only person on this island who can give flight."

A swift-moving current of air was coming toward them.

"Also . . . GET AWAY FROM MY SISTER!"

Peter turned just in time to see John hit him like a freight train. With a groan, Peter flew backward out over the sea, and John grabbed Wendy's arm. They leapt into the air. "Come on!" he screamed, flying toward the Teeth.

Wendy shook her head. "John! He'll kill you!"

"Probably!" yelled John in return, but the smile on his face said that in this moment, he didn't care.

"I'm proud to be your sister," she said softly. John gave her hand a short squeeze in return.

"Don't get all mushy on me, Wendy. It makes me uncomfortable."

"Abbott?" She closed her eyes, bracing for the worst: one more general dead at Peter's hand.

John grinned infectiously. "Caught him by two fingers, maybe ten feet off the ground."

"Thank God. And the others?"

"Most of them alive, I think . . . except the boys over the trees."

A moment of heartbreaking silence passed between them. Wendy's warm heart ached for the broken bodies lying somewhere underneath the trees, alone even at the end.

My warm heart. Wendy's body straightened. *My warm heart, because that's where the coin is.* She hadn't put it in the bag with the pipes—she had put it back in her blouse. In all the insanity, she had forgotten about the coin.

"My God, John! Take me down, immediately."

"Well, that was always the plan."

"John! Now!"

A rush of air passed around and underneath them as Peter circled somewhere near.

Her heart began pounding. "Where is he?"

They landed hard on the sand. Her brother stood protectively beside her, a sword in his outstretched hand.

"Where did you get that?" she asked.

John raised it up to eye level. "Hook gave it to me. I quite like him. He reminds me of Papa."

"You Darlings are by far the most ridiculous family I've ever encountered."

They turned to see Peter waiting behind them, his eyes bleeding black mist.

CHAPTER TWENTY-FIVE

"You made me do this," Peter snapped at Wendy, baring his perfectly white teeth. "You brought me to this place. You are forcing me to call it."

"No one makes you do anything," Wendy said, shakily stepping toward him. "Peter . . . the darkness inside you is of your own making. But I can help you if you let me. You can choose, Peter. Every morning, we choose the light or the dark, and every morning you choose—"

"Shut up!" Peter screamed. "And if I choose good, what then? Will that make you love me? Like you love him?" He gestured his sword out to the *Sudden Night*, where in her wildest hopes Booth still lived and breathed.

Wendy didn't say anything, and Peter's face distorted.

"That's what I thought. And why should the person who makes the sun rise in the morning have to choose anything? I am the light and the dark, and you . . ." The black mist was pouring off him now in great, freezing waves that enveloped Wendy and John.

"You never picked me, not once. You fancied yourself someone better than me, with your piety and your precious little devotion to your intolerable family. We're not the same, Wendy." Peter pushed up the sleeves of his tunic, and he was barely recognizable now as whirls of black licked over his flesh like a second skin. They danced with his body, distorting his movements into a spasm of quick jerks. Peter's eyes were black now, and even the curls of red hair that Wendy had once adored were licked with glistening black. "I'm not the same as anyone."

Wendy stepped forward. "Peter, don't . . ."

But it was too late. His mouth was open, and strange foreign words poured forth in a stream of smoke, words of an ancient time and place. Wendy swallowed and turned to her brother.

"John. Run."

But of course, he didn't.

Peter collapsed to his knees as the final word escaped his lips: "Come."

The black mist circled around him, draping itself over his shoulders like a lover's embrace.

The entire island of Neverland gave a shudder as the ground beneath Wendy's feet shifted violently. The sea pulled away from the shore, protecting itself from what had begun to move through the trees toward the beach. An unearthly howl sounded from underneath the canopy, shaking the branches as it went. Above them, a waterfall of dark mist plunged down from the tops of the Teeth. The island went silent; no birdcalls echoed through the trees, and it seemed to Wendy that even the sea was cowering in fear.

The black mist evaporated off Peter's skin, returning him back to the boy she knew; only his eyes remained black, like ink in water. Behind them, an inhuman screech echoed over the shore. An icy breath passed over her, and her heart felt as though it had been lanced with a cold wire. She needed to move—she needed to move *now*—but her feet were frozen in place as her eyes involuntarily closed, fear rooting her to the ground.

Words swirled through her brain as mist circled around her: *malice, death, decay, rot.* It wasn't that these words were used to describe the Shadow; the Shadow *was* these words. It was death, and it was the bringer of death, and it was moving toward them now. Wendy slowly made the sign of the cross over her chest before opening her eyes, and John's hand found her own. Then she raised her gaze, and a cry of terror escaped her lips.

It had the general shape of a human; in fact, it had the general shape of Peter Pan, but where its head should have been was an ever-shifting black mist that revealed a gaunt face. Crumbling white bone outlined the glowing black eyes carved deep into its skull. Inside its beak-like mouth, rows of razor-sharp teeth and a tongue spackled red with blood lashed noisily. Its neck turned slowly, its head swiveling all the way around to look at Wendy. Hook's words rang in her head: *When you pervert death, death becomes twisted.* When Wendy's eyes met the Shadow's, she saw the death of everyone she ever loved play out in her mind.

With a cry, Wendy fell to her knees in the sand, clutching the pearled granules in her hand.

This is real. This is real. This is real. She repeated the words, desperately trying to keep her grasp on reality. The Shadow moved forward toward Peter now, its foot stepping beside her head as she and John cowered. As it passed her by, the creature reached out and touched her hair with its crooked, skeletal hands, leaving Wendy shivering in its wake: its touch was like hollowed grief.

Peter and the Shadow were facing each other now, mirroring one another, Peter's body of flesh and color, and the Shadow's of white bone and black mist. And there: inside of the Shadow Wendy could see its black, beating heart. Even Peter looked afraid of it as he struggled to meet its eyes.

"Master . . . " the thing hissed, its words whining like steam from a kettle.

After a moment, Peter raised his head and pointed out to sea, where the *Sudden Night* was making its way to shore. Then he smiled the same smile that had once convinced Wendy to leave her nursery window.

"Destroy the *Sudden Night* and everyone on it."

The Shadow bowed before Peter.

"And bring me Hook."

At Hook's name, Wendy felt her body unfreeze, and she leapt to her feet, sprinting away from Peter, hoping to put as much distance between herself and him as she could. As she ran, she reached into her blouse and pulled out the coin, white heat scorching across her fingers. It pulled to her, and she sank to her knees in the sand. On the shore, the Shadow began to grow. Black mist swirled around it at a dizzying speed, and as it moved, it grew in size, and it howled as its legs extended and its body grew wider. Claws emerged as it grew upward, its body lengthening until it was as tall as the trees. With a scream, the towering monster looked out over all of Neverland.

"Go," ordered Peter.

The Shadow turned slowly toward the sea, which roared at its touch. An ebony vortex whirled around its feet as it passed over the waters toward the *Sudden Night*.

CHAPTER TWENTY-SIX

Wendy's breaths were coming short and hard as she knelt and spread the sand out flat in front of her. She tried to remember the notes that she had written out before, but it was useless; she would have to do it again. She looked at the coin and then back at the sand. Her hands shook as she drew the lines of the staff. If you unwound the rings on the coin, starting at the top, a line of music came spiraling out. The tiny skulls that decorated the money came to rest on the lines of the staff as notes, revealing a melody. Just offshore, she heard screaming and the sound of boats hitting the water.

Don't look; don't look.

The only way to save them was to call the Shadow.

"What are you doing, Wendy?" Peter launched off the ground toward her, but he was tackled in midair by John, who drew his fist back and punched Peter hard in the mouth.

The two flying boys spiraled up into the air, their blows landing hard as they bounced off trees. Wendy's eyes raked over the notes in the sand. *What happens if I make a mistake? Will I call another monster?* Cannons were firing on the Shadow now as it reached the *Sudden Night*, though the cannon balls passed through its body harmlessly.

Wendy looked one last time at the coin in her palm and said

a little prayer, and then she hummed the notes quietly, save the last.

One of the notes sounded off.

No.

Something was wrong. She didn't know how she knew it, but she did. Wendy silenced the overriding voice of fear inside of her with a low note, the one that had dropped a register from where it was supposed to be. Then she leaned forward in the sand and moved it one octave higher, to where it should be. She leaned forward on both palms, her body hovering protectively over the music; it was their only hope, and she took a deep breath.

That's when a foot met with her stomach, and she was sent sprawling, her hands clutched protectively over her ribs.

Peter stood over her, a cruel smile distorting his dashing face.

"Final prayers, Wendy?"

Lying on the sand, Wendy watched with blurry eyes as the Shadow reached the *Sudden Night*. With a howl, it brought its clawed hands down upon the deck, caving in the front of the ship. Men and boys were sent screaming into shards of black wood. The Shadow began ripping at the ship now, its claws tearing out the insides of the vessel as if it were pulling organs from a body. Pirates screamed as it grabbed their bodies and flung them into the sea, along with harpoons, treasure, and . . .

Wendy's heart sank as she saw the bone staircase yanked from the *Sudden Night* and dropped into the sea, the spine of a body that was now collapsing on itself.

Peter knelt over her, his fingers on her cheek. "Do you want to watch with me? The destruction of everything you love?"

When he attempted to pull her toward him, Wendy saw the notes on the sand; they were nothing more than mere scribbles to the naked eye. Suddenly she was thrust into her innermost memory of music: She was sitting at the piano in the drawing room as her mother stood over her, her hands on Wendy's shoulder. Wendy had been struggling with the piece—Moonlight Sonata, op. 27, no. 2 by Beethoven.

"Watch your hand position," Mother whispered, her thick tangle of hair brushing Wendy's collarbone.

Wendy got frustrated and brought her hands down hard onto the chord, a very unladylike action of which she felt instantly ashamed.

Mary Darling sat down beside her. "You're trying to make the music come out of here." She tapped Wendy's head with her pointer finger. "But it must come from here." She tapped her daughter's heart. "Make it sound like *music*. There is a richness that can only come from within." She leaned her head against Wendy's. "You're young and barely formed, dear heart. Someday, you'll find something that plays your heart just the right way, and only then will you be able to pull from that richness." She stood, her smile kind. "But you keep practicing, until the song is pulled from everything you are."

Wendy blinked at the memory, then set her jaw and shakily climbed to her feet, her eyes looking past Peter Pan and his bloodstained hands, past the shore where her brother lay still, out to where the Shadow was decimating the last remnants of the *Sudden Night*. The song was here, somewhere in the midst of this carnage, and when Wendy opened her mouth, it was *there*. The notes she had written in the sand were resting on her breath, pulled from the richness of who Wendy was, and who she was not. She began singing in crystalline tones, a song without words, the melody radiating out in otherworldly sounds.

Peter's eyes went wide, and he was moving toward her, but he was too late. Wendy was standing on the beach now, her arms outstretched to the Shadow, the song on her lips pouring out over the waves, power radiating from her. It was an intuitive melody, a stanza written in the blood of the fairies, and now it belonged to her alone.

Peter lunged at her, but he was yanked backward by an invisible thread, his body pulled away from her as if dragged by a hook. The Shadow spun around to face Wendy with an inhuman scream as the last note of the song passed over her tongue. Black mist rose up around it in violent chaos before shooting out over the shore, and a long line of mist hooked directly into Peter's heart. Writhing tendrils poured over his chest and hooked around him as they pulled him to the sea.

Wendy sprinted toward him, grabbing his ankle just before the mist pulled him under the water. Off the shore, the Shadow was changing form now, its high-pitched screams matching Peter's as black mist began snaking out of his heart. Wendy yanked him up, and his eyes met hers and were wide with fear.

"Wendy . . . I can't get it off!"

Without hesitating, Wendy plunged her hands into the swirling ebony pouring from his chest. Unlike the mist, this was solid, touchable. It swallowed her hands up to her wrists. Peter's screaming faded into the background as she wrapped her fingers around the tendrils, which slithered through her palms, wet and cold. The mist pulsed against her as Peter's heart clung to its dark passenger, but Wendy kept pulling, screaming as she exerted her strength to yank out each remaining strand until there was only one left.

It coiled above Peter's heart, hissing at Wendy. She hooked it with her finger and yanked hard, and Peter fell forward into her. Their foreheads pressed together as he slumped against her. She watched the black smoke writhe around her finger like a wedding ring before it evaporated into the air. She had pulled the Shadow out of Peter.

Now I have to kill it.

The tide at their feet rose suddenly, washing over them as Wendy dragged Peter's unconscious body back onto the sand. Once Peter was out of harm's way, she rushed over to her brother. John was unconscious but alive.

The ground shook as the Shadow tilted its head back and gave a painful roar, unhappy to be detached from its host.

"Stop," whispered Wendy, hoping in vain that the Shadow was

somehow called into *her* obedience now, but it wasn't, and Wendy closed her eyes, knowing that Hook's worst fear had come true: the Shadow was now freed. It shifted direction, its skull-shaped head swiveling curiously toward the Teeth and its giant body following. Something limp was hanging from its hand; peppered gray hair brushed the waves as the Shadow walked with it toward the white cliffs.

Hook.

"Leave him alone!" Wendy screamed, stepping forward, but her voice was swallowed by the wind. She took off running for the Teeth even though her steps were no match for the monster who passed over the seas, its wake of black mist twisting into images of corpses bent in half, screaming children, and licking flames. *Death twisted.*

The monster dropped Hook facedown into the water, leaving him to drown as it moved toward the Teeth. Wendy plunged into the waves, her strokes steady as she swam toward Hook.

"Captain!" Wendy shouted as she neared him. "Hook!"

She grabbed one handful of his coat and pulled his floating body toward her, turning his face to the sky. It was cold and blue, his cheeks ashen. She cradled him against her as she moved back toward shore.

"Please don't leave us," she whispered. "Please." Her feet found the sand and she yanked him onto the shore, falling to her knees to cradle his head. "You need to wake up, Captain."

Her fingers pushed the damp hair out of his eyes. Then there was a glorious cough followed by a beautiful sputter, and suddenly Hook was heaving, his hands on the sand. Wendy's heart felt as though it would explode with joy as Captain Hook took deep breaths. He hadn't even been conscious a few seconds before he shot unsteadily to his feet.

"The *Night*?"

Wendy shook her head. "Gone." She grabbed his arm. "Where is Booth?"

"Safe, I think. He took the children in a rowboat just before the Shadow . . . before it . . ." His eyes closed at the memory. "Ripped my men to pieces. Where is it now?"

"There." Wendy pointed. "It's headed for the Teeth, away from Port Duette, thank God."

"NO!" Hook took off sprinting up the beach, his face distorted in a look of wild fear. "Oh God, no!"

"Wait!" Wendy cried, chasing after him. "I think it's going home, back to the Forsaken Garden!"

"It's not!" Hook answered back, his dead sprint hard to catch up with. He turned back to look at her, and Wendy almost stopped running when she saw the terror in his eyes, his fear so deep.

His words decimated every good hope inside of her.

"The Pilvinuvo tribe. They're in there. In the Teeth. Lomasi!"

Wendy increased her speed, the screaming in her lungs no match for the screaming in her head.

Oh God. The Pilvinuvo tribe.

And Michael.

CHAPTER TWENTY-SEVEN

"You told me you didn't know where the Pilvi were!" yelled Wendy as they ran.

"I lied!" Hook yelled back. "Of course I lied! If I told you were Michael was, you would have tried to see him, and you probably would have led Peter straight to them!"

"You underestimate me!"

"Never bet against love!" Hook yelled.

As they raced up the shore, the Shadow paused in the sea, its nose sniffing at the sky. Then, to their horror, it began changing: its row of razor teeth elongated until it became a long beak, and its eyes narrowed to ebony slits. Out of its hands, two additional hands emerged, these ones peaked and shaped with sharp, ax-like ends.

It was changing to destroy the Teeth. To kill, and to eat.

Its black eyes focused on the white cliffs in front of it. Wendy and Hook were almost directly between it and the Teeth now, and Hook was screaming and waving his hands to distract it. The Shadow took another step toward the shore, but then it paused, its head jerking back and forth in confusion. It went to lift its foot, but nothing happened. It was stuck. The other foot tried to come up, but it was also stuck. Wendy paused to look closer, and she saw that both of the Shadow's feet were being pulled into a swirling vortex. The creature gave a hideous scream and fell to all fours, struggling to pull itself free from the violent water around it.

Finally, with a piercing scream that curdled Wendy's blood, it yanked free and leapt toward the shore. But suddenly, a huge geyser of water erupted in front of its face, blasting up with such force that it blew the mist-formed creature into a scattered, swirling haze. It quickly regrouped, looking confused and cautious. And then Wendy gasped, her eyes seeing something she could never have imagined to be true: the mermaid queen had come to fight.

Queen Eryne rose up out of the water, her huge, six-fingered hands spread out in front of her, her eyes as black as the Shadow itself. Her turquoise hair swirled around her as she called upon the sea's assistance, which bowed before her command. She saw Wendy on the shore and gave a slight nod before raising both of her arms, which sent a wall of water cascading up around the Shadow, encircling it from every side. Wendy heard the creature's scream as it was swallowed up in the salty blue, its eyes coldly focusing on the queen before it disappeared.

The mermaid queen swirled her fingers, and the cocoon of water shot out to sea, taking the Shadow as far from the shore as possible.

She is buying us time.

Up out of the cocoon, a black ribbon of mist emerged, swirling harmlessly into the air above the sphere of seawater before lashing out beyond its cage. Like a siphon, the Shadow sucked itself up and out of the water, regenerating its body next to the queen, who dropped her hands, leaving the sphere of water to helplessly dissolve. A violent wave rose up behind the queen to defend her, and she pushed the Shadow back from her, sending it screaming into the deep abyss.

A shout drew Wendy's attention, and she turned to look as Hook reached the bottom edge of the Teeth and screamed for

Lomasi. As if in a dream, the love of Hook's life—clad in daz-zling bronze armor—stepped out from behind what appeared to be a solid wall and spread her arms wide to catch her lover. They collapsed into each other in such a desperate tumble of love that it made Wendy's chest hurt. He whispered something into her ear, and she took his hand, rubbing it against her cheek just once before stepping back into the side of the cliffs.

Bells pealed from somewhere deep inside the rocky fortress, their sound muted by the cliffs that concealed them. The Shadow raised its head at the sound of the bells, watching with slit eyes as the Pilvinuvo tribe began to pour out of the Teeth. With a snarl, it whirled back on Queen Eryne, leaping into the air in front of her.

The queen sent a wall of water at it, but the Shadow dodged right at the last minute, clearing a narrow path for itself. A long tendril of mist, tethered to the Shadow by a thin strand, shot out of its arm like a spear. It pierced through the queen's abdo-men, and she gave a scream that shattered every piece of glass in Neverland.

After the mist passed through her body, the tendril changed forms, becoming flat and roughly the same size as the queen. Her sea-glass eyes were wide as the Shadow yanked her up and out of the water, her back pressed flat against the board made of mist. With a howl of victory, the Shadow curled its claws around her body and moved toward the Teeth.

No sooner than its feet had touched the shore, the Shadow opened its mouth as if to devour the queen, who was writhing in its grasp, her tail flapping madly against the monster's palm. Her final song passed through Wendy painfully as it traveled out to sea, where her clan waited in vain for their queen to return.

Wendy heard in it all the regret in the world, a deep lament that spoke of love and jealousy. Then the Shadow hurled Eryne into the side of the Teeth. Wendy watched in horror as the mer-maid queen of Neverland was splattered into blood and scales against the white rock. Wendy swayed on her feet, her stomach sickened as she ran toward the tribe.

What hope do they have if the mermaid queen—so strong she had seemed like a goddess—was just smote on the side of a cliff like it was nothing?

In front of her, the Pilvinuvo people were fleeing up the shore and into the jungle. A line of warriors—men and women armed with bows and swords—stood in front of their fleeing people. Lomasi and Hook stood together at the front of the line. The Shadow snarled and began making its way across the sand. When it came within firing range, Lomasi shouted a command and let her arm drop. The warriors behind her released their arrows, which flew harmlessly through the monster and landed with a volley of splashes behind it.

Hook reached for Lomasi's hand, a last comfort while she watched her people die. The Shadow stepped over them and started ripping at the Teeth, its claws digging into the cliffside, which crumpled like chalk under its powerful grasp. With its long beak, it tore at the holes and the small caverns that lined the outer edges of the cliffs. Seabirds and bats were plunging out of the cliffs now, their precious nests destroyed. The Shadow caught as many as it could in its teeth, tearing at the birds and swallowing the bats whole inside its black belly; it thirsted to kill any living thing.

Wendy was screaming at the Shadow now, trying to pull it away from the line of children that were streaming out from a cave on the side the cliff and racing for the shelter of the trees, all of them sprinting away from the Shadow. All except for one: a blond-headed little boy with bright eyes and red cheeks, who had seen his sister and was running toward her instead of toward safety.

His cries pulled at Wendy's heart like a tether attached to her soul, and he screamed her name.

"WENDY!"

"MICHAEL!"

Wendy screamed his name louder than she had ever screamed in her life, and then she was moving, everything around her a blur as she ran toward him. The Shadow sensed their desperation and turned, its terrible head jerking around to focus on the tiny boy running across the beach and the sister who was sprinting toward him. With a scream, it jerked its claws out of the Teeth and fell to all fours, leaping after the boy. A whip of black mist shot out toward Michael and yanked his small feet out from under him. He flew onto the sand and rolled to a stop.

"No!" screamed Wendy, who had almost reached him. "Michael!"

Without even thinking about it, her hand closed around the dagger pressed into the small of her back. It slid free effortlessly, and when she looked down at it, she was assaulted by memories: of the branches on Pan Island slithering back to reveal the dagger to her; of the way it always seemed to make it back to her; of Lomasi's words: "Your mercy will change the fate of Neverland"; of holding it against Peter's jugular but being unable to use it any further; of Hook, telling her that it had a little bit of fairy magic.

Wendy didn't even have time to breathe as the truth fell over her like sweet rain. She was stepping over her brother's body now, his screams echoing around her as the Shadow fell upon them both.

This weapon is meant to be used only once. And I am meant to protect it—to keep it pure, to keep it safe.

And then to wield it.

Above her, the pulsating black mist of the Shadow reared up, its eyes burning with malevolence. Somewhere far beyond them, Wendy heard someone screaming her name, but in this world there was only Wendy and the Shadow and the brother curled beneath her feet, his name on her lips.

"You will not take him from me," she yelled as the Shadow

closed its mouth over them both, the mist burning her skin while every dark creature of her nightmares reached to pull her under.

But Wendy would not fade to black, because she was the light.

Wendy opened her eyes and saw it ahead of her, the Shadow's mutilated heart, a black organ pumping the mist out from a bloody core, a diseased and wicked thing. She raised her hand above her head.

"Wendy?" Michael met her eyes, his small body trembling.

"Close your eyes and think of home."

Michael did, and Wendy, with all the strength left in her muscles and in her heart, plunged the ivory dagger deep into the heart of the Shadow, letting herself become the revenge of the fairies. She tore again at the heart, the gemstone blade ripping through the Shadow's tendons and bloody mass until the heart was torn in two. The two sides then began beating erratically as they ripped themselves into small, sharp shards that began whirling around her.

The dagger dissolved in her hands, and Wendy fell to her knees over Michael, protecting him from the black glass that was circling them now, the jagged pieces of the Shadow's heart. The scream that ripped through the Shadow pulled the skin back from Wendy's knuckles as she curled around Michael. She would make herself a shell; she would swallow this evilness and keep it from passing into him; she would make a shield of her love, of her body.

But it wasn't enough.

The Shadow's heart ripped into her skin, its fragments like razors. One pierced her calf while another sliced the top of her ear, but then . . . Wendy felt her body being pulled apart, a pulling that would rip both her and Michael into pieces. She held her brother, bracing for their painful end.

And then—it stopped. A light from above wrapped around them both, and swirling tendrils of white heat formed a protective husk around them. Wendy dared to open her eyes. Peter Pan stood in front of her, his arms raised up above him, his body encased in the glowing white light of flight. This time, however, Peter was pushing the flight downward and into the ground around Wendy. The flight reversed as it hit the ground and pushed upward, lifting granules of sand all around them as the cocoon of light flickered.

Peter was screaming with the effort as light poured from his eyes and every pore of his skin. He lit up like a lantern, Peter Pan, the boy who had caused such pain. Peter, who was reversing *gravity* to save her life. Peter, who, in the end, still loved his Wendy.

Black specks like cut glass hurtled toward them but were caught up in the cyclone of flight and sent spinning harmlessly upward. The last throes of the dying Shadow echoed as it pushed itself against Peter's flight, but Peter let out a roar, and flight whirled around them like a maelstrom.

Finally, the last tiny particles of black gathered themselves into the shredded heart above Wendy as the Shadow collapsed on itself. Then the small pieces of black knitted together as the Shadow pulled itself into a circle, no larger than a drum. It soared upward, moving into the sky above them like an eclipse. Peter's protective shield of flight collapsed, and he fell exhausted onto the sand, his ribs heaving.

Wendy raised her head, her body still curled over Michael. The Shadow shuddered once as a crack of golden light peeked through its black surface, and a new feeling swept over the shore; it was a breath of peace, a reminder of what the Shadow had once been. With one hand on Michael, Wendy watched as the watery sun rose past the clouds and into the stars above Neverland.

Then, without warning, the world exploded.

It sounded as if Neverland itself were tearing from its core. The sound ripped through Wendy, and she covered Michael's ears and pressed her own head against his shoulder. A huge breath of wind cleaved off the shore and whirled up into the sky, and Wendy felt gravity shift, just a little, as her stomach pulled against itself. Prayers tore through her as she held on—held on to Michael as if he were the only solid thing in the world, held on until the evil lifted . . . and then it did.

When she looked up, the sky had returned to its normal blinding blue, and the sea below it lapped quietly. There was no hint of the Shadow, save the tiny cuts that covered her bare skin in almost every place.

"Wendy!" John fell to his knees in front of her and threw himself at his family, and Wendy wrapped him up against them; she and her brothers were all together at last.

Booth burst through the growing crowd and encircled the Darling family with his long arms. Tears of relief fell from Wendy's eyes, and Booth's gentle hands wiped them away.

"It's okay," he whispered to her. "It's okay. Wendy, you did it. You killed it. It's over."

Finally she raised her head, lingering on Booth's jubilant face, one of her favorite sights in all the world.

John's voice burst through the crowd. "Wendy, the sky!"

Wendy uncurled herself from Michael, her eyes following the same path that the last breath of the Shadow had taken, just past where the clouds broke . . .

She leapt to her feet, her eyes disbelieving what she was seeing. There, in the fabric of the sky, was a tear, and beyond it, a celestial gateway peeked out in hints of blues and purples. Through the middle of the tear, stars from other worlds sparked and glimmered in a changing, prismatic light.

What had Qaralius said? *The Shadow committed an act so violent that it tore the sky.* Perhaps this was its apology.

"The passage," she whispered. Her head jerked up to meet John's teary eyes. "Home."

"Not yet," snapped Hook's deep voice, just before he buried his hook deep in Peter's shoulder and dragged him up the beach.

CHAPTER TWENTY-EIGHT

"Stop!" Wendy yelled as she chased after them, her body trembling with the effort. "Captain!" Hook was dragging Peter through the surf now, and Peter was too weak to fight him. "No!" Wendy wasn't close enough to stop him, and she watched in horror as Hook pulled Peter's sword out of his own belt and held it against his throat. "Hook!" The captain looked up at Wendy for a second, his eyes apologetic but unrelenting.

"I'm sorry, Miss Darling," he said, and then he brought the sword arching down toward Peter's neck. But one minute he was striking with a mortal blow, and the next he was sent flying backward through the air, splashing into the sea ten feet beyond.

In front of Peter, Tink snarled, her bright blue wings beating furiously.

"Get away from him, filthy pirate!"

Peter let out a low chuckle from the sand, where he was slowly climbing to his knees. "Dear Tink, loyal to the very end."

Lost Boys and Pilvinuvo Indians were rushing up to them, a large circle forming around Peter on the shore. Wendy veered away from the cluster and stepped into the waves, her feet sloshing through the water toward Hook. When she reached him, she found him drenched and furiously searching in the waves for

Peter's sword, and she extended her hand. Hook batted it away. "I don't need your help, girl."

"Please don't do this. Peter saved us."

"He ordered the murder of an entire race," replied Hook, wiping the water from his face. He'd found the sword, and he raised it again. "And my father, and hundreds of others. He took my hand. And if I have to go through a fairy to get my revenge, so be it. Get out of my way, Miss Darling."

"No." Wendy stood her ground. "Justice will be paid, but not with blood."

Hook lunged, and Wendy continued to stand in front of him, blocking his way.

"No. Where does it end?"

Someone stepped up beside her, and an unearthly sense of calm washed over her. Lomasi had walked out into the water, and she'd left her bow on the shore.

"Listen to her, James. It's time to stop fighting. Revenge has taken you far enough. Look at him. He is beaten. The Shadow is dead. When will it be enough? When you kill him? When you punish those boys? Peter will pay for his crimes, but let's choose to stand against this cycle of violence and blood. You and I. Together."

Hook's face melted as he looked at the woman he loved. "Until when?"

Lomasi stepped forward, taking his hook in her smooth hand. "Until forever."

Hook looked as though the words broke him. "He can't be free."

"No. You're right. He can't be free." Lomasi shook her head. "But he can breathe, and if you give my tribe enough time, I believe we can teach him to how live."

The pirate captain raised his face to the sky, leaning his head back to the sun, tears falling down his worn cheeks. A moment passed as Wendy watched his chest rise and fall; he took one deep breath: a surrender. And then, he exhaled and dropped the sword, freeing himself from his dark fate, from his quest for revenge. His hand reached out, but instead of reaching for Peter's sword, he reached for Lomasi. For his future.

They made their way back to beach, where Peter was still kneeling in the sand, his body drained, but the color returning to his face. His emerald eyes lit up as he watched Wendy walk in from the waves, and there was no sign of the navy that had once swirled there, but his mischievous smile remained. Tink hovered protectively over him, the bruises that Peter had left on her arms still visible. When Lomasi stepped onto the shore, her people bowed before her, and some of the Lost Boys followed with confused but awed looks on their faces.

"May I speak with you?" She gestured to the fairy. Tink nodded and stepped away from Peter, toward an old alliance that had once been the foundation of Neverland.

It was then that Wendy saw him moving through the crowd, his maroon cloak and hood pulled up over his face; he slid between people like a ghost, moving quickly, desperately.

She didn't even have time to scream his name.

Abbott stepped out of the crowd in front of Peter, and without saying a word, he buried a sword deep into Peter's heart.

Peter slumped forward against Abbott's blade, his hands reaching out for Abbott but grasping only empty air. Abbott twisted the blade, and Peter cried in pain.

"For Felix," Abbott hissed. "For Kitoko. And Darby. For Oxley and Zatthu and a hundred Lost Boys. And for the parents you took them from." Abbott's face was calm as he pulled the sword back out of Peter.

A piercing scream erupted from Tink's throat, and a blast of white heat passed through Wendy. The fairy whirled quickly, grabbing Abbott by the throat and hoisting him into the air. Abbott remained still, impassive.

"Are you going to kill me, Tink?"

The fairy's face twisted into a mask of pure pain as her hand closed around Abbott's neck . . . but she didn't squeeze.

"So many boys," Abbott whispered, and star-streaked tears fell down Tink's face. "No more. No more dead boys."

Peter fell backward onto the sand, and the crowd surged forward. With an anguished cry, Tink dropped Abbott and fell beside Peter, taking his hand in hers while with the other one she tried desperately to stop the bleeding. Peter whispered something, and Tink leaned forward. At his words, a sob fell from her lips, but she looked up, her eyes meeting Wendy's.

"He wants you. Even now, he wants you."

Wendy's heart broke for Tink, who'd been betrayed until the very end, but she stepped forward after giving Michael's hand a reassuring squeeze. She wove through the crowd, all eyes on her as she made her way toward Peter. He was lying on his back on the sand, his breaths coming short and hard and Tink's hand across his chest. Blood and fairy dust stained the sand underneath him.

"Wendy Darling."

She smiled gently and laid her hand on his cold cheek. "Peter Pan."

He shifted, a moan of pain escaping from his lips. "Will you do me one small favor?" His lips trembled, and his body straightened as a tremor of pain ripped through it.

"Of course."

"Take me to the sky."

He grabbed her hand in his—a fit so perfect she had once marveled at it—and Wendy felt flight pass through his palm. She heard the voices of pirates rising out of the crowd now; the survivors from the *Sudden Night* had their swords drawn and were looking for revenge.

Wendy looked down at this broken boy and took him protectively in her arms.

And they soared.

The voices fell away from them as Wendy flew upward with Peter cradled against her. Up, away from the bloodstained shore and the decimated cliffs of the Teeth. Away from the pirates and the Lost Boys and the floating remains of the *Sudden Night*. Away from it all, until the clouds parted and it was just Peter and Wendy.

Peter gave a dry laugh.

"Abbott. I never would have guessed that Abbott would be the one who would end it all. It's funny." He gave a cough, and blood flecks covered his hand. "I quite liked Abbott. This might make me like him even more."

Wendy said nothing, but she wiped away the line of blood that was seeping from Peter's mouth with her fingers. Peter reached out and grabbed them, and he pressed them to his lips.

"I'm sorry. For all of it." His eyes filled with tears. "I wish that I could do it again, and this time I would be the hero. The boy everyone loves."

"I loved you," whispered Wendy, the anger in her heart fading with each last breath of Peter Pan. "I loved you until you made it impossible."

Peter's face crumpled.

"Wendy, my one good thing. I did many bad things—many of them quite fun—but loving you . . ." He took a ragged breath. "That was something pure. Perhaps it will have to be enough."

Wendy pulled him hard against her, their bodies encircled by the damp gray sky.

"Do you remember the first time you kissed me?" she whispered. "Here in the clouds?"

He nodded. "It's my favorite memory."

Her hand reached up and gently stroked his fiery red hair, and her words were gentle. "Mine, too." She smiled. "You changed my life that day. I was lost somewhere inside myself, and you pulled me free. By your good—and by your evil—you called me out of the girl my parents wanted me to be and into my own self."

"Well . . ." That charming, selfish Peter Pan grin that she desperately loved returned. "You're welcome." His face twisted in pain, and he clutched her hard. "I want to give you something."

Wendy shook her head. "What could you possibly give me right now?"

Peter's eyes met her own. "All the world." He grabbed her hand and spread his fingers wide, lacing them with hers. "Consider it my apology and my last gift."

It wasn't just *a gift*. It was *his gifts*. *Tink's gifts*. White magic exploded from underneath his palm and began pouring into hers. It was different than flight; it was more powerful and consuming, and it electrified every single cell within her. Her heart pounded wildly, pumping against her chest as it tried to escape the magic snaking around it.

"Peter!" she gasped, but it was too late. The magic was in her body, setting fire to every part of her.

"I know it hurts," he murmured as he veered on the edge of unconsciousness.

It wasn't that it hurt. It was that it was killing her from the inside out, pushing every human thing out of her and filling it with fairy magic, with marrow made of stars and skin bursting with flight. There was a moment where she could feel her human soul pushing back, but the magic was stronger, older, and it burst through Wendy's mortal being like a broken dam.

Her body flickered once, twice, and then it was over. An anguished cry left Peter's mouth, and his body went slack. Wendy raised her hand in front of her, marveling at the tiny tendrils of white that she could see lacing underneath her skin. Then they faded, and her hand returned to normal.

"Speed. Strength. Flight," muttered Peter, his own glow receding from him. "And immortal life . . . if you want it."

She turned to him, shocked at his gift. "Why?"

He grinned. "Well, one, so you don't fall to your death after this. But also . . ."

He coughed, and blood splattered her cheeks. "Someone good should have it this time. Please tell Tink I'm sorry . . . that I wasn't worth her gifts."

Peter's spine arched, and he let out a cry of pain. "It's happening. It's coming." His chest began seizing up and down. "I'm afraid!"

She pulled him close and felt the gradual slowing of his heart. "It's okay, Peter, I'm right here."

"Wendy?" Peter whispered, his face terrified. "Is this goodbye? I don't like goodbyes, because goodbye means going away, and going away means forgetting."

Wendy leaned forward and pressed her face against his, desperately wanting to keep this boy to herself for just a few more minutes.

"I promise, no one will forget you, Peter Pan. Least of all me."

A sob escaped from him as he struggled for breath, and Wendy's words dropped to a whisper. "You know that place between sleep and awake? That's where I'll always love you, Peter Pan. That's where I'll be waiting for you."

Peter's face crumpled at her words, and tears fell from his eyes and dropped into the sky. "That day in the nursery, when I saw your face, I knew I would die with your name on my lips. My only love."

She kissed him, their lips dancing across each other's once more, here in this tiny piece of sky that would always belong to them. "You lived grandly, Peter Pan."

His body gave a shudder, and his eyes looked past her, into somewhere far beyond Neverland, where the stars themselves could not hold him.

"Wendy . . ." It was the last time she would hear her name on his lips. "To die will be an awfully big adventure, don't you think?"

Tears streaked down her cheeks as she held his body close. "I do, Peter."

But he was gone.

Wendy bent over his body with a sob, and his skin, which had always burned like fire, grew quickly cool. She pushed the hair back from his forehead and closed his green eyes for the last time. It felt so strange to be flying on her own, to be the tether to Peter as he had once been to her. If she dropped him, he would fall.

But she wouldn't.

As she sank down through the clouds, his body slumped against her, and she knew that she couldn't return him to the beach. The pirates would want his body to be desecrated, and the Lost Boys would have to look upon their dead leader—stripped of all his glory—one more trauma to endure. No, his body didn't belong to them. His body belonged to Neverland. And maybe just a little bit to Wendy. So Wendy flew downward, her body now fine-tuned to each changing pattern of the wind and the sky.

While they sank down, Wendy took one last look at his beautiful face, carving it deep into a memory that she would reach for often. Peter Pan, the most beautiful boy in the world, a contradiction, a monster, a lover. The sea appeared below her, and she drifted down until they hovered just above the breaking waves. Wendy leaned over and caressed Peter's cheek, her feet brushing the water. Then she gently lay him face up in the waves, his body bobbing with the current.

While floating in the air above him, Wendy reached up and pulled Joseph's ring dial from around her neck. A curl of her hair was tangled in it, and she winced as it yanked free. The waves had already begun to swallow Peter's body when she bent over him, lifting his head with loving hands. Wendy Darling slipped the necklace marked with a piece of her hair over his head before kissing his lips softly.

"May it lead you home, Peter Pan." She squeezed his hand one last time and rose up above the water, watching silently as the Neverland Sea slowly pulled his body underneath its waves.

CHAPTER TWENTY-NINE

When Wendy landed back on the shore, Hook was waiting for her.

"He's dead," said Wendy before he could ask.

"Are you sure? Without a body—" He stopped speaking when he saw the sorrow in her eyes. "Ah. Dead."

Wendy wiped a tear off her face. "His body is out there. A part of Neverland, as it should be."

Hook put his hand on her shoulder. "The world will never see another one like him. Lord knows it probably wouldn't survive it."

Wendy wiped her face and shook her head sadly. "I loved him, you know. For all the good possibilities that never came to pass."

The tip of his steel claw tipped her chin up. "I understand better than most."

Wendy turned to him, her heart aching at all they had lost. "Poor Smith."

Hook's face crumpled a little at his name. "Smith. Redd. Wu. And probably twenty others. There will be a time for a deep mourning for us all, but . . ." His face lifted to the sky. "I think it's time for you to go home, Wendy Darling. I promised that I would see you home, and I intend to see it through. The Shadow's death ripped the passage open, but who knows how long it will stay that way."

Wendy was silent, her eyes filling with tears as Hook sputtered. "If we don't get a chance, then, let me just say . . ."

But Wendy was walking away from him, her dress flapping in the Neverland wind that was passing not around her, but through her. Goodbyes were too painful.

In the center of the crowd, Tink was curled up in a ball on the sand, rocking back and forth and sobbing Peter's name. Wendy knelt beside her and put a hand on her back.

"He's gone. It was peaceful."

A wail escaped from Tink's lips as she tore at her blond hair. Tears filled with stars splattered onto the wet sand as she clutched desperately to herself, trying to fill the void that Peter had left. Wendy's heart broke for her, but as she reached out to comfort her, Tink swatted her hand away.

"You . . ." Her words spilled out over Wendy, cruel words of jealously, and Wendy just sat silently as they pummeled her. Wendy didn't deserve it, but she knew what she had taken from Tink: Peter's last moments, a treasure that she would always carry with her. The fairy was raking lines in the sand now, her words growing hysterical.

"He gave them to you, the gifts! I can feel it in my bones. Who are you to deserve such gifts?"

Wendy shook her head. "Nobody. I'm not worthy of them, Tink."

She looked up at Wendy then, her lip curling back to reveal her gritted white teeth. "Maybe I should kill all of you. Maybe Peter was right." She collapsed onto the sand as Wendy held her. "What do I do?" she moaned. "What is left for me?"

The air vibrated around them, and Wendy felt him before his feet touched ground. The magic inside of her amplified, its roar so loud she could feel it from her toes to the tips of her hair. The crowd around them froze in shocked silence as Qaralius's feet landed beside them on the sand.

He was unrecognizable. Whereas before he had been ancient

and withering, this Qaralius was the opposite; this was the Qaralius that Wendy had *felt* but not seen. He had gone from an old man to a young one, his hair golden and pressed back from his face in a smooth sweep. His amber eyes flashed with a wizened intelligence that had measured the years in centuries, their compassion unmatched.

And these eyes were on Tink.

She raised her gaze, gasping at his beauty.

"You." Qaralius knelt beside her.

"Me. I'm here."

He took her small hand in his; the two fairies, the last of their race, were reunited at last.

"I have much to apologize for, but if you'll let me, I would like to spend the rest of our time in this life restoring you to the fairy you were meant to be. I can be . . . whoever you need." He knelt before her and kissed her hand, and Wendy swore that she saw a flutter of silver blush rush up Tink's face.

"But, Peter . . . " she muttered.

"He will be grieved for," Qaralius answered gently. "We will mourn him for as long as you desire." He took her hand. "If you loathe me, you can always change your mind."

Wendy almost laughed. The idea of anyone being able to resist the fairy king was ludicrous.

"I'm not worth it," Tink whispered, so quietly that only Qaralius and Wendy heard it.

Qaralius put both hands on her shoulders. "Don't you know? You are worth everything in Neverland to me. Everything." He reached gently around her neck. "May I?" he asked.

Tink nodded shyly, her eyes overwhelmed with emotion as Qaralius reached up and ripped the brown shroud that covered her wings in half, letting it fall to either side of her. Wendy stepped back, shielding the light from her face. From underneath the shroud, Tink's beautiful gossamer wings burst forth in all their glory. Beating in time with the fairy king's, they flapped behind her, funneling fairy dust into a vortex that whirled around the crowd's feet.

Over her body a glittering short green dress was revealed, lighter than air and made of some similar substance. The shimmering pale green moved with her body, shifting its shape as she moved: in one moment it was a flower, and in the next it was a twisting vine.

Tink stood shyly, her arms clasped over her chest.

Wendy stepped forward and put a hand on her shoulder. "It's okay. You're beautiful."

Tink grabbed her hand so hard that Wendy gasped in pain. "I'm not this person," she hissed as Qaralius looked proudly on.

"No." Wendy leaned forward and kissed her cheek. "But someday, you will be. Tink . . ." She leaned closer and whispered in Tink's ear, "It's okay to be free. You can still love him and be free of him."

A sob erupted from Tink's throat, and she turned to Qaralius in such a natural way that Wendy knew someday she would be more than free of Peter.

Qaralius smiled at her. "I want to show you where you came from, and when you're ready, you can decide where our future lies. Here in Neverland or elsewhere." With that, the fairy king turned to Wendy. "Use your gifts thoughtfully, child. You've surely earned them; now deserve them."

Wendy watched silently as the fairies rose into the air together, Tink's body still shaking with sobs. Wendy noted that even though her tears fell freely, her spine was straight, and her wings loomed large. The combined power roiling off the fairies' bodies was so potent that the air carried a burning metallic scent. Wordlessly, they took to the sky, leaving the chaos of the beach far behind them. As Wendy watched Tink disappear into the clouds, a whisper passed through her:

Thank you.

Then they were gone.

Booth took her arm. "Wendy . . . the passage. It's time."

She let her fingers trace over his cheek. "Are you sure about this?"

Booth nodded before kissing her softly. "I meant what I said on the *Undertow.*"

Wendy smiled and walked toward her brothers, her heart clutching with every step at their joyful faces. She looked up at the passage, the cut in the sky smaller than it had been before. Wendy shook her hands out in front of her and stared at them. "This is my first time trying this, boys, so . . ." But she didn't need to do anything; the mere thought of sharing flight caused a chain reaction inside of her. The white heat raced from her heart and passed into her veins.

"Clap your hands," John whispered. "Just a small one."

Wendy reached above her, her palms shaking with the power passing between them, and she clapped once. Flight exploded out from her palms, swallowing not just the boys, but everyone on the beach. The pirates and the children screamed as the wave passed over them, swallowing them up in the white rush of heat. Wendy turned back to John and laughed with delight.

"It's quite strong!"

The beach exploded into giggles as pirates and Pilvi children began playing. Voodoo was kicking his legs to go higher and gesturing to Hook—who stood with both feet on the sand, rebuking Voodoo's efforts.

"You look like an idiot. You all look ridiculous!" He shook his head, grumbling. "Absolutely not. I am a man for the ground." He surrendered, though, when Lomasi floated up beside him, her face dizzyingly happy as she reached for him.

"My love." She took his hand. "Come kiss me in the sky."

"Well . . . just this once. But I'm bringing my sword."

The Lost Boys were floating up as well, but they were decidedly less happy; their eyes were afraid, their expressions lost.

Wendy reached a hand out for her brothers. "Say goodbye to Neverland."

Michael turned his face to the sky. "Mother," he whispered. "I'm going to see our mother." Then he was flying upward, clumsily kicking his little boy legs.

John took a moment longer, his gaze trailing over the beach and all its inhabitants. Tears gathered in his eyes. "Will I remember it, do you think? Or someday will we convince ourselves that this was all a dream?"

Wendy smiled quietly at him. "I think Neverland will be whatever we want it to be, John."

With a last look, John leapt into the air, followed by Wendy and finally Booth, who lagged far behind. The Darling family soared upward, passing out over the sea. Together they climbed, clouds passing above and then below them as the temperature around them plummeted. Wet mist began pattering their faces, and Wendy knew they were close. Above them, the passage loomed. Inside its depths, stars leapt and played.

Wendy could feel the passage distorting the gravity around them; it felt thicker, like flying through water rather than air. The place were the sky had been shoved apart had a strange glass-like texture to it, and Wendy saw herself reflected in its prism and almost laughed.

She was almost covered head to toe with the ash of the Shadow. Her eyes burned bright with Peter's gifts, and her hair was a wild tangle. She was nothing like the girl that had come through this passage the first time, and somehow she was exactly that girl and would always be. The passage pulled them toward it now, and Wendy hung back carefully.

"Boys!"

The boys turned and flew toward her.

"Wendy! I think its closing. We have to hurry!" John's glasses were foggy, and Wendy reached out, wiping them with her fingers.

Michael tumbled into John's back, his flight not as controlled. He giggled happily. "Sorry, John! Wendy! Did you see the swirling lights? So pretty."

A sob escaped Wendy's lips, and their faces fell. John's eyes narrowed as he watched his sister try to compose herself.

"Wendy?"

It was the first time she had heard her brother use that careful voice, and it made her come undone. Tears fell unbridled from her eyes as she reached for them, pulling them both into her arms. Understanding dawned on John's face.

"You're not coming."

"What?" Michael's face crumpled. "What does he mean, Wendy? John, that's not true. Don't say mean things."

John reached out for his brother. "I wish it were only that, Michael."

Wendy buried her face in her hands. *This is so much harder than I thought it would be.* John kept watching her as Michael cried and finally reached out for his sister. Wendy pulled them both into her arms, holding them as close as she could.

"The Lost Boys. You're staying for them," John said with terrible finality.

Wendy nodded, and Michael clutched to her neck so hard that he was hurting her. Wendy buried herself in Michael's shoulder, her voice cracking.

"Yes. The Lost Boys."

She had known it when she returned to Pan Island and had seen their hungry faces and the raw betrayal of her leaving them fresh in their eyes. She had known it when Oxley had died, leaving them without anyone in the world who truly cared about them. She had known it when they stood on the beach, their eyes on Peter, who had hurt them right up until the very end of his life. And she had known it most when she had looked into Peter's eyes as he died in her arms. She knew that the best way to love him was to make sure none of these boys ended up like him.

She would stay for the Lost Boys, some of whom had never known the love of parents, some of whom had never once been held. That night on the *Undertow* she had whispered to Booth what she had feared, the words that she didn't even want to say out loud: that she needed to stay. And when he had looked down at her, his eyes so full of love and sadness, she had known then something else: that he would stay, too.

Wendy let out a cry and touched John's face.

"Take care of Booth's father. Help him run the store. Tell him how brave Booth was. Tell him I begged Booth to go, but . . . that his son knows no other way to do things than the right way."

Tears filled John's eyes. "I'll look after him, I swear it. But our parents . . ."

Wendy took a deep breath, thinking of all the things she would like to say. "Tell them the truth. Father will believe you, and eventually he'll make Mother believe it too."

John looked away for a moment. "Mother will never forgive you for staying."

"Neither will I!" choked Michael, angry now. "If you stay, I'll hate you, Wendy! I'll hate you!" His tiny fists began pounding on her back, each gentle strike causing more pain than a knife to the heart.

"Michael," she said softly, pulling him around her body so that their faces were pressed together. John flew back a few feet, giving them space. As he moved, the passage closed a bit, the prisms on the side crackling as they pulled toward one another.

The boy who had at times felt like her very own nuzzled his blond head against her shoulder. "You can't stay, Wendy. You can't. Not without me. We're . . ." He sniffled, his tiny hands on the sides of her cheeks. "We're a family."

Wendy nuzzled his nose, pressing her forehead against his.

"We will always be a family, Michael. I won't be far. Second star to the right and straight on till morning." Michael let out a wail, and Wendy tried to shush him but ended up crying herself. "Shhh. I love you, Michael!"

"The passage, Wendy!" John's panicked voice cut into their sobs. "It's closing!"

"Come here!" Wendy cried, and she wrapped her arms around both of her brothers, crushing them tight, hoping to remember everything—John's brown curls and the way Michael's pudgy hands clutched her cheeks, how they smelled of seawater and proper English tea.

"I love you forever," she whispered.

Together the three of them flew toward the portal. John bent in, looking through the crack that was now no wider than his body and was closing slowly. "I see the window of our nursery! And a gray sky! London!" He looked back to Wendy, his eyes sad. "Are you sure you won't come? You'll break our parents' hearts." He took a long breath, his face twisting a little. "And mine."

Wendy faced both of her brothers, their hands clutched in her own. "This isn't goodbye forever. But someone has to love those boys, to fix the parts that Peter broke. Do you understand?" She turned to Michael, taking his face in her hands, softly kissing his nose. Her baby brother looked up at her, and Wendy found herself moved by the strength in his eyes. "You're going to find them, the Lost Boys," he said.

A sob burst through her lips. "Yes. I'll find them. For you, and for John." John wiped his nose, one eye on the passage as it shrank another few inches.

"Peter once said it opened every thirty years."

Wendy nodded. "I hope that's true. John . . ." She looked long and hard at her brother. "Be good."

He nodded once, tears dripping down his face. "I will. I swear it."

Michael curled up in her arms. "But, Wendy . . . my heart hurts without you."

Wendy lowered her face to his. "All my life," she whispered, "I will be your sister. And every day I will watch the stars and think how much I love you."

"Okay," whispered Michael. John reached for his hand, and together her brothers turned to face the passage.

"I love you! I love you!" she cried as they made their way into the crack in the sky, turning sideways so that they could slip through. Michael turned, and she saw one last glimpse of her brother. He waved silently, and Wendy mouthed goodbye, unable to make actual sounds without screaming. The passage closed, the crack sealing before her eyes, and blue sky covered up where there had once been a vortex of stars and color.

Her brothers were gone.

Wendy buried her face in her hands, and racking sobs bent her shoulders forward as she struggled to breathe, each cry tearing through her like broken glass. But then, between her violent cries, she heard something just on the other side of the blue sky: Michael's happy voice—always too loud—drifted past her on a breeze.

"MOTHER!"

Wendy reached out her hand to her family for one last time. Then there was only silence.

Something passed behind her, and she turned, for a moment expecting green eyes accompanied with a smile that a girl would give the world for, but it wasn't him. It was someone else, someone who wanted to give *her* the world.

"They're gone," she whispered to Booth as he floated in front of her.

"I know," he responded, taking her up in his arms. His eyes were red and blotchy, and Wendy was reminded that Booth had lost something, too.

A father. A legacy.

"Are you going to be all right?" he asked, his fingers wiping away the tears that fell freely from her eyes.

"Someday," she whispered. "Just not right now."

"Well, there are plenty of people here who love you. Present company included."

She smiled quietly. There was no shortage of work before them: to give flight freely, to raise hundreds of boys, to rebuild the lives that had been ruined, to build a Neverland that was safe, to mourn those that the Shadow had taken. But that would not happen today.

They sank down through the clouds until the island appeared beneath them, Neverland looking exactly the same as it did when Wendy had first burst through the clouds with Peter Pan: an emerald paradise, whispering of untold adventures and the possibility of burning hearts.

Wendy turned to the boy she loved. The sun caught his hair, and for a moment she was blinded by his beauty, the shadows on his face reminding her of the boy who never had to grow up. Wendy squeezed Booth's hand, and they began flying together down toward the shore, and hopeful words filled her mouth at the dawn of a new world:

"To live will be an awfully big adventure, won't it?"

Wendy smiled.

"The biggest adventure of all."

Song of the Shadow

Music by Nicole London

EPILOGUE

Exactly thirty years later . . .

Mr. John Michael Barrie (John Darling's pen name, one that he thought sounded quite official) was working on his manuscript in the small attic apartment above the bookstore when the phone rang. The bookstore was empty at this time of night, but John still enjoyed retreating to this quiet corner to work; it was much more preferable than his other large dwelling down the way.

With furrowed brows and an ink-stained hand, he wrote as fast as he could, calling forth long-buried memories and spilling them onto the page. He ruffled through the soft paper until his eyes rested on the title: *Peter and Wendy*. A good title, probably, for such a strange story. No one would read it, of course, but it served two purposes: it kept him from being lonely on these long nights, and it helped him process the parts of his life that he still couldn't quite believe.

The phone rang again, and John frowned with frustration as he reached for it: it was probably his shrill mother, who would beg him to join her, his father, and his considerably younger sisters for dinner tonight. There would be much laughter, but those nights always left John a little exhausted, and he had to be in court early the next morning.

Running a bookstore while also being Kensington Garden's top legal counsel was exhausting, but it was worth it in the end.

Where his colleagues mocked his strange hobby, John knew the truth: Being a lawyer was his hobby. Being a bookseller was his *true* job. He snatched up the phone with an annoyed sigh on the third ring, his glasses slipping down his nose.

"What is it?"

But it wasn't his mother's voice; it was Michael's.

"John," he whispered softly. "I think it's time."

John's mouth went dry as he stumbled over his desk, his hands frantically searching for his calendar . . . the one with the date and time written in red.

"No, it can't be. I would have known . . ."

"You've been busy." In the background, Michael's young children shrieked happily. "Shhh . . . " Michael shushed them gently, and then he returned to the phone, his voice low. "I'm positive, John."

John didn't answer him because he had found his calendar and was staring at the date, swallowing hard.

"You're right. By God. You're right." He took a deep breath.

"Hurry," said his brother, but the phone had been left on the desk; John was already pulling on his coat as his feet pounded down the stairs.

Twenty minutes later, John silently let himself into the house on Kensington Street. Down the hall, he could hear the sounds of his parents and sisters having dinner, his father's voice—so much older now—reprimanding one of the girls for her lack of decorum, and his sisters laughing in return. His parents had no control over those girls whatsoever, but their delight in them more than made up for their lack of discipline.

John quietly slipped up the stairs to the second level, turning left at the staircase and making his way down the hall to the long-abandoned nursery. He pushed the door open and shut it quietly behind him. It was dark inside, but thanks to the moonlight, John was able to make out a shape standing in front of the window, his head bent forward.

"Michael?"

"Of course."

John stepped forward, removing his hat and holding it beside him. His heart pounded nervously as he moved through the nursery. As he walked, John let his hands trace over the old nursery furniture—the rocking chair where he had read a lifetime worth of books, the broken chair that had been Michael's and his pirate ship, and finally . . . a bed at the corner of the room that had sat empty for years, his mother unwilling to move it. He slowly pulled off his coat and laid it across his own small bed and stepped forward beside his little brother, who was now the handsome dean of a local parochial school.

"Are we mad?" Michael whispered, his blond hair still as bright as it had been thirty years ago. "This feels mad."

Perhaps we are, thought John, but he didn't say anything out loud, protecting his brother as he always had. Michael began fiddling nervously with the books on the shelf.

"Remember this one? She used to read us this one all the time."

John leaned over and looked at the title. "Ah. Yes. She loved that silly little book."

"Speaking of books . . . how is yours coming along?"

John nodded. "Slowly but surely."

"I'll never understand." Michael shook his head, his tone heavy with disappointment. "Making *him* the hero."

John bit the inside of his cheek, not knowing himself. "I have to, Michael. Otherwise, it's too painful, because it's the truth. My Peter will give children something to believe in."

Michael nodded thoughtfully. "I guess it's not a bad thing, letting children believe they can fly."

John smiled, wiping his glasses with a cloth. "No, it's not a bad thing at all—" But he was cut off by a strange creaking sound.

"What was that?" Michael looked up at him.

"Just the wind, I imagine . . ."

It sounded again, and both men stopped breathing as the

window transformed before their eyes into a moving prism of light and color. After a moment, John stepped forward, his fingers reaching out to touch the trembling glass. It came off on his fingers like liquid.

Michael's hand grabbed his own before the world in front of them exploded into whirling blues and purples. It was then that John witnessed the most beautiful sight he had ever seen: his brother's face lit up with stars, with his sister's name on his lips when she appeared on the windowsill. She was here.

"Wendy?"

ACKNOWLEDGMENTS

It's over.

The *Wendy Darling* series has come to a close, and I find myself both relieved and heartbroken at the idea at never returning to Neverland. Wendy was a wonderful character to inhabit for the last four years. After writing for so long about a dark, villainous heart, I wanted someone lighter for the next turn. Someone good at their very core, who could stand against a great evil. Wendy embodies all the best traits of those around me: She is kind without wanting reward, strong without being violent and loving, even at the cost of her own heart.

I am lucky to have loved and been loved by such people all my life.

Wendy is lit by your best qualities, and in return I hope that she can spark the same light in others.

Thank you to my agent Jen Unter, who has helped *Wendy Darling* take flight in so many ways. Thank you to Crystal Patriarche and the team at Sparkpress, who have supported my words from the *very* beginning. Their hard work has helped craft this series into something both other-worldly and accessible. To my writing partners and dear friends Brianna Shrum and Mason Torall; thanks for the late-night laughs and the rock-solid advice. I can't wait to see what creative enterprises await us and what new magic phrases we can stitch onto pillows.

To the friends who love this strange writer-creature just the way she is: Karen Groves, Kim Stein, Elizabeth Wagner, Katie Hall, Nicole London, Erin Chan, Cassandra Splittgerber, Katie Blumhorst, Emily Kiebel, Amanda Sanders and Erin Burt. To those voices who have helped the creation of *Wendy Darling* through three books: Erin Armknecht and Patty Jones—I'm talking about you.

To readers who have spoken words of love to me, to those who identified with Wendy or Tink or even Peter . . .

To those who have created beautiful art of the series, or those bright souls at TeenCon, or NTTBF or FIL Guadalajara who welcomed me with open arms. This series belongs to you.

Finally, to my remarkable family, who continue to astonish me daily with the love they pour out so willingly. To Ryan Oakes, who has always been my biggest supporter and my voice of reason when the storm drags me under. You are a rock to all who know you, my very own Sybella who calls to me when I can't hear my own thoughts. To Maine—I didn't know it at first, but it turns out I was saving all my best smiles for you. I'll give them forever. For Cynthia, I feel bad for anyone who doesn't have a sister as wonderful as you are. To my parents: Ron and Tricia McCulley, who told me that no dream was too big. To Denise McCulley, Butch, and Lynette Oakes: thanks for all the babysitting and the love. You're marvelous.

Psalm 95:5.

About the Author

© Erin Burt

Colleen Oakes is the author of books for both teens and adults, including The Queen of Hearts Saga and The Wendy Darling Saga. She lives in North Denver with her husband and son and surrounds herself with the most lovely family and friends imaginable. When not writing or plotting new books, she can be found swimming, traveling, and totally immersing herself in nerdy pop culture. She is currently at work on her third YA fantasy series, a children's book, and a stand-alone YA novel.

SELECTED TITLES FROM SPARKPRESS

SparkPress is an independent boutique publisher delivering high-quality, entertaining, and engaging content that enhances readers' lives, with a special focus on female-driven work.
Visit us at www.gosparkpress.com

Wendy Darling, by Colleen Oakes
$17, 978-1-94071-6-96-4
From the cobblestone streets of London to the fantastical world of Neverland, readers will love watching Wendy's journey as she grows from a girl into a woman, struggling with her love for two men, and realizes that Neverland, like her heart, is a wild place, teeming with dark secrets and dangerous obsessions.

Wendy Darling: Seas, by Colleen Oakes
$16.95, 978-1940716886
Wendy and Michael are aboard the dreaded Sudden Night, a dangerous behemoth sailed by the infamous Captain Hook. In this exotic world of mermaids, spies and pirate-feuds, Wendy finds herself struggling to keep her family above the waves. Will Wendy find shelter with Peter's greatest enemy, or is she a pawn in a much darker game, one that could forever alter not only her family's future, but also the soul of Neverland itself?

Within Reach, by Jessica Stevens
$17, 978-1-940716-69-5
Seventeen-year-old Xander Hemlock has found himself trapped in a realm of darkness with thirty days to convince his soul mate, Lila, he's not actually dead. With her anorexic tendencies stronger than ever, Lila must decide which is the lesser of two evils: letting go, or holding on to the unreasonable, yet overpowering, feeling that Xan is trying to tell her something.

Red Sun, by Alane Adams
$17, 978-1-940716-24-4
Drawing on Norse mythology, *The Red Sun* follows a boy's journey to uncover the truth about his past in a magical realm called Orkney—a journey during which he has to overcome the simmering anger inside of him, learn to channel his growing magical powers, and find a way to forgive the father who left him behind.

Running for Water and Sky, by Sandra Kring
$17, 978-1-940716-93-0
Seventeen-year-old Bless Adler has only known betrayal—but then she falls in love with Liam. After a visit to a local psychic and a glimpse of Liam lying in a pool of blood, Bless now has 14 blocks to reach Liam and either beg him to fight for his life, or say good-bye to the first person who made her want to fight for her own.

ABOUT SPARKPRESS

SparkPress is an independent, hybrid imprint focused on merging the best of the traditional publishing model with new and innovative strategies. We deliver high-quality, entertaining, and engaging content that enhances readers' lives. We are proud to bring to market a list of New York Times best-selling, award-winning, and debut authors who represent a wide array of genres, as well as our established, industry-wide reputation for creative, results-driven success in working with authors. SparkPress, a BookSparks imprint, is a division of SparkPoint Studio LLC.

Learn more at GoSparkPress.com